VALOR UNDER Siege

Elizabeth Boyce

Avon, Massachusetts

Published by
Crimson Romance™
an imprint of F+W Media, Inc.
10151 Carver Road, Suite 200
Blue Ash, OH 45242. U.S.A.
www.crimsonromance.com

ISBN 10: 1-4405-8505-9
ISBN 13: 978-1-4405-8505-0
eISBN 10: 1-4405-8506-7
eISBN 13: 978-1-4405-8506-7

Cover art © Inara Prusakova/123RF.

Chapter One

December 1817, London

In every crisis, there is a moment when catastrophe can be averted, a moment when it cannot be, and an indiscernible filament separating the two. The Honorable Mr. Norman Wynford-Scott, of Gray's Inn, feared the Christmas revels had tripped beyond that ineffable point of no return when he observed that the punch was on fire. This development was brought to his attention by the cries of fright issuing from the throat of a first-term Fellow, whose festive medieval costume of hose, doublet, *et cetera*, was somewhat spoiled by the flames crackling merrily in the plumes of his velvet hat.

Whether the conflagration began in the punch or on the young man's head, Norman could never say with certainty, for at the moment when spark met alcohol (or ostrich feather), he'd been occupied elsewhere in the hall, coaxing a stupendously inebriated Lady Fay down from where she danced atop one of the bench tables gifted to the Venerable Society of Gray's Inn by Queen Elizabeth.

"Elsa," he hissed as she shimmied her shoulders and hips in time to the musicians bleating a merry, seasonal tune, "come down from there at once!" He made a grab for her hand, but jerked back when she spun and kicked up her heel, flashing the flounce of a black petticoat beneath her rose-red satin gown as she nearly sheared the nose from his face.

She might be forgiven for not hearing him, as the normally staid hall was this evening bursting with the sounds of feasting and music and laughter, but her beguiling indigo eyes cut to his, communicating defiance—and something dark—in the instant before she spun away. From the neighboring table came the sonorous drone of Mr. Yelverton, the aged Serjeant-at-law who, for the last several decades, could be found in his customary seat pontificating upon various points of legality to his nightly bottle of port and whichever wide-eyed first-termers happened to be caught within earshot. Obviously, he was not about to be put off his routine by anything as trifling as Christmas revels.

"Consult the Book!" Yelverton declared now, jabbing a gnarled finger against the table. "We abandoned these absurd revels nigh on a century ago, and for good reason. This buffoonery diminishes the dignity of this institution. You'll not find the Fellows of Lincoln's countenancing a strumpet like that in their midst." Even as his condemning words were hurled in Elsa's direction, his gaze tracked her sinuous motions, like a snake entranced by its charmer.

The venerable elder was not the only gentleman who had noticed Elsa's display. Two barristers and a former Solicitor General gathered around, eagerly watching as the raven-haired beauty in red tossed back her head and slowly lifted her skirts.

"Elsa, stop this," Norman demanded as her ankles appeared.

"I say, isn't that our hostess?" asked one of the men who had joined the burgeoning throng.

"Yes, that's Lady Fay. Used to be quite the political hostess for her late husband. No wonder her invitations were coveted." Someone landed a friendly jab in Norman's ribs. "Good show, sir. The old man knew what he was about, naming you master of revels."

More than having been named *magister jocorum, revellorum, et mascarum*, resurrecting the Christmas revels had been Norman's bloody stupid idea to begin with. Somehow he'd gotten it into his head he could leave his mark on this grand and ancient school of law not just by excelling in his studies, but by livening the place up a bit with a call to bring back some of the old traditions.

He was responsible for it all, for the invitations issued to every member of the Inn and distinguished guests. For the decorations and music and food. For choosing the lady who served as hostess.

Like a curtain rising on a bawdy spectacle, red satin and black muslin inched past that same hostess's shapely calves encased in sheer silk and revealed two pretty, dimpled knees. Appreciative whistles and hoots of encouragement accompanied every inch of progress, while appalled ladies formed a tight knot across the room, silk fans kicking up a wind of umbrage. Elsa tipped back her raven-haired head and laughed, sinful and loud.

This was hell. Like the men around him, Norman couldn't help but respond to the slow uncovering of the luscious woman on the table. But even as his heart pumped desire-thickened blood through his body, his mind went cold with panic. Not only was this a scandal for all of Gray's Inn, Elsa was not in her right mind, drunk beyond sensibility. She was his responsibility; he had to get her out of there.

"Lady Fay," he said in a commanding tone, "you will stop dancing at once."

Wonder of wonders, she did. Her skirts dropped back into place, and she lifted her head, confusion crinkling her brow. Norman's shoulders relaxed a fraction. Now then, if he could quickly escort her from the hall, perhaps the evening could be salvaged.

That's when the cry went up behind him, pulling Norman's attention from Elsa to the bowl of flaming punch and equally blazing gentleman. Additional shouts of alarm joined that of the human torch.

"Oh, good lord," he blurted. There would be no salvaging the evening now. Discarding his typical, careful manner when stepping through a crowd, Norman set his broad shoulders at an angle and plowed through revelers. The man's companions seemed more amused than concerned, clutching their middles and guffawing at their beleaguered comrade.

Snatching a banner festooning the beverage table, displaying the Inn's golden griffin device, Norman tossed it over the head of the *avocat brûlée*, smothering the flames. He plucked the cloth—and the burning hat along with it—off the man, threw it to the ground, and stomped his large feet upon it for good measure. The costumed man was a little crisp around the edges, but no lasting harm done.

Beside Norman, heat radiated from the still-burning champagne punch. How the hell had such an innocuous libation caught fire? Like a witch's cauldron, blue and orange flames undulated across the liquid's surface and set the crystal bowl aglow with eerie light. The scent of caramelizing sugar filled the air.

Curious onlookers gathered around and murmured excitedly. Many seemed to think the punch was another of the revel's entertainments, like the dancing dogs that had performed earlier, or like Elsa's erotic display.

Half turning, he easily looked over the heads of the crowd to where he'd last spotted her. She was no longer on the table. He'd not believed things could get worse, but now she was sandwiched between a barrister and the former Solicitor General. One of her discarded long, black satin gloves was cast around the neck of one of the men like a scarf. Elsa clasped the ends, holding herself tight to the man's chest. His hands were upon her waist, while the other man stood behind her, trailing a finger down the side of her neck, his other resting proprietorially upon her hip.

Norman's heart dropped. Elsa was in a mood for trouble, but in no state to engage in what those two so obviously intended. "Elsa," he called, but his voice was swallowed by the roar of the assembly and the frenetic music still blaring from the little band in the corner.

He took two brisk steps toward Lady Fay. A hand gripped his sleeve. He wheeled around to find himself face-to-face with Mr. Turton, one of the Master Benchers of Gray's Inn, and one of the most vocal opponents to Norman resurrecting the Christmas revels. Defying his wishes had been a calculated risk on Norman's part, one he thought would pay off when the party's success gave Gray's an edge of prestige above the other Inns of Court.

"What the blazes is going on here?" Turton demanded, without a hint of irony even as the flickering punch fire reflected in his pale eyes. "I knew this was a terrible idea! You've turned this hall into a pagan bordello."

There was a blast of cold air, which Norman attributed to Turton's icy disdain whipping around the room.

"I'm sorry, sir." Norman extended his hands in a placating fashion. He towered a foot above the Master Bencher, but Norman was intimidated by the man, nevertheless. Turton could scuttle his career as a barrister before it even began. "This wasn't meant to happen," he nodded to the bowl, which issued an ominous groan. He bent to pick up the banner with which he had smothered the fire on the first-termer. Turton's eyes widened at the abused coat of arms, then narrowed dangerously as Norman assured him, "I'll get this extinguished straightaway."

As he moved to smother the punch, he heard a feminine battle cry. He turned just in time to see Elsa hurtling his way, clutching a bucket. He hooked an arm across her waist before she fell headlong into the fire. Her arms extended. Icy water doused the table.

The tortured punch bowl shattered; its burning contents spilled across the table and onto the floor. Greedy flames met airy buntings and lace doilies and quickly found the table's legs. Faster than Norman could have believed possible, the entire table was engulfed in fire. The burgeoning conflagration took hold on the ancient wooden floor in several places.

Instinctively, he hauled Elsa back from the fire. "Everyone out!" he bellowed, herding panicking Fellows and their guests toward the door without taking his hands off of Elsa.

Someone else shouted for the men to form a bucket line. "Save the hall!" went up the cry.

Still sitting at his regular bench table, old Mr. Yelverton's chin trembled, and the silvery tracks of tears stained his lined cheeks. The fire was heading right toward him.

Biting back a curse, Norman set Elsa on her feet and pointed her in the direction of the door through which she'd come with her bucket. "Go outside. I'll meet you at the Field Court, by the garden entrance."

She blinked glassy eyes, swayed on her feet, and swatted off Norman's steadying hand. "Let off. 'm fine," she scolded, taking tottering steps toward the door.

"Wait for me," he called after her. "Field Court, in front of the garden."

She waved a negligent hand and was swallowed up in the stream of evacuees.

Norman quickly crossed to where Mr. Yelverton sat and stared, stricken, at the fire consuming his beloved hall. His gnarled fingers clasped tightly in front of him on the dark, aged table, his bottle of port still resting at his elbow.

"Mr. Yelverton, we must leave." Norman took the man's arms.

"Where will I go?" the old man wailed. "This is my home!"

"It will still be your home," Norman assured him, struggling to maintain equanimity while the fire licked steadily closer, "but we must get out of the way of the bucket line so they can do their work."

Rheumy eyes twitched from side to side. "A captain goes down with his ship," he said, voice tremulous with indecision.

Growling, Norman restrained himself from pointing out that this was not a ship, and Mr. Yelverton was in no way a captain. "We can always rebuild, but what would Gray's Inn be without you, sir?"

As though insensible of the smoke curling tendrils into the air, the old Serjeant-at-law lifted his eyes to the soaring, Gothic beams spanning the hall, his gaze coming to rest on Cromwell's coat of arms. "Rebuild?"

"Of course, Mr. Yelverton. Now, if you'll permit me—" Norman scooped the man up into his arms, the fire leaving no time to preserve Yelverton's dignity. Bombastic the old buzzard might be, but there was little left of his wizened form. He weighed no more than a slip of a maiden. Norman, being larger than most everyone else in existence, had no trouble carrying the old man out into the fresh night air.

Depositing Yelverton on a stone bench a safe distance from the fire, Norman returned to the hall to aid in the evacuation, plucking from the fray a lady with a snapped slipper ribbon, assisting a gentleman suffering from exposure to the smoke, and then rescuing a musician pinned beneath a table upended in the chaos.

By the time the hall was fully evacuated, the fire was out, the bucket line having efficiently put a stop to the threat.

Norman stared at the sad, soggy ruin of his Christmas revels. The hall was a mess of smoke-stained wood and charred fabrics, many of them laying in wet heaps on the floor and bearing the imprints of the feet that trod upon them in panic. There was a surprising quantity of mud, a combination, Norman supposed, of dirt tracked in by the bucket line and soot churned with the water.

Mercifully, Queen Elizabeth's bench tables had been spared, and none of the portraits, coats of arms, or stained glass windows on the room's perimeter had been harmed. Cleaning this mess would take some effort, but the damage wasn't too extensive. A good scrubbing and a few new floor planks would set most of the disorder to rights. Fully cognizant that he was ultimately responsible for the fiasco, Norman was musing over where he could obtain scrub brushes and lye first thing tomorrow morning when he sensed an ominous presence at his shoulder.

"Mr. Turton," he said to the Senior Bencher, "I was just thinking over what should be done. I think the hall is still usable—once it's had a good airing and sweeping—so there shouldn't be much disruption to daily life here while repairs are made. I will personally oversee the recovery."

"You'll do nothing of the sort."

Norman shifted his weight from one foot to the other. "I beg your pardon, sir?"

"You have overseen your first and last undertaking at Gray's Inn, Mr. Wynford-Scott."

Two more Senior Benchers appeared, flanking Turton, making it clear he spoke for them, as well.

Norman licked his lips, found them dry and cracked. "I quite understand, gentlemen." He bowed his head. "I beg you'll accept my sincere apology for what has transpired here tonight and allow me the opportunity to assist in making it right again. I'm capable with a broom and a hammer and have no qualms about dirtying my hands with honest labor, if it means—"

"We insist you depart the premises of Gray's Inn," cut in Mr. Turton. "You will be summoned when we have decided what's to be done with you."

"But my rooms," Norman protested. He'd lived at 23 Gray's Inn Place for the past seven years. This wasn't just the institution where he learned the King's law and assisted barristers with their cases and debated with his fellow Fellows—Gray's Inn was his home. Without it, he would be just as lost and adrift as Mr. Yelverton feared he would be.

"Leave an address where you may be reached." Mr. Turton was merciless. "I expect your father has room for you. A cot in the nursery, perhaps?"

Norman's face heated. His long-widowed father, Mr. William Wynford-Scott, third son of the Earl of Littleton, had instigated something of a scandal when he took a dairymaid for his second wife, shortly after his only child had departed for university. As if their marriage wasn't shocking enough, the couple was persistently, almost distastefully, in love. For the past decade, Norman's father had added to his second family with alarming regularity. After growing up an only child, Norman now had six younger half siblings.

"As you say, sir." Norman bowed stiffly. "I expect you will be able to reach me at my father's house. Good evening, gentlemen."

Outside, Norman was suddenly struck with a wave of dizziness and exhaustion. Bracing hands on his knees, he coughed, back heaving, eventually bringing up thick, gray phlegm. His temples throbbed, and his eyes were gritty. It was like the worst morning-after head he'd ever experienced, without the consolation of at least having enjoyed a night of carousing.

Speaking of drunken nights, he must meet Elsa and see her home. Straightening, Norman took a deep breath of the cold night air and winced at an ache in his lung. Clutching a hand to his ribs, he slowly made his way through Field Court. Most of the evening's guests had departed, but a few stragglers and many students still milled about.

"Excuse me," Norman said, gently pushing past bodies blocking his way, careful not to tread upon toes with his oversized feet. "May I get by, please? I beg your pardon." He stopped only once, when he was waved down by the old Serjeant-at-law. "Yes, Mr. Yelverton, the fire has been extinguished. The hall survives. Oh, don't weep, sir. There, there. Keep it, please; I've other handkerchiefs."

At last, he reached the entrance of Gray's Inn Gardens. Elsa was nowhere to be seen. Exhaling wearily, Norman craned his neck, peering into the dark garden. The mid-December night was cold; surely she hadn't wandered in there? Perhaps she'd grown tired of waiting and had summoned her carriage.

But no, that was preposterous. When last Norman had seen Elsa, she was swaying on her feet, her words beginning to slur. She was wickedly drunk. Besides drinking who-knew-how-much of the devil's brew in the punch bowl, Elsa kept a flask about her person at all times and, usually, a reserve in her reticule. If she'd consumed any more liquor after leaving the hall, she'd likely lost consciousness somewhere. She might be behind a hedge, being nibbled upon by an opportunistic fox. She might be drowning facedown in a puddle. She might be in the garden after all, he mused, insensible of the temperature and at risk of death from exposure.

Norman's weariness slid away. He turned in a circle, his eyes darting to every shadow and crevice. No Elsa.

"Have you seen Lady Fay?" he demanded of a passerby. The man shook his head. "About so tall," Norman pressed, his flattened hand extended at his lower chest. "Dark hair, red dress." The man shook his head once more.

"Lady Fay, have you seen her?" he asked of whomever he intercepted. No, no one had seen her. One lady even berated Norman for daring to mention *that Jezebel's* name in her presence. At last, he cornered the young Fellow whose hat had caught fire. Still sporting their silly medieval costumes, Human Torch and his friends looked anomalous slouched against a wall of the kitchen behind the great hall, puffing on cigarillos, as if they hadn't had enough smoke for one evening.

"Have any of you seen Lady Fay, our revels hostess?"

At his anxious query, one of the gentlemen snorted; another snickered. Human Torch elbowed his companion and cast a guilty look at Norman. "It's not our place to tell tales about a lady, Mr. Wynford-Scott."

Norman swallowed, his throat tight. "Lady Fay is ... she's ill. I have reason to believe she needs help, may even be in danger. If you know where she is, for the love of God, say so."

One of the men coughed and looked at his toes. Another regarded Norman with a mocking smile. "She has the kind of sickness a man likes, hasn't she? I shouldn't worry too much about her, old man. She's in good hands. Lots of them."

"Lots of..." His lips tingled, then numbed. Those men, the two who'd been groping her brazenly in the hall before she'd made her foolish attempt at dousing the fire. "Where is she?" he ground out.

"Well, if I know Brograve," said the insolent bard, or whatever he was meant to be, "she'll be on her hands and knees, taking it—"

A fist Norman didn't remember making landed on the side of the man's face with the satisfying *snap* of something giving way in his jaw.

Good. *Good*. Norman, who had never—not once—struck another man, hoped to God this one would be a long time in regaining the use of his odious mouth.

The man slid along the wall as he collapsed, velvet doublet rasping over the brick. When he'd come to rest on the ground, a brief, shocked silence fell over the scene.

"She's in there, Mr. Wynford-Scott, sir," blurted Human Torch, pointing to the kitchen door. "And thank you, sir, for coming to my aid this evening, sir. If there's anything I can do for you, sir, you've only to say the word. Sir."

Human Torch and his friend made good their escape, deserting the one Norman had pummeled. A soft groan arose from the unconscious blighter. A twinge of guilt pricked Norman's conscience, but it was quickly wiped away when a woman screamed inside the kitchen.

"Elsa!" he roared, bursting through the door. The glow of banked coals on the brick hearth provided the room's only light. He turned in a circle, desperate to find her. "Elsa, where—"

He heard her again, not a scream, but a laugh. "Here, Misser Wynfor'-Scah. Join us, do."

Rounding a preparation table, he found her. Them. On the floor.

In short order, he'd plucked Elsa from the floor and tossed her, kicking and hissing like an angry cat, over his shoulder.

"Put me down!" she demanded, the toes of her little red slippers thrumming against his sternum.

"I think not, my lady."

Her fists drummed his back. Over the last ten years, Norman had grown adept at ignoring infantile tantrums.

Just outside the hall, Norman flagged down a servant and summoned Lady Fay's carriage. Then, heedless of gawking onlookers, he strode swiftly across Field Court to his rooms at Gray's Inn Place. Bringing a woman to his chambers was strictly forbidden, but he'd already been evicted; what worse could the Senior Benchers do?

He kicked the door shut behind him, locked it, and pocketed the key. Then he deposited the screeching Fury on his worn old sofa, from which she continued her angry diatribe. "Wha's the matter wif you, Misser Wynfor ... Misser Wyn ... Norm? Do you've some problem with *fun*? Are you a ... are you a *monk*?"

Through his friend Lord Sherian Zouche, Norman had been acquainted with Elsa Fay for years and had appreciated her beauty and vivacious spirit from afar. His direct dealings with her had been limited until last year. At the betrothal ball honoring Sheri and his lovely bride, Norman had been called upon to assist with a powerfully intoxicated Lady Fay, who was wreaking havoc at the ball (a truth he should have, perhaps, taken into consideration when choosing a hostess for the Christmas revels; but there exists no system of logic powerful enough to overcome the heart's desire, he had lately discovered, to his eternal regret). Though she was as lovely as ever, it had become evident to Norman at that time that Elsa was deeply troubled: Her lively behavior had turned manic, and what was once an infectious joie de vivre now manifested as recklessness bordering on self-destructiveness.

On that night, Norman's admiration had shifted to something else. He'd lifted her into his arms (well, slung her over his shoulder) to see her safely home, and some protective instinct had emerged. No one else in Elsa's sphere—not even Sheri—seemed to notice how frequently she overimbibed on spirits or how her previously circumspect affairs had become more and more indiscreet. Norman had despaired to witness such an intelligent, sparkling woman throw herself headlong into ruin. He'd wanted, powerfully, to help, to save her from herself.

It was that chivalrous streak that had prompted him to invite her assistance with the Christmas revels. Once, Elsa had been the toast of London's political circles. While he'd never attended one of her suppers or soirees, he'd often overheard barristers and judges bragging at having received an invitation or rhapsodizing about the glories of an evening spent at her table.

These days, a man was more likely to rhapsodize about the pleasures of an evening spent in her bed.

Naively, Norman had hoped that reminding Elsa of her glorious past would nudge her in the direction of more moderate living. Greater fool, he.

Norman dragged his traveling trunk from a closet and quickly filled it with clothes, other essentials, and, after a brief, tortured moment at his bookshelf, a history of the Roman Senate and the latest edition of *British Courts and Law: A Quarter in Review*.

After donning his frock coat and hat, Norman deposited the trunk outside, then returned to his small sitting room. When Elsa spotted him, she fell silent. Her hands curled around the edge of the cushion, and she glowered up at him, her eyes fathomless pools of deepest blue.

"Can you stand, my lady, or shall I carry you?"

"'Course I can," she muttered. Her full lips puckered in concentration as she shoved to unsteady feet. Norman wrapped her in his own cloak. The dark wool swallowed her and dragged on the floor. He lifted the hood, covering the shining silk of her mussed hair. Her delicate features looked small and frail in the immense garment.

Lady Fay leaned heavy into Norman's side as they made their way outside. When she stumbled over a loose paving stone, he tucked her against his side; his large hand fit neatly in the curve between her ribs and hip. They walked in silence, he guiding her toward the waiting carriage while she doggedly fought for every listing step. Unbidden, he found himself remembering the vision she'd been dancing on the table, powerfully alluring even as she'd maddened him.

He felt her ribcage expand on a sharp inhale. "Fire?"

"Out," he assured her. "No serious injuries or damage."

"Tha's good," she mumbled. "I told 'em be careful wif Uncle Seamus's whiskey. No open flame or drinkin' it straight." She chuckled. "Wicked stuff."

Something in Norman's head snapped. Or broke. Came loose. Went wrong. Stopping short, he yanked her around to face him. "*You* did that?" he demanded, pointing to the now-dark hall. "Turned harmless champagne punch into a lethal potion? And then you threw cold water onto hot glass, spreading a fire that could have brought down the entire hall. How could you be so foolish?"

She blinked slowly, her head drooped. Norman gave her a shake, bent low, and crowded her. Embarrassed by his unseemly six-foot-nine height, he'd always tried to be smaller and quieter than his body allowed, hoping a reserved disposition would make up for him occupying more than his fair share of space. But now ... now he hoped—wanted—to intimidate her. Wanted her to tell him what the bloody hell had been going through that pretty head of hers. "Do you have any idea what you've done, Elsa?" he boomed, his voice cracking off the brick walls of the surrounding buildings. "Do you? The entire hall might have been lost. People could have died. You've cost me—" He cut himself off, biting his tongue until he tasted blood. No good would come from venting his spleen, not with her in this state.

He trembled all over, caught in the grips of the fiercest anger he'd ever known. Her stupid stunt and her unforgivable love of drink had cost him his home and other repercussions yet to be determined by the Master Benchers. When he should have been celebrating his imminent call to the bar, Norman instead found everything he'd worked for about to be snatched from his grasp.

He towed her to the carriage. After several failed attempts to navigate the step, Elsa started laughing. "My foot won' go!"

Norman hoisted Elsa, still laughing, onto the seat.

She swatted his arm. "Oh, don' be dour." Her plump lips, red and moist, twisted in her flushed face. She fell against his chest, knocked his hat to the floor, and played her fingers into the shaggy hair over his ear. Her fingernails scratched lightly at his scalp, as though she were petting a dog. "I liked being with you tonight."

What the devil was wrong with the woman? She was unrepentant about the damage she'd done, blissfully unaware of his ire.

"Regretfully, I cannot say the same." He brushed her fingers aside. He never should have asked her to be hostess of the revels, knowing as he did her weakness for drink.

"Oh, don' say you're angry at me." She clung to his hand, her eyes pleading. "I was jus' havin' fun. I din' mean for it to happen. An' I didn't mean to be so ... I tol' myself only one drink."

She sniffled; an overabundance of liquor had her mood staggering about as much as her faltering steps. Despite himself, her crestfallen expression tugged his heartstrings.

"Elsa ..." He sighed. "Don't fret over it tonight, all right? We'll talk about it tomorrow."

She dried her eyes against his sleeve. "You're good, Norman. Sheri always says so. He's right."

Shaking his head, Norman turned his gaze sightlessly to the window, Mayfair's houses and streetlamps passing in a meaningless blur.

Though her tears had ceased, Elsa still rubbed her face against his arm, back and forth. Her hand found his chest and slid up to hook around his neck.

"Elsa, what are you—"

She pulled his mouth to hers. She was warm and soft and inviting, tasting of whiskey and the promise of sex. Her tongue swept into his mouth on a moan, invading his senses with her scent.

He was a man of flesh and blood, and she was a temptress like no other he'd encountered. His body responded, even as his mind insisted he do the right thing. Never had he been so at odds with himself.

Gently as he could, Norman pushed her away. "No, Elsa," he rasped.

She blinked up at him, bewildered. "You don't want me?" she asked in a small, pitiful voice.

Sinking back into the squabs, Norman dragged his hands down the sides of his face. "You would hate me in the morning."

"I could never hate you."

"I would hate myself."

Her face darkened. "Because I've been with other men? Not played the pious widow? Fine. I've other *friends* who'll keep me company." She pounded on the ceiling to signal the driver to stop.

He didn't doubt there were any number of men who would be more than happy to take advantage of a lonely, inebriated widow. "Now see here," he said darkly, "I'm not about to let you jump into bed with one of your ciscebos—not in this state. Drive on," he called out the window.

In a flash, Elsa's defensive glower turned to a sneer. "Jealous?"

Undoubtedly. How often had he watched her turn the head of every man in a room, then take her pick of them for a night's dalliance? So many nights, he'd secretly ached, foolishly wishing she'd chosen him.

But longer than he'd desired Elsa, he'd known this: A woman who couldn't walk a straight line or speak a straight sentence was in no frame of mind to choose to go to bed with a man, and any male who did so anyway was a piss-poor excuse for a man.

"You aren't my keeper," she railed. "You've no right ... none."

"You're scarcely more your own keeper than I am," he retorted sharply. "You've no control over yourself."

Her face screwed up in anger. "You ain't so good, affer all, just a sad little man threatened by a woman unafraid of pleasure. Find us threat—threat'nin'."

The coach stopped. When he saw Elsa's townhouse through the window, he sagged in relief.

When the door opened, Elsa half tumbled out; it took both the driver and Norman to get her onto the front walk. With his arm around her waist, Norman steered her to the front door. "Fetch Foster," he instructed a footman. "Her ladyship isn't feeling well."

While the man went for the lady's maid, Elsa pushed away from Norman. She swayed alarmingly in the center of the entry hall. Her coiffure listed to the side, dark strands dangling lank around her pale face. She looked, he thought, like a banshee. Or a sad, drunken fishwife. He reached for her, but she held him off with a warning hand.

"How dare you judge me?" she hissed. "You think I never seen how you lookit me?" She jabbed herself in the chest; the tip of her finger disappeared into her cleavage. "An' the time I offer you a fuck out of pity, you're sunnly too good for me? Well, *Misser Norman Wynfor'-Scott*," she sneered, imbuing his name with a healthy dose of scorn. "Well, maybe ... Maybe you're not good 'nuff for *me*."

"I've no doubt that's true," he clipped off, the sarcasm dripping from his words seeming to pass right over her muddled head.

Foster hurried down the stairs. Taking in the sorry state of her mistress, the maid let out a gasp of dismay. She wrapped a protective arm around Elsa and guided her toward the stairs. "Thank you for seeing her home, sir."

"And don't come back," Elsa yelled. "You hear that? I'm rejecting *you*. I've got no time for fools."

She didn't mean it. It was the liquor talking. When she'd slept it off, they'd once more be friends. But when she became drunk again, as she inevitably would, her mood would be unpredictable, and he'd be powerless to resist the need to protect her from herself.

As he watched her slowly ascend the stairs, Norman had a realization: The night was lost to catastrophe long before the punch caught fire. Disaster was inevitable from the moment he'd become entangled with the beautiful, ruinous Lady Fay.

Chapter Two

Light sliced through her eyelids. Elsa, the dowager Viscountess Fay, winced. "Closed, Foster," she croaked, flapping her hands in the general direction of the parted curtains and their skull-splitting blades of yellow death. Her stomach lurched alarmingly, so she stopped flailing, instead pressing her fingers to eyes pounding in time with her heart.

"It's gone one, my lady." Foster's tone bristled with disapproval. "Here's tea for you." There was the sound of liquid pouring into a cup, the neat *snick* of the teapot placed precisely where it belonged on the tray. "Cook's kept kidney pie warm for you. Have your tea while I fetch it up." She paused, adding as an afterthought a slightly pitying, "Milady."

Insolent biddy, Elsa silently remonstrated. None of her friends tolerated such managing from their abigails. She heard Foster's brisk steps cross the room and disappear down the hall. A draft from the corridor soothed Elsa's heated cheeks. If she lay very still and took shallow breaths, the bed didn't spin quite so crazily. She drifted.

Footsteps again. Heavy. A man's.

Elsa startled out of her drowse, confused and cold with fear. *Harvey.* He disapproved of her lying abed beyond sunrise. And she'd had her courses. Without child once more. She'd failed. He would be angry—

A hand on her shoulder. For a few terrifying seconds, she was paralyzed, waiting for the grip to turn punishing.

"No use feigning sleep. Foster told me you're awake."

Not Harvey. She knew that voice. Elsa opened her eyes and her lips, air flooding her lungs on a gasp. A handsome man stood at her bedside, splendidly attired in perfectly tailored weskit and tailed morning coat. His left hand still rested on her shoulder. In his other, he twirled a silver quizzing glass.

"Sheri?" Her hands trembled as she swiped a damp strand of hair from her forehead. What was Lord Sheridan Zouche doing in her bedchamber? Sheri was married now, wasn't he? Why couldn't she remember for certain?

"Here, allow me." He made quick work of gathering pillows to prop her up, handling her gently but efficiently.

Elsa disliked being made to feel like an invalid, but her limbs did not seem inclined to cooperate. "Where's your wife?" she asked, as Sheri turned to the tea tray.

"Here, my lady," said a rich, musically accented voice. Elsa glanced past Sheri to see Arcadia Zouche just inside the door.

Sheri handed Elsa her tea. Ignoring the liquid sloshing over the rim, she buried her face in the fragrant cup, hiding her disquiet. In other circumstances, she'd be delighted by a visit from her dear friend and his lovely bride, but why were they in her bedchamber? Something was not right. Something was, she suspected, terribly wrong.

Shame twisted her gut. Last night. The memories were piecemeal, but what she recalled was reason enough for embarrassment.

Mr. Wynford-Scott, one of Sheri's cabal of Honorables, had asked her to serve as hostess for the Christmas revels at Gray's Inn. He was overwhelmed by the undertaking, he'd said, and since she had experience with such things ...

Once, she'd been a political hostess for her husband, holding weekly salons and fortnightly dinners during every session of Parliament throughout the six years of her marriage. She had charmed the nation's mighty and powerful, knowing whether to employ a pointed observation or a flirtatious remark to best advance her husband's interests. She'd been good at it, too, so good. It was the only way in which she'd not been a failure as a wife, Harvey had often remarked.

And so she'd been secretly delighted to be needed once more. She'd swooped in and rescued poor, fumbling Mr. Wynford-Scott. He'd had a few rough ideas that she had honed to perfection. She'd made sure the food would be prepared in ample quantities, chosen the most amusing entertainments, and hired the liveliest musicians.

She was in high spirits, drunk on her success and proud to once again have felt part of a team. But soon, that natural euphoria wasn't enough. She'd sworn she'd only have one glass of wine with supper, and only a bit of punch elsewise, but then she'd given those boys a bottle of Uncle Seamus's homemade Irish whiskey, the fumes of which curled the hairs in one's nostrils, and had to prove to those green fellows that she could keep up with the rest of them.

After that, the evening was a blur of music and dancing and— Her cup clattered into the saucer. *Dancing.* She'd made a proper fool of herself dancing on the tabletop. That must be why Sheri had come, to chide her for the lewd display.

"Do you remember setting fire to Gray's Inn last night?" he asked in a light tone.

The question caught her off guard. "Fire?"

There had been the drinking, and the music, and some more drinking, and then the dancing, another nip of whiskey ... She'd enjoyed teasing Norman, loved the heated look in his eyes when he watched her, not caring that she was tormenting him. But then he'd left, and she'd followed with her gaze, spotting the fire in the punch bowl. And then she'd—

"Cold water on hot glass. My fault." She twisted a hand into the ends of her loose hair. "Was anyone hurt?" she asked in a pained whisper. If someone had been hurt—God, *killed*—because of her stupidity, Elsa didn't know how what she'd do.

Yes, you do, said a strange double voice in her head.

Shame and guilt, guilt and shame. Guilt and Shame. Like mythic twins, they resided somewhere inside her, twirling in gossamer robes until her middle knotted, their voices twining in a haunting melody that condemned her foibles and frailties. Guilt and Shame's song now raised in crescendo until her ears rang.

Elsa's mouth tasted terrible. Her stomach roiled. She felt the all-too-familiar battle between the muscles in her torso, her lower belly forcing her gorge upward, the ones below her ribs fighting to keep the contents of her stomach contained.

Long ago, she'd learned to hide her next-day vomiting. To a vigilant husband, it was too easily mistaken for a pregnant woman's morning sickness.

"Mercifully, there were no serious injuries," Sheri said. "A flutist with a twisted knee and a few cases of chest complaints caused by the smoke."

None dead. No one too badly hurt. Elsa sagged, the relief easing her stomach, too.

"... some minor structural damage that will necessitate repairs, to say nothing of the fright you gave all those people."

His soothing voice droned on. Her lids slid shut.

"Elsa!" He clapped in her face. She jerked awake, her fingers flinching tight on the cup she'd somehow managed not to spill.

"Sheri," said Arcadia, coming to stand beside her husband. "Her ladyship is tired. Perhaps we should come back another—"

"No," came another voice from the door.

Norman Wynford-Scott entered, his long legs eating the distance from the door to the foot of her bed in three hungry strides. He was absolutely tremendous, the tallest man she'd ever known. It was his height that distinguished him, of course, for his face was nothing remarkable, pleasing but not strikingly handsome. Wavy brown hair of a regular, middling hue shagged around his ears and flopped across his forehead. His eyes were ...

well, Elsa didn't know for sure. She'd never paid much attention to them. His lips were full in a masculine way; on another man, they would be good for kissing, but Mr. Wynford-Scott was such a dull humdrum, preferring his studies to livelier pursuits.

If possible, he seemed larger just now than he usually did. His jaw was tense, bracketing those wasted, sensual lips in hard lines.

Those lips.

It came to her then, all at once. The carriage. She'd kissed him. Tried to lure him to bed.

He slashed a look of accusation at her, and she realized why he seemed larger than normal. Mr. Wynford-Scott had quiet, gentle manners. He was good-natured and soft-spoken. Even at full volume, his rich voice was sonorous and even, a trait cultivated, she assumed, to carry throughout a cavernous courtroom in a dignified fashion.

But now, even in his stillness, she could see agitation frothing just below the surface of his skin. He wasn't merely angry; he was hurt. Justifiably so. She'd spoiled the revels and kissed him and—

He had told Sheri, of course. Why did she only now realize it? After leaving her last night, he'd gone to Sheri, tattled on Elsa as though she was an ill-behaved child. But had he told all? Did Sheri know that Elsa had tried (and failed) to seduce one of his closest friends?

And where was Foster with that kidney pie? It dawned on Elsa that she'd been set up. Even her maid was involved in orchestrating this gathering.

The teacup shook in her hand, spilling tawny liquid onto her coverlet. She cut a glance at her adjoining dressing room. Carelessly dropping the china cup onto the tray, she hurled herself out of bed. "I'm going to be sick," she blurted. Sheri made a grab for her; she gripped his sleeve and pushed him away. "Go," she begged, darting past a stunned Arcadia and lacking the courage to assess Mr. Wynford-Scott's expression.

She slammed the dressing room door behind her and yanked open the vanity drawer. With shaking hands, she sifted through jars of powder and pots of rouge. She dropped to her knees and pulled the drawer out, upending its contents onto the floor, scattering small brushes and rabbit fur poufs across the light blue carpet.

"Where?" she gasped. "Where?" Her eyes darted about the space while she crawled on hands and knees, desperate for a glimpse of the silver flask with its beautiful mother-of-pearl inlay.

"You'll not find it," said Mr. Wynford-Scott. When had he entered the dressing room? She'd not heard the door open. He filled the small room with his immense size and the force of his presence. She backed away, her eyes trained on his glowering face, until her bare heels touched the leg of the settee.

"Where?" she repeated.

From the pocket of his somber brown coat, he withdrew her flask, clasped in his long, thick fingers.

Her nostrils flared, as if scenting the juniper fumes of the gin inside. She lunged. He raised his arm, easily keeping it beyond reach. "Give it to me," she demanded, clutching his lapel with one hand and grasping the sleeve of his raised arm with the other. Even on tiptoe, extending to her full length, she couldn't touch his elbow. "That isn't yours. You've no right." She clawed and grappled. When that didn't work, she grabbed his arm with both hands and let herself drop, in a play to pull him off-balance.

He remained stubbornly vertical.

Her breath came in pained, sobbing gasps, and her stomach heaved in earnest. Releasing his arm, she stumbled around him and returned to her bedchamber, catching a glimpse of Sheri's pained, pitying face as she dropped to her knees before the chamber pot.

As she vomited and cried, she sensed the three of them closing around her, not even granting her privacy in this low moment. Every contraction of her abdomen was compounded by the mortification of their presence. Animal noises escaped her as her body made a valiant attempt to turn itself inside out.

After, she slumped over the pot, too weak to move. She imagined how she must look to her pitying friends: a woman undone, sick and deranged for want of drink. It wasn't as though Elsa didn't know she drank too much. No other ladies of her acquaintance tipped gin into their morning tea or put away neat scotch with Elsa's practiced ease.

She'd tried to curtail her consumption. She'd tell herself she'd only have one flute of champagne at a ball or one glass of wine with supper. Sometimes she kept her promise, but more often, one drink had a way of turning into two. The line having been crossed, there seemed little point in stopping at just two.

Why is this so hard? she'd silently wail. *Why is it harder for me than others?* All around her, ladies enjoyed their fair share of inebriating beverages without becoming disastrously drunk.

It isn't harder for you, said Shame. Or Guilt. She could never tell those two harpies apart. *It's just that you're so much weaker than everyone else.*

"I'm sorry," she cried, lifting her head, strands of hair clinging to the mess of her face. "I can't. I can't." Her lungs heaved fast and faster, her head growing giddy.

Arms were around her then. Not Sheri's, as she'd have expected, but Mr. Wynford-Scott's. Those great, long arms of his held her together when she should have fallen to pieces. He brought her to his chest without a hint of the anger or recrimination she could have expected from him, by all rights.

"I've tried to stop," she confessed into the protective shield of his embrace. "I can't. I can't. There's something wrong with me."

The tears fell hot and fast now, beyond Guilt and Shame, as her darkest truth was brought to light. She was broken. Wrong. Weak. A failure as a wife and an embarrassment to her friends.

"You *can* do this." Mr. Wynford-Scott's lips murmured against her ear, the rumble of his voice a soothing vibration.

"Elsa." It was Sheri speaking then. She opened her eyes as far as her tear-swollen lids would allow. Was surprised to find that Mr. Wynford-Scott had relocated to the window seat and that she was cradled in his lap.

Sheri's hand rested lightly on his wife's back. "We've taken the liberty of asking Mr. Dewhurst to join us."

Elsa's puffy eyes widened at the name of the surgeon, another of Sheri's Honorables. "Why? No! I don't … Sheri, please send him away." She didn't notice she'd begun trembling until Norman's hand rubbed soothing circles on her back.

"What could he do for me?" she pressed. "Send me to an asylum?" It had happened to one of Elsa's older cousins, who had been sent away for unspecified "female trouble" and never returned. "No, Sheri, please. I … I just want to go home, to Berrybrook. Some time in the country will do me good."

Sheri and Arcadia exchanged a look. Elsa felt her temper start to rise. "Well, it isn't your decision, is it? You can't come into my home and start ordering me about, Sheridan Zouche."

"We only want what's best for you," he insisted.

"And who's to say what's best for me, better than I?" she rejoined.

Eyes wide in an expression of disbelief, Sheri shook his head. "My dear, only moments ago, you behaved like a starving dog going after the world's last cutlet, trying to get your hands on that flask. Elsa …" He raised a hand, then let it fall uselessly to his side.

His silence said what words could not. She was not fit to make decisions regarding her own care. Maybe it was true. Shame—she was sure this time—raised her voice in agreement.

"Knock, knock," a voice said, rather than did. "This seems an opportune moment to announce my unwanted presence." Mr. Brandon Dewhurst smiled genially. "No one is ever happy to see the surgeon," he explained. "Grimly relieved, perhaps, but never happy."

"And have you brought along your wife, as well, Mr. Dewhurst?" Elsa asked testily. "My bedchamber is as busy as Bond Street."

The dark-haired man set his leather satchel of horrors on the foot of her bed and drew off his gloves. "I'm afraid Lorna couldn't join me today, as there was an emergency with a tenant out at Elmwood. But she sends her compliments, my lady."

Elsa nodded once, her neck stiff. "My compliments to Mrs. Dewhurst," she returned, chagrined by the gentle reminder of Lorna Dewhurst's kindness. Elsa really was not in control of herself. Her manners had fled, along with her composure.

Foster chose that moment to reappear, probably wagering Elsa would not flay the maid for her defection in the presence of so many witnesses. Her arrival seemed to serve as a cue to Sheri and Arcadia to slip out of the room. With a final squeeze of reassurance, Norman slid Elsa from his lap to the window seat cushion and followed his friends, leaving only Elsa and Mr. Dewhurst behind, with Foster discreetly chaperoning from the dressing room, where she began gathering up the cosmetics Elsa had flung about.

"I couldn't help but overhear your earlier discussion." The surgeon pulled up a chair to sit facing her. "You're right, madam, that leaving Town would be for the best."

An anxious flutter buffeted her ribs. "Not an asylum?" she ventured.

He shook his head. "Your own home will be fine. Country air will do you good, and the quiet will be helpful. Rest, daily exercise, these things will see you through this crisis. As well as abstaining from any alcoholic beverage whatsoever, naturally."

He made it sound ... pleasant, almost, as if she was just going to recuperate from a minor illness. "It cannot be that easy."

His lips turned up in a humorless smile. "I said nothing about easy. The cure is simple, my lady, but never doubt that it is hard work—perhaps the most difficult undertaking of your life." He leaned forward, resting elbows on his knees. "But hear me speak,

Lady Fay: You are fighting for your life. Habitual drunkards are given to diseases of the liver and have trouble recovering from illnesses. Not to mention an alarming tendency to bleed to death. I shouldn't like to think of you attempting childbirth in this state. How old are you, Lady Fay?"

"Nine-and-twenty," she woodenly reported. "Assessing my risk of falling with child?"

He chuffed a laugh. "Rather considering the harm you may have already done your liver and the chances it has of recovering."

Silence fell between them. There seemed little to say. Other than her womb, Elsa had never given much thought to the state of her inner organs. The only liver she had passing acquaintance with was whichever one appeared on her plate. She'd no knowledge of the function of the one inside her. To think: all the time she'd been chugging spirits with abandon, she'd been abusing the poor thing.

Guilt, this time, had the honor of twisting Elsa's middle.

"This isn't a moral failing, you know," Mr. Dewhurst stated.

"Then why does it feel like one?"

He tilted his head. "I was in the Army. Spain. Saw too many good men fall prey to opium and the bottle to ever think such an affliction is a character flaw."

"Then what is it?" she asked, shaking her head slowly.

Mr. Dewhurst lifted one shoulder in a shrug. "It's a condition, Lady Fay. An affliction. Of the mind, I believe, though others of my colleagues hold differently."

"Like madness, you mean?" she asked pointedly.

His lips tightened. "If you like, although not everything that afflicts the mind is madness. You're coming back around to asylums, aren't you?"

She was acutely aware of her wild appearance, of her bedraggled hair and bare feet and white night rail stained with tea and other, unmentionable fluids. She ached and sweat, and she wanted to sleep forever. Perhaps she belonged in an asylum, after all.

"Go home, Lady Fay," the surgeon instructed. "Rest and recover your health, but keep yourself occupied. Reading, charity, gardening—whatever activities you prefer. It's going to be difficult, the early days, especially. You will feel sick, and you will want to drink like you want your next breath, but you must resist the temptation."

Even as he spoke of it, her throat dried and she felt the familiar impulse for a sip of something strong. She swept her tongue across her lips. "For how long must I persist? When shall I be cured?" It would be hard to abstain, but she could do it. A few months of convalescence, and by spring, she'd be back in Town and able to enjoy her claret like everyone else, like a sane person.

"Unfortunately, there is no known cure for drunkenness. The best way to avoid suffering a relapse of your condition is to avoid drinking for the rest of your life."

Elsa's heart stopped. The rest of her life? When Mr. Dewhurst had spoken of fresh air and exercise, it had sounded easy. When he brought up the terrible longing she'd have to confront, she felt daunted, but determined. But the rest of her life? She quailed at the prospect. How could she ever hope to succeed?

She must have spoken her fear aloud, for the surgeon took her hand and gave it a sympathetic squeeze. "It must be done day by day, my lady. Hour by hour, and sometimes minute by minute. It seems impossible now, but with time, you will become accustomed to a life of sobriety. When did you last imbibe?"

She swiped the back of her wrist at the corner of her eye, surprised to find her eyes wet again. *Hopeless*, Guilt and Shame wailed in unison. *You cannot do this impossible thing. Why even try?*

Why, indeed. Foster may have confiscated all of Elsa's liquor, but there was bound to be more in the kitchen. If not, any inn, tavern, public house, or apothecary could sell her what she needed.

Her mind already on procuring her next bottle, she shifted impatiently, willing the interview at an end. "About eleven o'clock last night, I believe."

Mr. Dewhurst regarded his pocket watch. "Fifteen hours already without a drink. Can you make it twenty-four hours?"

She blinked in surprise. Fifteen hours? When had she last gone so long without alcohol? When had she ever bothered to quantify her time without? She smiled down at her hands, absurdly delighted by this information. The tiniest seed of gumption found an infinitesimal plot of fertile soil somewhere at the base of her spine and began to germinate. She straightened, her back a little firmer than it had been since she'd awakened.

"Yes, Mr. Dewhurst," she promised, "I can make it twenty-four hours."

Chapter Three

Ensconced in her sitting room with a cup of tea warming her hands, Elsa watched a thin rain drizzle down gray windowpanes. In the small fireplace, the wood cracked and popped and hissed, the sounds a cheerful rebuttal of the morning's gloom.

She'd gone to bed early last night, figuring it would be easier not to drink if she was asleep. And so she'd crossed the finish line of Mr. Dewhurst's twenty-four-hour challenge without even trying, and set off on her second sober lap around the sun. By the time she awoke, she was already seven hours to the good. Maybe not drinking wouldn't be as hard as she feared.

"Lady Fay. Good morning."

She turned from the window. Yesterday's overabundance of emotions had subsided, for Mr. Wynford-Scott was once more the placid fellow to whom she was accustomed.

"May I offer you tea? Anything to eat?"

He waved off her offer. "Thank you, but we should be on our way."

Carefully, she set her cup into its saucer on the side table. "You needn't do this, sir. I'm quite capable of traveling home by myself. I've made the trip unaccompanied on countless occasions."

"Brandon was clear it would be better if you had … company."

A minder, he meant. A keeper. Someone to ensure she did not consume any of the alcohol on offer in the inns she'd be staying in during the two nights she'd be on the road. Foster had already written ahead to have Berrybrook Cottage emptied of inebriants, but the road was fraught with liquid peril.

Sheridan had suggested Mr. Dewhurst for the task, but the surgeon had obligations to his patients.

"I'll go." Norman had stepped forward with the bleak courage of a soldier volunteering for a suicide mission.

She'd tried to put him off, but Mr. Dewhurst endorsed the idea, in turn winning the support of Sheri and Arcadia. Elsa hadn't the fortitude to put up much of a fight.

Now that the moment had arrived, she felt anew all the reasons why she did not want to spend three days traveling with the gentle giant. Bad enough she was deemed incapable of looking after herself, but Norman Wynford-Scott had seen Elsa at her absolute worst on that terrible night.

Looking at him now, standing there so calm and sensible, he was Guilt and Shame incarnate, a physical manifestation to remind Elsa of her myriad sins.

Clasping her hands around a knee, she worked her jaw from side to side. "Foster will look after me," she said.

"Foster is just one person," Norman returned. "She cannot be expected to tend you 'round the clock." He lifted a brow. His eyes were a soft brownish green, she noted. "Furthermore—"

"Oh, there's more?"

"Foster has not managed your behavior very well to this point."

Elsa drew back. "She's my maid. It's not her place—"

"Precisely." His eyes flared with an excitement she'd never seen in him before. "It is *not* her place. Foster is but a servant."

How dare he? What did Norman know of Foster's time in Elsa's service, of the six long years the faithful abigail had dried Elsa's tears when her courses arrived, or of the bruises she had tended without comment?

"If you demand drink from her, will Foster not feel obligated to carry out your wishes, fearing for her livelihood?"

Queasily, Elsa realized Norman was employing some courtroom tactic upon her. She'd fallen into his rhetorical trap. "I wouldn't ask that of her."

"So you say," he snapped, "and it is to be hoped you would not. But what if you procure a bottle for yourself? Would you tolerate Foster taking it away from you?"

"Well, I—"

"And if you find yourself in the taproom," he pressed, looming ever closer, one slow step at a time, "cozied up to a glass of your favorite scotch, and Foster suggests you remove yourself from the room, what would you say then?" He towered above her now, the shadow of his large body cutting her off from the light and warmth of the fireplace.

She lifted a hand. "I would say—"

"In fact, Lady Fay," his voice rose, reverberating through every particle of air in the sitting room, "you don't know *what* you would say. Before two nights ago, would you have imagined yourself capable of setting fire to one of the Inns of Court?"

Her cheeks flushed hot. "That was an *accident*," she pressed, stomping her foot for emphasis. "And if you hadn't—"

"But it happened, did it not?"

She pressed her lips together, her chin trembling.

His nostrils flared. His lips quirked in the smallest of smiles. "And so, Lady Fay, we return to Foster. Despite your stated intentions, none of us—you, perhaps, least of all—can know of a certain how you will behave once you are actually confronted with the object of your temptation. Foster is in an untenable predicament: If she capitulates to your demands, she will further your ruin; but if she defies you, she risks dismissal, leaving her without employment and you to drown in your own folly."

That would never happen. Elsa would never send Foster away; Foster wouldn't let her. The maid's loyalty ran deep. But when her maid had poured sweet almond oil into Elsa's bath to soothe the welts on her thighs, there had been no conflict of loyalty. Her place was with her lady, providing for her needs in the face of a difficult marriage. However, Elsa herself was the villain now—as well as the one who still needed protecting. So to whom did Foster owe her loyalty: Elsa the drunkard, or the Elsa struggling to break free of that demon?

After allowing his statement a moment to sink in, Norman spoke again. "But I, Elsa," he said quietly—it was the first time he'd ever said her given name, and the sound of it in his deep voice trickled over the nape of her neck— "have no such fears. I will refuse you. I will defy you. I will insist you leave the taproom, and if you do not, I will remove you bodily and let bystanders gawp their fill, damn your pride and mine."

Truth rang in his words, even as she recoiled from the image he evoked. He meant what he said and was more than capable of carrying out his threat. If she put up a fight, he could easily put a stop to it by plucking her up in those great paws of his, the same ones that had held her so tenderly just the day before.

She was defeated and they both knew it, but she could not allow him to think she would be so easily vanquished. "You sound as if you quite relish the idea of thwarting me, Mr. Wynford-Scott. Do you wish to punish me? Is that what this is about?"

He tilted his head thoughtfully, as though giving her question due consideration. "For what would I wish to punish you, Lady Fay?"

Just that quickly, he'd talked her into another corner. She was exposed, her misdeeds reflected in his steady gaze.

Elsa turned from those damning eyes to pour herself a sherry. Her feet stuttered when her eyes landed upon the bare spot on the sideboard where the crystal decanter had been. Her throat convulsed. It was just that simple—stunningly so—to forget, to go wrong again. Her eyes would not leave that blank space. Guilt and Shame crowed in triumph.

Silently he came to stand behind her, his warmth on her back echoing the heat blooming on her cheekbones.

Finally, she tore her gaze loose with a sharp turn of her head. "Let us be on our way," she said.

• • •

The problem with travel was that it was boring. Reading in a carriage nauseated Elsa, and she'd abandoned her needlework after she'd stabbed her finger when the coach hit the first big rut in the road. Foster had never been one for idle chat, and so Elsa had nothing but empty hours and nothing to do but think.

For a woman in her position, she soon learned, thinking was dangerous. Inevitably, her mind turned to drink. She sat with her craving and came to know it intimately, felt the way it affected her body. It wasn't just a thirst in her throat and mouth; her hand itched to curl around a heavy tumbler of whiskey, and her bones felt wrong inside her skin. Too, she was afflicted with a hunger that gnawed painfully at the underside of her ribs. At breakfast this morning, she'd fallen upon a plate of scones like she'd not eaten food in a month and devoured the entire platter. Already, just three hours later, she was ravenous again. Visions of oven-fresh loaves with crackling crusts and dripping with butter had her mouth watering. Or maybe something sweet, a pot of chocolate or cake swimming in ganache ...

Elsa's toes tapped anxiously against the floor. Her palms went clammy. She flexed and released her fingers. From the facing seat, Foster eyed her carefully. "My lady?"

"I'd like to walk, I think." Elsa pounded the roof. The carriage lurched to a stop, and she hopped out, her foot skating on a slick of mud. She caught herself on the coach door, then pushed away, and began a determined march.

"My lady!" Foster called after her. "Come back! You'll take a chill."

"Drive on," Elsa instructed her puzzled coachman. "Wait for me at the next posting inn."

"But that's not for three miles!" he protested.

"Drive. On," she ground out through clenched teeth.

"Go on," said a deep voice accompanied by the steady plod of hooves. "I'll accompany Lady Fay."

Pulling his behemoth of a horse to a halt with a quiet "Whoa there," Norman dismounted. Because of his considerable size, he'd claimed sitting in a carriage for any length of time was uncomfortable, and so he'd ridden the entire trip thus far.

The coach rumbled away, leaving them in the middle of a road bordered on both sides by desolate fields impaled by the stiff, dead remains of the previous season's wheat, cut down and left to mummify in the autumn sun before moldering and melting into nothing before next spring.

She felt his gaze, but could not bear to meet his eyes. "Are you all right?" he asked, his voice careful.

Suddenly, her throat was tight and her eyes were full and it hurt to breathe. *Everything* hurt. No longer pleasantly muffled with drink, her senses were overwhelmed by the world—the earthen stink of rot and shit rising from the fields, the wheezing bray of an unseen donkey, even the way the cotton of her shift grated against her sensitized skin—and cried out for her to *do something* to make the agitation end.

There was one solution only, and it was no solution at all. How was this all-consuming need her life? How was this *her*?

A keening cry-moan rose in her throat. Norman turned her around, softly shushing her. "There now," he said, tucking her against his side, his arm heavy across her shoulders like Christ's own cross. "Brandon said you need exercise, yes? And you've been cooped up in that coach for more than a day. A good walk is just the thing. I should have thought of it myself."

She dashed a hand across her eye and laughed bitterly. "More than anything, I need—"

"A walk," Norman insisted. "Fresh air."

His vehemence caused her to look up at him. His eyes—how had she never noticed what a pleasing color they were? more gray-green than hazel, she decided—held a note of pleading, a soft counterpoint to the resolute set of his chin.

His horse peered over his shoulder at her as if in agreement with his master. Slowly, the great chestnut head eased forward, velvet lips quivering, and began to delicately nibble at the brim of her straw bonnet.

"Apple, no!" Norman shouted, aghast. "Leave Lady Fay alone, you bounder."

Elsa laughed, all at once feeling lighter than she had in days. "That monster's name is Apple?"

Norman gave her a rueful smile, boyish and endearing. "He came with it." He wrapped the reins around one hand and patted the horse's neck with the other. "He used to be a draught horse at a brewery, and that's what the stable master called him. He was already low from the death of his teammate, Dumpling. Didn't wish to worsen matters by changing his name."

"Apple and Dumpling." She tossed Norman a wicked grin. "I don't suppose the stable master meant to pay tribute to his favorite pastry." She took one step forward and then another. If she was going to walk three miles, she had best begin.

"By no means," Norman agreed amiably, falling in beside her, shortening his stride to keep her pace. "All the horses at the brewery were named for parts of the female anatomy."

"Really?" Elsa asked, reaching across to pat Apple's shoulder. "How charming."

He laughed at her wry tone. "Indeed. Besides Apple and his friend, there were Bubby and Diddey, and Bumbo and Water-mill."

"The creative spirit will find a way, I suppose," she drawled. Elsa slanted a look up at her companion. "You speak to me as if I were a man."

Delightfully, Norman's ears reddened. His eyes cut to her, then bounced away. "Beg your pardon, Lady Fay. I should be more mindful."

She scoffed. "Please, Norman. You don't mind if I call you Norman, do you? Wynford-Scott is quite the mouthful, and I'd like to think you and I have become friends over the last number of months." She tucked a strand of hair behind her ear. "It's refreshing, is all I mean. Besides Sheri, you're the only man who speaks frankly to me outside of bed. Social niceties grow wearisome."

The silence emanating from the giant man carried a quality of alarm. He cleared his throat, readjusting his hold on Apple's lead. "Still," he blurted at last, "I know better, and I shall do better in future, my lady. Elsa."

Smiling, Elsa lifted her face to the sun. The demon nipped at her heels, but she could outrun it. She was strong. And if she grew weak along the way, she knew the man at her side was strong enough to carry her through.

• • •

After their trek, Elsa and Norman rejoined the coach at an inn, where she guzzled water and stuffed herself silly with roasted potatoes, rolls, and plum pudding. Back in the carriage, she fell asleep almost instantly, not stirring again until they'd stopped for the night.

The supper laid out in the private dining room held no appeal, and the sight of yet another pot of tea made her stomach turn. Maybe a glass of watered wine or a mug of small beer would be permissible, just to have with her food. Those beverages were mild enough for children. She couldn't see any harm ...

"The kitchen is preparing hot cider for us. Fresh, not fermented."

From across the table, Norman regarded her with that steady gaze.

Were her thoughts so obvious? Guilt and Shame, those wicked twins, stirred in her belly. "There's no need for them to trouble themselves on my—our—account."

He shrugged, his massive shoulders rising and falling like a gentle swell of the sea.

It was a good mulled cider, as it happened, and she sipped slowly at her mugful. Of the food, however, she partook only a little. Soon enough, the room felt suffocating and she wanted only to get away. Norman's efforts at conversation put her teeth on edge.

"Anything amiss, Elsa?"

Lips pinched, she glanced at Foster, whose attention was determinedly fixed on the pigeon on her plate. Norman shouldn't be so familiar with her in front of Foster. It would give the maid the wrong impression. Lord knew Foster was used to Elsa bringing home the occasional paramour and always exercised utmost discretion, but this wasn't that. She wasn't sure why it mattered, but it did. It just did.

His brows lowered. "You look a bit peakish."

Elsa touched her upper lip, surprised to find her fingers trembling and her skin damp with perspiration. Just like this morning, her pulse galumphed inside her chest and beat against her temples from within. Her hair hurt.

"If you'll excuse me, Mr. Wynford-Scott." She shot to her feet, and he quickly fumbled to stand. Foster, too, got up. "No, no," she waved the lady's maid back. "Finish your supper, Foster. I'm fine, I just ..."

Nothing to say, she turned sharply, feeling their eyes boring into her back as she left the dining room, cutting off their questioning gazes by firmly shutting the door behind her.

The stairs she had to take to reach her room were adjacent to the common room, at this time of day filled with travelers and locals enjoying a pint or glass of their favorite libations.

Her belly was a hard knot of wanting and dread as she approached. The innkeeper stood at a wooden barrel, pulling on the tap to fill a mug. He gave Elsa a welcoming smile. She was choking for want of a drink. Just one.

With a strangled cry, she turned and darted up the stairs, running all the way to her room. Slamming the door behind her, she leaned her back against it and cried.

The night did not improve. Foster helped her bathe and change into her nightclothes before removing to her own cot in the little dressing room, but sleep was out of the question for Elsa. She'd slept all afternoon and thought she might crawl out of her skin, besides. She paced the length of the small chamber, back and forth, back and forth, desperate to reclaim the relief she'd found earlier while walking with Norman.

Elsa twisted her fingers tight and tighter, trying to wring from them the need to touch a bottle. Then her hands were in her hair at her temples, clenching, pulling, and seeking to distract herself with pain.

Distraction. Distraction. What was it Mr. Dewhurst had said? Something about keeping herself busy, distracting herself with her favorite activities. She barked a bitter laugh. Her favorite activities were drinking and fucking. One was forbidden, and as for the other—

She halted in her pacing. As for the other ... Norman found her physically appealing. A woman intuited these things, but she'd seen the evidence for herself when he'd watched her dance on the tabletop at the Christmas revels, seen desire writ plain across his face. As for her, she found him intriguing. Compelling. He was so tall. Enormous, really. It would be pointless to deny her lusty mind had pondered his manly asset, wondered if its size was commensurate to the rest of him.

Her lower belly quivered, and her nipples perked against her thin night rail. "Oh, God," she moaned, lifting her hands to her cheeks. This was hellish. Norman Wynford-Scott? Was she really going to do this? Then again, if she did not, how would she live through the endless hours stretching from here to dawn? If something did not give, Elsa would find herself downstairs gulping the first potent drink she could get her hands on; of this, she was certain.

But, Norman was ... well, he was kind and considerate and noble of spirit and ... a bit boring, really. So upright and proper all the time. Except when he made her laugh with his story about a brewery with a stable full of horses with naughty names, of course. And when his voice rang with command, there was something rather thrilling about it. All the same, he didn't seem the sort to countenance a tumble in a roadside inn with a notoriously immoral woman.

Elsa swallowed. Drew a deep breath. Now that the idea of sex was in her head, her body thrummed in anticipation. She would take care of her own needs, was all, as she'd done many and many a night. Decision made, she crossed to the bed. Her knee sank into the mattress.

A soft knock. "Elsa? Lady Fay?"

Her lids slid home on a soft groan. It was as inevitable as that first snifter of brandy turning into a second.

She jerked open the door, and there he was in only dark breeches and a rumpled white shirt. How broad his shoulders were, she marveled, and how wide his chest. She could spend hours exploring it, give her mouth an occupation beyond demanding liquor. Her heart hammered.

Norman's gaze slipped down her length, then pulled back to her face. She'd neglected to put on a wrapper before opening the door, she realized.

"I just wanted to look in on you," he said in a low voice. "You left supper so abruptly, and—forgive me, I didn't mean to eavesdrop—but I'm just in the next room, and I heard you pacing and crying even, I thought. Is there ... may I be of assistance?"

Without allowing herself time to think, she grabbed his hand and tugged him to his room. When they were inside, she shut the door, and tipped her forehead against the beveled panel. "I'm suffering. I didn't know it would be this hard."

Behind her, he sighed. "What can I do to help, Elsa?"

"I need ..." Turning, she let her eyes travel meaningfully over his body, from tip to toe. He had a hand buried in the muss of his brown hair, cupping the back of his skull. He was utterly delectable. How had she never seen it before? "I need a distraction." She sauntered to close the distance, allowing her hips to sway and her hand to trace the valley between her breasts. "Distract me, Norman."

His eyes widened. "You mean ..." His tongue darted out, a flash of pink swiping across his bottom lip. "I've a deck of cards." He jerked his chin toward his valise standing by the foot of his bed. She saw his pulse leap in his neck, knew he wasn't unaffected.

"I want you to take me to bed," she stated bluntly.

He grimaced as if in pain, kept his eyes averted.

"I want to undress for you, and I want you to undress for me." She plucked at the shirt tucked into his waistband. Norman drew a sharp breath, but made no motion to stop her. Rising on tiptoe, Elsa dropped her voice to a sultry whisper. "I want to look my fill at this most impressive body of yours, and then I want you to put it to good use."

"You said you were suffering," he accused, his voice strangled.

She gave a laugh-cry. "I am. God, you don't know how much. I need ... *I need*, Norman." Her fingers closed on his bicep. "The wanting is driving me mad."

"Wanting for drink?"

"Yes, yes, but you, too. It's all tangled up, don't you see? Just a dreadful ache that's killing me. I swear to God, Norman, I'll be drunk or dead by morning if I can't have *something*."

Frowning, he took a step back. "This isn't fair, Elsa. You can't lay that at my feet: If I don't do this with you, you'll drink?"

"Would it be such a hardship?" she cried. Hands shaking as if she were palsied, she managed to untie the ribbon at her neck and pull her nightgown over her head. She swept her arms wide, presenting her naked form. "Does this not please you? I have seen you look at me with longing. Will you stand there and tell me you do not want me?"

For a terrible moment, she feared he would tell her exactly that. His eyes caught on her raspberry nipples, swept the curve of her hip, halted on the triangle of black hair at the apex of her thighs. But he said nothing, gave no hint of his thoughts.

Then he groaned, the sound rumbling in the depths of his massive chest, echoing her own pain. "Damn it, Elsa, yes," he rasped. "Yes, I want you. There's not a man who looks at you and doesn't want you. Is that what you want to hear?" His pupils were wide, nearly obliterating the soft green of his irises. With jerky movements, he fisted his shirt, pulled it over his head, and dropped it to the floor.

Elsa's lips parted on a soft gasp. Her eyes were level with his sternum, and she had only to raise them the barest fraction to see flat, berry-brown nipples surrounded by a little fringe of tawny hair. He was well formed, obviously took care of himself, but not overly muscled like some of her prior lovers had been. The skin of his torso was nearly as pale as her own, making the thatch of hair on his upper chest and the line of it beginning at his navel show all the more starkly. His belly pooched just a tad, and she remembered that this was not a man with hour upon hour of idle time to spend riding or fencing or boxing. Norman was a scholar, his days filled with whatever it was barristers-in-training did.

Altogether, he gave the impression of strength and reliability and, maybe too, a touch of vulnerability. It was the skin, she decided, so white she could see the blue of his veins in places. Like the inside of his elbow there. Touching him would be heaven, heavy and solid, with just enough softness to sink her hands into as he rode her. Or she rode him.

She reached out to the indentation below his ribs. His hand covered hers, removed it from his person. "Elsa, we can't," he said. "You're not well."

Her eyes snapped to his. "I am as well as I can hope to be— perhaps as well as I'll ever be. Am I too damaged for you?"

"No, that's not what I—" Both hands delved into his hair this time, and he growled. "That's not what I mean."

"Well, then what do you mean?" she pressed. When he gave no reply, she retrieved her night rail. Coming here like this had been a mistake. She kept her eyes downcast, not wanting him to see the pain his rejection caused. She turned to go, heedless of the fact that her clothes dangled from her hand.

A grumbled curse, the sense of movement, and then his arm was around her, pulling her back tight to his chest. "Don't go," he whispered, cupping her breast in his palm. His other hand ripped the night rail from her grasp and dashed it to the floor. And then his hand was in her braid, wrapping it around his fist as he'd done Apple's reins earlier in the day. He tugged her head to the side, exposing the sensitive place where her heart's beat throbbed, and he covered it with his mouth. Just a brush of lips at first, but then he tentatively tongued her there.

Elsa moaned. He was so strong, sheltering her in the curve of his great body. His hand shifted on her breast to circle fingertips around her nipple, then moved to the other side to palm and pluck. The hard ridge of his erection pressed between her buttocks, and Elsa canted her hips, undulating to stroke his length.

Norman's grip tightened on her breast; his breath was hot in her ear. Then his hands were on her hips, and he was holding her even closer as he pressed against her, a sort of helpless moan escaping his throat.

Elsa brought one of his hands to her belly. "Touch me," she pleaded.

"I haven't …" he started. "I don't know … That is, I've never …"

Elsa turned in his arms, took in the desperate, lust-crazed look of the man, eyelids heavy and hair tangled about his ears.

"Never? No one?" The seam of his breeches must have been sorely tested by the heavy press of his impressive cockstand. His chest heaved like a bellows, and his hands gripped her waist. He was utterly scrumptious, and the notion that no woman had yet laid claim to him boggled her mind.

He shook his head. "Not that I haven't wanted to." Color crept up his chest. "I mean, there have been—"

"It doesn't matter," she assured him. The last thing she wanted to do was make him feel self-conscious about himself. "I'll tell you what I want, where I'd like you to touch me. But you must promise to do the same and tell me what you'd like."

He nodded.

She smiled. "Kiss me, Norman. Please."

His mouth covered hers, and she reached her arms around his neck—and it *was* a reach. Even though he bent low, she was obliged to stretch long, arching her full length against him and relishing the way he planted his hands just so on her back, gentle but firm. He explored her mouth, and she drank him in, sucking hard on his tongue.

She broke away, panting. Needy flames lapped up her legs and between her thighs, and Elsa was going to combust herself if she did not get the release she craved. "Here," she said, pulling him to the bed. This would be easier for them both if they were horizontal. She climbed onto the mattress on hands and knees, giving him a good view of her arse and aching flesh.

When she rolled onto her back, he followed her down. She took his hand and brought it between her legs. "Like this," she said, guiding his fingers between the slick folds, rocking her mound up to meet his palm. Then she released his wrist and let him explore on his own.

"You feel incredible," Norman rasped. "So soft. Wet. And hot. God, I've never felt anything so hot."

He gave her a firm stroke, and Elsa purred, then arched off the bed when he brushed over her clitoris.

He made a fretful sound.

"No, no, so good," she rushed to explain. "Some men go their whole lives without ever touching a woman there. Just take care. Easy does—oh!" He pressed down lightly as he rubbed a circle, then ran his finger once more down the length of her wet slit.

"Inside me, Norman. I need it inside." Her entire body shook, desperate for release.

His finger pressed inward, giving her a hint of the delicious stretch she craved.

"Now," she said between pants, "use your thumb to rub here again while you— God, you're a quick study!"

He chuckled, the corners of his eyes crinkling with humor and lust, and something in her chest melted, even as she pulled her knees up and widened her legs. "Another. Two."

He complied at once, her clever man, filling her more, giving her more of that glorious slow burn. She tipped her hips and he met her rhythm and the flood rose up inside her, drowning out everything else: her anguish and her wanting for drink and even the hateful voices of Shame and Guilt. There was only Norman, sure and steady as he touched her exactly the way she needed. She pulled his mouth to hers, tongues darting, teeth nipping. All the while, the beautiful agony rose and filled, the pressure building more and more until she could not contain it and she came, the overwhelming pleasure knocking her legs out from under her, catching her in a riptide of ecstasy that tumbled around and through her and went on and on, until she was gasping, drowning in pleasure.

And when it was over, Elsa felt scoured on the inside, raw and tender but clean all the same. Clean and pink and maybe even a little bit new.

He nuzzled her hair, kissed her damp forehead. Then the soft green of his eyes clouded and a frown twitched at his lips. "Why are you crying, Elsa? Did I hurt you?"

She'd not noticed it until he asked, but now she felt the tears flowing down her temples. She cupped his jaw and exhaled a watery laugh. "Not in the least. That was gorgeous, Norman. Exquisite. It just takes some people that way, the little death."

He still looked uncertain so she added, reckless but true, "But not for me. Never before. That was beyond anything I've ever experienced."

She saw in his eyes as the fog of doubt lifted. Belief and pride kindled in its stead, took root, grew until he was grinning down at her like a deliriously happy puppy, and she couldn't help but return his smile. Where she had been crushed by the oppressive weight of her demons, now she felt buoyant, free.

Affectionately, she pulled his head to her chest. She toyed with his brown hair, humming softly to herself. When had she last been so sated, felt so utterly relaxed? And only from the ministrations of his hand. Oh, but she couldn't wait to experience the rest of him.

For the time being, though, she was content to simply rest beside him, to feel the rasp of his whiskers on her breast and the warm blanket of his chest pressed to her body. Her knee tucked snug between his thighs. And his arms—those marvelous arms— wrapped about her and hugged her close, offering sanctuary where the desolation of her addiction held no sway.

"I haven't forgotten my part of the bargain," she promised, sleepy. "Only give me a moment to recover."

His reply was lost in the sleep that abruptly took her, a rumble in his chest that melted into her dreams.

• • •

Elsa awoke to familiar sounds: Foster neatly arranging the tea tray on the bedside table, then crossing to the window and crisply parting the drapes. The light was weak, early yet, but Elsa didn't mind being stirred. She stretched, long and comfortable, then opened her eyes. Her stomach dropped.

This was not her room. She'd come to Norman's bed last night.

"Good morning, my lady." Foster's neutral tone betrayed nothing, but her careful blankness was itself a condemnation. Foster was only so assiduously without mien when Elsa had spent the night with a gentleman.

Sitting up, Elsa saw, on the corner of the tray, a small bottle of vinegar and a sponge—a precaution against falling with child. Usually, she appreciated Foster's quiet competence in these matters, but at the sight of those tools, a cold pile of worms writhed in her belly. Last night, she didn't ... Norman hadn't ...

But of course Foster would believe they had—anyone would. Norman must have told Foster where Elsa was, but he was gentleman enough not to divulge what they had or had not done. Now Foster would judge Norman as no different from any of her past lovers. Her abigail's loyalty was such that she believed every man Elsa'd brought home over the last four years had taken advantage of a lonely widow. She didn't understand what it had meant to Elsa to reclaim this part of herself, to be a sensual woman and not just a failed broodmare.

Yet knowing that she'd diminished Norman's reputation, even if only in the eyes of her maid, hurt.

Guilt and Shame lifted their voices in terrible harmony. The bitches. The creeping tendrils of their song wrapped around the solace she'd found last night and pulled it to the ground. Last night, she'd behaved like a cat in heat, driven mad by her need for distraction, for release. She'd thought her days of inappropriate drunken behavior were behind her, but it seemed she did not even need the catalyst of alcohol to make a spectacle of herself. On the periphery of her consciousness, she was always aware of the unspoken threat of the asylum. How could she explain herself to Norman in a way that did not make her sound crazed?

After preparing for the day, she made her way outside, her dread of facing Norman causing her palms to perspire in her gloves. She found him in the stable yard, securing an unsaddled Apple's lead to the rear of the coach while the beast churned the ground with one shaggy hoof. Norman was dressed in a dark jacket, nankeen breeches, and camel waistcoat. His well-worn riding boots must have necessitated an acre of leather to cobble, she mused. His attire, serviceable but without pretension to fashion, stood in stark contrast to her own emerald traveling costume of sumptuous velvet.

"Do you not ride today?"

She needn't have bothered worrying about meeting his gaze, for he steadfastly refused to meet hers. "I've given Apple a hard go of it the last couple days. He could use a break," Norman said, his eyes fixed somewhere over her shoulder. "We've only a few hours' travel to Berrybrook, I believe?"

"Yes."

"Well then, I'll cozy up with the driver for the duration of our journey."

The driver? He'd rather cram himself onto the edge of the driver's box than share the carriage with her?

Did he believe himself too good to breathe the same air as a wanton? Or did he fear she would become clinging and simper after his attentions?

Elsa did not *simper* after any man. She raised her chin a notch, forced her mouth into a rictus imitation of a smile. "Last night was great fun, was it not?"

Startled, his eyes jerked to hers before skidding to the side again.

She dropped her voice to a conspiratorial whisper and touched his forearm lightly. "I apologize for falling asleep. You should have woken me. I'd have been happy to service you with my hand. Or mouth. Or any of the rest of me."

His face flushed, then paled, at her deliberately crude words. He looked back and forth, as if to make sure no one overheard.

"Thank you for the very excellent orgasm, Norman. What a good friend you are."

Mouth hard, he jerked a stiff bow. "Lady Fay." Then he strode to the front of the coach and clambered to the driver's seat.

There. She'd saved some face, even if inside she was small and sad.

Hours later, she caught her first glimpse of Berrybrook Cottage from the drive. It was an adorable house, like something from a storybook, with its white walls, dark beams, and a thatched roof topping its two stories. In the springtime, flowers of every sort spilled from the window boxes and filled the garden with a riot of color and scent and bees drunkenly bumbling from blossom to blossom. Even now, with the rest of the garden fast asleep, a rosemary shrub was defiantly green. Mr. or Mrs. Whittle, the caretakers, had hung a bundle of holly sprigs from the door. Cheery puffs of smoke rose from the chimney, cozy and inviting.

When the coach drew to a halt, Foster climbed down. The front door opened. The Whittles spilled out, both of them round and dumpling-faced and darling in their exuberant welcome. Elsa held back. They would have had a letter from Foster, warning them. There would be no alcohol of any sort in the house. Their mistress was a drunkard.

Norman appeared at the door of the coach and offered his hand. With a sigh of resignation, Elsa took it. She accepted a hug from Mrs. Whittle and a bow from her husband and introduced them to Norman. Elsa clung to his arm all the way to the door, but when she went to cross the threshold, he did not budge.

She regarded him in unspoken question.

"I must be on my way."

A knot formed in her throat. Norman had been her stalwart companion these last several days, keeping her sane and sober when nothing else could. She didn't know if she could do this without him. "So soon? But we've only just arrived. Come in," she insisted, "have some tea."

His face was stone. "Thank you, but I've pressing matters to attend in London." He bowed and turned, then hesitated. "Good luck, Elsa," he said over his shoulder. "God be with you." And then he was striding back to the carriage, retrieving his saddle from the coach, and readying Apple for departure.

Elsa blinked. Abandoned, she went into her house to battle her demons alone.

Chapter Four

Elsa made a tally mark. Her sixty-seventh. The brief line, glistening wet, represented another twenty-four hours without drink. Inspired by Mr. Dewhurst, she'd begun keeping count in her journal the day after arriving at Berrybrook. Each night she fell into bed exhausted from waging a battle no one else could see or understand, with nothing to show for it. Marking the days on paper provided Elsa something she could look at and hold, a meager token of triumph. Because her eleven o'clock finish line came after she'd gone to bed most nights, she'd taken to adding to her reckoning first thing in the morning.

She watched the ink dry, the glossy black gradually becoming dull. "There," she whispered as the last bead of moisture sank into the paper. Proof that she'd accomplished something yesterday. Not drinking had been the sum of Monday's achievements—was the only thing she managed far too often—but it was something. It was hers. She had brought her drunkenness to heel and kept her foot on its throat with grim determination.

That she felt her boot was on her own throat was a philosophical quandary she tried not to dwell too much upon.

Besides, today would be better. Though spring was still a long way off, a turn in the weather had lifted the temperature enough that she intended to make the most of it.

After breakfast, Elsa bundled up in her heaviest pelisse, wool cloak, and stoutest boots. She stepped across her threshold, a border she'd crossed but infrequently these last months. Outside, she drew a deep breath, thrilling at the prickle of cold air in her lungs. It enlivened her, proved she was still here, still winning the fight. A knot between her shoulder blades eased. *You see, you are getting better*, she told herself.

Though not particularly cloudy, the sky had a white, blank look to it, as if the sun was huddled in a blanket somewhere, hoarding its light for itself. The air held the dampness of winter about to come undone. One good swat of warmth would melt all these patches of snow that clung to the shadows and low places, releasing the water to swell the mill creek and the lake. In the meantime, everything was black and brown and a dingy, exhausted white, with a few bursts of green provided by a holly or pine.

She set off without a destination in mind, only wanting to stretch her legs and shake off the dust of a long winter spent tucked inside her house. The gravel drive of Berrybrook Cottage let out onto a narrow track traversed most often by farmers and their cattle, and so she kept a close eye on her footing, skirting icy puddles and droppings. A prickle of unease at the nape of her neck had her moving faster than she had in ages to outrun the unseen foe that dogged her. Two months ago, she would have been too drunk to dodge ruts and sheep pats.

"Can't get me," she hissed into the steel-gray air. Drunkenness would never have her in its power again.

Soon, Elsa had a stitch in her side and her breath came in shallow little huffs that clouded in front of her cold-stung nose. The feeling of being pursued did not dissipate. She pumped her arms, worked her aching legs harder. A forlorn, sheepy bleat sounded from a nearby hill. Sweat popped out on her temples and instantly chilled, causing her to shiver.

Thud. Thud. Thud. Pounding in her ears, as if her heart would punch through her chest.

"Elsa!"

Gasping hard, she clutched her hands to her chest and spun about. A gentleman saddled on an elegant palomino approached, coming from the direction of Berrybrook. Elsa's gaze dropped to the horse's hoofs striking the frosty ground.

Thud. Thud. Thud.

Rolling her eyes at herself, Elsa forced her fists to relax, then lifted a hand in greeting to the rider.

Mr. Oliver Fay was her cousin by marriage, younger brother of Rollo Fay, who had inherited the viscountcy from Elsa's late husband. Oliver brought the handsome gelding to a stop, then swung out of the saddle, caped frock coat swirling around his legs, and sketched a brief bow. Though nearly forty years of age, Oliver retained the trim physique of an avid sportsman. He wore the country gentleman's uniform of buckskin breeches and tall riding boots. A perfectly knotted white cravat peeked above a dark brown waistcoat striped with rich green. Straightening from his bow, he stepped forward to place a brotherly kiss on her cheek.

"Good morning, Oliver, you're looking well."

"And you, my dear." The lines etched around his eyes and brow deepened. "I rode by Berrybrook this morning, determined to flush you from your warren, only to learn you'd already bolted."

"I'm hardly a rabbit to be run to ground, Oliver," she said breezily, waving a dismissive hand. "I fear you're suffering a lack of good hunting, if you think to make quarry of me." She turned away, ensuring her profile would be seen at its elegant, serene best. Completely at odds with the nervous queasiness roiling in her middle. She hadn't expected company. She preferred to be alone.

With a few quick strides, Oliver was back at her side. Gripping his gelding's reins in one hand, he offered her his other arm. As she slipped her hand into the crook of his elbow, Elsa could not help but recall walking just this way with Norman and his behemoth, Apple. She stomped down the pang of regret the memory elicited.

"Come now, Elsa," Oliver coaxed. "I've scarce laid an eye on you since you returned from Town. You've declined all of my invitations, have been 'not at home' most every time I've called.

You didn't even bother attending the Fleck Seed Exchange and Assembly, despite having organized the blasted event the previous three years!"

Elsa felt his slightly-too-close-set eyes upon her. She turned her head, feigning intense interest in lichen clinging to the trunk of a winter-nude elm.

Oliver's complaints tugged at her heart. Whenever Elsa and her husband were in Fleck, Oliver had been a regular fixture while Harvey tended to his duties as paterfamilias and lord of the manor. She'd not seen her cousin-in-law as frequently since Harvey's death, but Elsa always made it a point to visit with Oliver whenever she was at Berrybrook. Though their familial relationship existed merely through marriage, Oliver and his often-absent brother, Rollo, were the only family Elsa had left. Her avoiding him these last months must have been puzzling to Oliver—if not hurtful.

Always hurting, always disappointing ... Guilt and Shame's whispered words swirled and coalesced into a stone that lodged behind her sternum. Elsa rubbed the spot, trying to massage the pain away.

"Forgive me, Cousin." She cast a glance to him. "We did have tea—"

"Once," he interjected. "Soon into the new year. I seem to recall you burst into tears over the crusts on the sandwiches."

Elsa winced. Things had been so hard then, when sobriety was new and unwelcome. It was still hard, and still unwelcome, but she'd grown accustomed to the wearying grind of it. "I told you I hadn't been well. I've been ill much of the winter."

Oliver handed her over a puddle. "Were you not a most respectable widow," he said, his light tone belying the bite of his words, "I might suspect your emotional outburst and subsequent refusal to see me—indeed, to see anyone, from what I've heard—indicated a ... condition, shall we say, rather than an ailment."

Elsa choked back a gasp. Caught in her throat, it transmuted into something else. Thirst. Thirst that crept up onto her tongue, binding it, forbidding her words.

No matter. Guilt and Shame had plenty. *No baby. No child. Hurt Harvey by refusing to give him an heir.*

If she had a drink, she could wash those mean thoughts away, swallow and swallow until only the burning of the liquor and comfortable numbness in her soul remained—

Ruthlessly, she next checked her craving. *You will not drink. You. Will. Not. Drink.* Biting the inside of her cheek, hard and harder, the electric twang of pain finally overwhelmed the urge.

Not my fault, she then mentally snapped at the tutting monsters. *I did my part. It's not my fault there was no child.*

She drew a breath. Another. Forced her face into a placid mask of composure. Dropping Oliver's arm, she turned to face him full on. Holding his gaze, she loosened the frog of knotted silk at the neck of her cloak. Head held high, she drew the garment off, allowing it to fall heedlessly to the ground at her feet.

Oliver's eyes remained locked on Elsa's. She raised a brow in challenge. Color spread across his cheekbones. All at once, his gaze raced down her front to her midsection, where it lingered while his face continued to redden.

Slowly, he stooped to retrieve her cloak. Shook it out. Settled it on her shoulders. "Forgive me, Elsa." He spoke haltingly. "There have been ... unkind rumors. Since Cousin Harvey's passing." He shifted his weight, dark eyes focused several inches to the left of Elsa's head. "Some friends passed through the village last week, on their way from London to Martlesham. One of the gentlemen asked after you, and when I said you hadn't been well ..." Oliver's mouth twisted. "I should have known better than to listen to Town gossip. I should have ignored them, the way I've always done until now. Forgive me. Please do." He offered a sheepish smile.

Elsa blinked, her thoughts and emotions in such a disordered state she could scarcely formulate a response. Oliver had probably heard nothing about her that wasn't true, excepting the conclusion the busybodies drew. Far be it from her, however, to dissuade Oliver from talking himself out of believing sordid tales. Briefly, she wondered what he would say if he knew the truth, that she was so lost to drunkenness that she had spent the winter drying out and scared to leave her house, lest she confront temptation.

The man removed his tall beaver hat and scrubbed a hand through short, dark hair frosted with silver. "Are you better now?" he asked when she neither gave nor denied forgiveness. "I trust you are, else you wouldn't be out like this. I can see now that you've been unwell. Your eyes are tired ..." His voice trailed away. The horse huffed impatiently. Oliver glanced at the beast, then back to Elsa.

At last, she managed a wan smile. "Better now, yes. Thank you." She started back in the direction of home. It was time and more for this outing to end. The fresh, cool air, which had initially enlivened, now darted painfully up her nostrils to needle behind her eyes. The wholesome exertion of muscles had become fatigue.

She took Oliver's arm once more, experiencing a distance from him, though less than a foot separated them. While Oliver spent his days in idle amusement, Elsa engaged in daily battle against herself. He knew nothing of her trials. To be sure, she wouldn't want him to, would fight to conceal her shameful secret, even as she resented him for not knowing. Why didn't he get on his horse and go away? Their meeting was spoiled, didn't he see? Ruined by his unkind allegation, which skirted all too close to the part of herself she never indulged in Fleck. Ruined by the truths she would never tell.

Only one man had known her secrets, had seen her for the shattered woman she was, had witnessed and known and still had given her kindness. Had offered his strength. Had sheltered her in his arms.

Until he washed his hands of her at the earliest possible moment.

If Norman Wynford-Scott, with his gentle eyes and tender heart, had been driven away at the last by her licentious nature, there was no chance Cousin Oliver would ever accept the whole of her. He was family, yes, and he was a friend. But how true a friend was he, really, if she could not confide in him? And family relationships, she knew all too well, were never as simple as one could hope. And so she would go on in her loneliness, waging her private war.

As they neared the stone pillar that marked the drive of Berrybrook Cottage, Oliver asked, "Have you heard the news about Mr. Jonson?"

Elsa tilted her head. "Ben Jonson? Our MP?" Oliver nodded. "No. What of him?"

"He's dead. My groom told me this morning, before I rode out. They found him yesterday in the old boathouse."

That startled Elsa from despondent thoughts of her own woes. "Oh no," she said, mournfully. "He was such a dear." As one of Fleck's two members of Parliament, Ben Jonson had frequented her suppers and salons in London. The older man had a wicked sense of humor and a boyish gleam in his eye. He'd reminded her of an elderly Sheridan Zouche, in fact, and she rather suspected the resemblance was a large reason why she'd taken so to the irascible MP.

"That leaves just Mr. Trumbull in Commons for our borough," Oliver observed. "There will have to be a by-election to fill the seat."

Elsa scowled, bothered that instead of reflecting on the man who had died, Oliver instead chose to dwell on a hole left in Parliament.

"Who do you suppose will take the seat?"

With a sigh, Elsa shook her head, her eyes scanning the green shoots nosing their way up through the black soil on either side of her drive. Were they daffodils? Crocuses? She remembered discussing new bulbs with Mr. Whittle last autumn, but couldn't recall what she'd told the caretaker to plant. Sobriety had revealed many such blank places in her memory, unnerving voids where her life was supposed to be.

"Oh, Oliver, I don't know." Her tone was more cross than she'd intended. "I've not been involved in politics for years."

"But ..." A shadow crossed his face. "Our family ... Cousin Harvey, that is ..."

Yes, yes, Cousin Harvey. Elsa's late husband had dominated the political scene here in Fleck. Besides his seat in the House of Lords, Harvey had used his influence in the borough to handpick the representatives he wanted elected to the House of Commons. And he got his way. Always. As had every Viscount Fay before him, going back as far as anyone could remember. And as his wife, Elsa, too, had held sway with the villagers. Were Harvey still alive, he would have pulled Elsa aside this morning so that, between the two of them, they could determine the best choice for filling the vacancy. Harvey always said Elsa had the political instincts of a man. It was the only thing he'd liked about her. The only thing she was good at.

But that was all over now.

She crossed herself with one arm, propped her other elbow on her wrist, and idly stroked her throat, back and forth, as she once more regarded the mystery plants. "You should be having this discussion with Cousin Rollo. It's Lord Fay's duty to lead the way in this matter."

An exasperated sigh was Oliver's only response, but it said everything: *Rollo is not here. He's out of the country, God knows where, and I've no way of reaching him. Even if I could, what would be the point? He takes no interest in his own seat in Lords, much less Commons.*

This had been the situation almost since the moment Rollo stepped into his inheritance. He'd dipped into the very considerable

Fay fortune and embarked on the life of travel and luxury to which he'd always believed himself entitled, with scarcely a backward glance for the responsibilities tied to his newfound affluence. The once-strong Fay dynasty had dwindled down to two: a younger son and a widow.

The widow in question shivered inside her cloak. Loitering at the top of the drive had allowed the damp cold to seep through her layers of clothes. She was ready for the coziness of her little house, for Mrs. Whittle to fuss over her a bit with a warm brick under her feet and a cup of tea tucked into her chilled palms. She lifted her face to Oliver, a practiced smile-grimace firmly in place, the one that communicated, *It's been lovely, but I really must go*, only to find him watching her with a pained look of his own.

"I thought I might stand for the seat myself." He cringed as he spoke, as if anticipating derision.

She did nothing more than cock her head. Oliver? In Commons? The idea sparked something that had lain dormant inside her for a long time, part of her mind that quickly analyzed Oliver's suitability for the post. Certainly, the Fay name still carried weight in this borough, and Commons was a, well, common destination for younger sons who wished to make themselves useful. But Oliver had always been one for country living, hunting and fishing and gadding about in the woods. He'd spent little time in London. Being a big name in a small town suited him fine. He'd done very well as a minor member of the prominent family in the neighborhood.

"Why?" she asked, tilting her head to the other side, peering at her cousin in a new light. "You've never expressed interest in politics before."

Still, if she squinted her eyes and leaned in close, Elsa could almost see potential in the notion. With the viscount's prolonged absence dragging into its third (or was it fourth?) year, Oliver might be feeling pangs of duty, a sense that he should Do Something to serve the people upon whose backs the Viscounts Fay had made their fortune.

Oliver pulled a face. "Politics?" He said it like a dirty word. "No, my dear. No. I fear the political mania that infects our family bypassed my branch of the tree, as I share my brother's antipathy for all things civic." He wiped his palms against his waistcoat.

Pinching the bridge of her nose, Elsa took a deep breath and let it out slowly. "Then why in heaven's name would you stand for the seat?"

"Because I am a Fay," Oliver pronounced solemnly. "And even if I care nothing for the government, I do have a care for my family. Maintaining our prominence requires that we hold prominent positions."

Well. Not quite a burning in his bosom to serve king and country, but it was something, she supposed. Something heartfelt, at least, if not noble. She clasped his hand. "I wish you luck, cousin."

When she moved to pull her hand away, he gripped harder. "I thought I'd have a little reception. To announce my candidacy to the local gentry, you know. And I hope you'll do me the favor of acting as hostess."

Elsa stilled. A thrill shot up her spine at the words *politics* and *hostess* once more being placed in close proximity in regard to herself. But a reception would involve alcohol. Her blood leapt even as her mind panicked.

"I don't, I'm not ..." she stammered, shaking her head.

"Please, Elsa." His eyes were all desperate imploring. Like Norman's had been when he'd asked her to help with the revels.

And see how that turned out.

"Please."

Her breath stuttered. How long could she and her sobriety hide in her cottage? Unless she meant to become the crazy old hermit lady children whispered scary stories about, she'd have to face this eventually. And she was stronger now. Even if the sheer effort of not drinking was nearly all-consuming, she was doing it. Most days without tears.

She bit her lip, considering. Oliver clasped his hands to his chest, begging. Maybe praying.

"Very well," she relented. "I'll help you with your reception."

Oliver grinned, and Elsa tried to ignore the dreadful voices. She could do this.

We'll see, they trilled anyway. *We'll see how this turns out.*

• • •

That very day, she sent invitations to all the important families in Fleck and even dashed off a letter to Mr. Trumbull, in London. He was already back in Town ahead of the opening of the spring session of Parliament, and while he would almost certainly decline the invitation, she hoped he would send a letter in reply, endorsing Oliver's candidacy. While no Whig stood against Oliver, a vote of confidence from the remaining member of Parliament for the district would be news worth sharing at the reception.

With the invitations out, she turned her attention to preparing Oliver's house for the event. Little Beeswick was a small establishment situated on a hundred acres that had been carved away from the primary Fay estate, Beeswick Hall, at some point in the distant past. Enough land to mollify a younger son or stray relation, allowing him to dabble with running an estate-in-miniature, but not enough to build fortune or power to rival the paterfamilias. During Elsa's time as viscountess, Rollo, Harvey's heir, had occupied Little Beeswick. Once he inherited and moved into the big house, he passed the small one on to his brother.

The house had been built three-quarters of a century ago, replacing one lost to fire. Though only about twice the size of Elsa's house, Little Beeswick had been built in the style of a much grander home, with tall ceilings and an abundance of windows. A colonnaded portico welcomed guests into a spacious entryway, and the several public rooms adjacent to it made a fine setting for the reception.

What the house lacked in architectural imperfections, it made up for with bachelor barrenness. Over the course of a week, Elsa rode on a tide of decorating mania, calling upon neighbors and friends she'd not seen all winter to beg and borrow plates, glassware, and linens. Her friend, Lady Laura Beaufort, even loaned Elsa her second-best silver, so the spoons would all match. Elsa pulled together a menu of hors d'oeuvres and miniature desserts, not even slowing down when she rattled off the wines and liqueurs the party would require. She didn't have time to crave the alcohol for herself. She barely had time to think.

It was marvelous.

In the midst of her planning frenzy, she even found herself playing nursemaid, soothing Oliver's fits of nerves.

"Perhaps this isn't a good idea, after all," he'd fretted one afternoon. "What if my brother's absence from Lords turns opinion against me?"

Elsa had adopted a falsetto voice. "What if the other boys at school don't like me, *maman*?" she'd teased good-naturedly to break his sulk.

On another occasion: "What if I don't win?"

At that, Elsa had planted her hands on her hips. "This is an uncontested election, Oliver. You can't *possibly* lose. Even if no one comes to the hustings to cast a vote, you'll win by virtue of being the only candidate in the running."

He'd looked stricken. "Are you sure?"

"Certain," she'd assured him.

Men, she knew, had very tender sensibilities. And they called *women* the weaker sex. *Bah.*

And so the evening of the reception arrived. The doors of Little Beeswick were thrown open, and the great and powerful of Fleck descended to hear Mr. Fay's announcement—and to take a gander at his cousin, Lady Fay, who had been missing from their little society since Christmas. In the case of a borough with the overall consequence of a persistent rash, those illustrious persons consisted of several squires, a handful of gentleman farmers, two industrialists of independent means, one dotty scholar, the vicar, the ladies attached to this fine array of males—and Mr. Denny, the village barkeep, who was providing libations for the reception, as Oliver's cellars were as woefully stocked as his linen cupboard.

Elsa stood at Oliver's side, once more in her element as she greeted guests, chatting and laughing while nimbly directing the staff as needed. The first hour passed gaily as neighbors discussed the coming growing season and swapped the latest gossip.

And it was easy not to drink. So easy. Elsa was far too busy tending to her guests, ensuring everyone was comfortable and amply fed and watered, to even think of imbibing. The faint perfume that drew her toward Mr. Denny's beverage station, the tugging she felt inside her head, those weren't thoughts. She wasn't thinking about drinking at all.

In politics, as in theater, timing is everything. Elsa gave her guests time enough to arrive, to enjoy a bite and a drink, to have a bit of a chat—but not enough to become bored with the company or dull from food and drink. While the merriment was still at its zenith, Elsa nodded at Mr. Denny, their predetermined signal for him to begin pouring the champagne.

The *pop* of the first cork elicited a startled laugh from someone standing near the table. Several heads turned to see what Mr. Denny was about.

Elsa watched, too. But while others merely registered the man pouring drinks and then returned to their own conversations, Elsa was riveted. Mr. Denny tipped the bottle and poured a measure into each glass. Elsa's throat felt parched. *You've been so good,* whispered a seductive voice. *Learned your lesson. Things got out of hand, but it'll be different this time. You won't let it happen again.*

And she *had* learned. She'd seen the underbelly of drunkenness, experienced the hell of deprivation. She would not go back to that. Not ever. But suddenly, the idea of spending her entire life without ever again tasting champagne seemed absurd. There were moments in life—special occasions such as this—that called for a celebratory libation. Was she to sacrifice her culture, her very way of life, on the altar of abstinence? She thought not.

As the footman loaded up his tray and began distributing the glasses of champagne, Elsa's knees trembled. She tracked the servant moving from guest to guest. Her heart pounded. What did her friends and neighbors know about her? Did they suspect? Was it plain to them that she was not supposed to have a drink stronger than milk? It felt to her as though the truth must be branded on her face. Couldn't they hear her teeth chattering, see the way her limbs were limp and stiff all at once?

Plainly, she could not get away with this. Someone—the vicar, probably—would step in. Would stop her from taking a glass. But then, suddenly, it was in her hand. The footman nodded and turned to Lady Beaufort, and no one looked twice at Elsa clutching a glass of champagne. Just that easy.

Then Oliver had the attention of all, obliterating the possibility of anyone noticing Elsa and her forbidden nectar. She stood at his side, smile pasted in place, hearing not a word of his brief speech. He must have said something about her, thanking her, maybe, for now all eyes *were* on her. Demurely, Elsa dropped her gaze.

The liquid inside her glass was the palest gold, the purest morning sunshine streaming over the Suffolk hills. Through the thin crystal, she felt the effervescence, the sensation of a million tiny bubbles swimming to the surface to release their heady aroma. She brought the cup to her nose and inhaled, relishing the way the fumes unfurled in her nostrils and drifted into her brain, making her a bit giddy before she'd had a sip. Her mouth watered in anticipation.

I really shouldn't …

It's a special occasion.

Mr. Dewhurst said never again.

Just this once.

My count! I'll have to start all over again.

The tiniest taste. Not enough to do any harm. It wouldn't signify. Your journal would never know.

In the space of a second, a dozen arguments and counter-arguments tumbled through her mind. Panic spiraled through her as she was seized with a craving almost violent in its intensity. She didn't *want* the drink. She had to have it. She *would* have it.

Elsa felt heat bloom in her cheeks, her mood suddenly soaring. Oliver had concluded his speech and glanced at her. "To Mr. Oliver Fay," she toasted, lifting her glass in salute. "Our next member of Parliament."

"Mr. Fay," chorused the assembly.

She brought the glass to her lips, her blood fizzing right along with the champagne.

Suddenly, Elsa knew a terrible truth: She craved this drink more than she wanted Oliver to win, more than she cared about the good opinion of her neighbors. She'd ignored them all these last long moments, her entire being utterly fixated on the champagne.

Numbly, she allowed the liquid to touch her top lip, tightly sealed to the rim to prevent it from entering her mouth. Then she set the glass down. Meant to do it gingerly, but her arm jerked and it tipped, splashing wine onto the floor.

Oliver's brows drew together in unspoken question.

A bead of champagne clung to the bow of her lip. Elsa felt it there, like a fly, a ticklish presence that consumed her attention.

"If you'll excuse me," she murmured out of the corner of her mouth, straining to keep the liquid balanced.

Ignoring her neighbors' stunned expressions, she all but ran out the door. She dashed away from the house, then scrubbed her mouth on the back of her gloved hand until the drop of champagne was gone, scrubbed until she could no longer smell it, scrubbed until she tasted blood.

She turned for home and stumbled blindly up the darkened drive to the lane. What manner of unnatural creature was she, to desire drink more than anything else?

Failure, keened Guilt and Shame. *Too selfish to be a good wife. Too selfish to become a mother. Too selfish to help your friends.*

A sticky residue of old regrets clung to her hands. She wiped them on her thighs.

Failure and a fraud. Not a lady, not a hostess, but a wanton and a drunk. That's what you are. That's all you are.

"Shut up," Elsa croaked through a constricted windpipe. She swiped wetness from her cheek. "Just shut up!"

In a nearby pen, a sleepy cow lifted its head to mark her deranged progress with a liquid brown eye.

Sobriety wouldn't be such a challenge if those horrible voices would just go away. Alcohol was the only remedy she'd ever known for silencing them, although she had enough clarity to recognize that her drunkenness only gave those demons of self-loathing more ammunition to use against her.

What was she to do? *What was she to do?*

Sobriety was killing her by inches, locking her in a hopeless battle against herself. She couldn't even spend an evening in company without nearly careening back into her old habits. All she did was not drink, and the effort of it left her spent. Elsa's struggle was relentless, incessant, with no sign of abating, no promise of respite, and no hope that her life would ever be anything but this hell.

Her wanting for alcohol had not ebbed. She'd been a fool to believe otherwise. The anguish of it lashed her mind like the crack of a whip across her back, demanding she give in to the craving. "Don't drink," she sobbed. "Don't drink, don't drink, don't drink ..."

Elsa didn't remember arriving home, but at some point, she became aware of Foster hovering nearby, her face creased in concern.

"My lady, you're unwell. Are you ...? That is, did you ...?" Were those tears in the redoubtable abigail's voice? Odd, that. Elsa had never seen Foster cry.

A bitter laugh escaped her dry lips. "No, I'm not drunk," she said dispassionately. "But I wish I was. Oh, how I wish it."

Foster regarded her in a kind of shocked silence. Then, with a trembling touch, she guided Elsa to the vanity stool, took down her mistress's hair, and began combing it. The nighttime ritual soothed Elsa's fevered nerves a bit, the sensation of the comb passing through her black tresses something to focus on besides her unfulfilled longing.

Foster divided Elsa's hair to braid it for bed. "If you don't mind my saying so, milady, I do not believe Mr. Dewhurst's country air cure is working."

"That wasn't all. He said ..." Squeezing her eyes shut, Elsa fought to retrieve her memory of the conversation with the surgeon. Like much of that day, like too much of her life these past several years, her recollection was spotty.

"He said you were to distract yourself." None too tenderly, Foster tugged as she plaited. "You've kept busy—didn't hardly sit down this whole last week—but still this happens."

Elsa opened her mouth to argue, but she was too tired to fight. When she had been able to stir from her room this winter, she'd engaged in a litany of mindless pursuits around the house: needlepoint, paper quilling, rearranging furniture in the parlor—anything to keep her hands busy. The problem was that all of these activities bored her to tears. She'd not yet found something to engage both her hands and her mind.

If only Norman was here. The thought did not surprise her; it was one she'd had often enough. *No,* came the quick reply. *He may have provided a distraction, but he left you.*

He'd abandoned her in her hour of need, but her body would not forget the exquisite, searing release he'd given her. Neither could she ignore the sense of stability and care she'd felt during their journey—before he'd ditched her on the doorstep, of course. If he appeared right now, she would hotly inform him what a cad he'd been ... but she would probably take him to bed right after. She was pathetic.

No, Norman was not the answer—not him, nor any other bedmate. Elsa was in no state to have an affair. Though it would be diverting, there was always the risk of her emotions being left in worse a shambles than they were at present.

Elsa needed something that was hers, something that gave her a feeling of purpose and a reason to maintain her sobriety. Something like her old days of political hostessing, when she could charm a recalcitrant aristocrat into supporting Harvey's agenda in the House of Lords or help broker a coalition between rival factions in Commons. She'd been useful then; she'd made a real difference.

This past week, this evening, hostessing for Oliver had given her a tiny piece of it back, and it had been wonderful. If only ...

With a sharp gasp, Elsa's eyes met her own startled blue gaze in the mirror. A smile, the largest smile she'd smiled in months, stretched across her face.

"He needs a hostess," she exclaimed in wonder. "The election is the easy part." Uncontested it might be, but her mind was already racing to plan campaign events to coax franchised men to the hustings to vote for her cousin. This past week had proved that doing something she cared about eased her desire to drink, and so she'd do more campaigning, unnecessary it may be. And then, *oh then* … "Once he's in London, he'll *have* to have a hostess if he's any hope of making a name for himself. He'll need me."

She could have it again. She could have it all again. All she had to do was win that seat.

Chapter Five

The killing blow, when it came, was delivered in the afternoon post. Norman eyed the letter warily. He should rip it open, he thought, get it over with. He snatched it from the top reaches of the stack of unopened post in the entrance hall. Neglected letters accumulated on an antique console table like a snow drift until either his father found his way to opening them (his stepmother could not read), or one of the maids got tired of tidying the heap and quietly shuffled it off to a fireplace.

Several floors above, a thundering herd of children shrieked and screamed as they galloped from one side of the nursery to the other. The lone governess for all those hellions attempted, in vain, to assert herself as the voice of authority. A girl child made a sound of derision; the others laughed. He heard something that sounded rather like begging, followed by an immediate resumption of the whooping and running. A door shut and then, closer, the soft weeping of a life gone awry.

To N. Q. Wynford-Scott, Esq.

stared up at him, the coal black letters formed in the even, impersonal hand of a clerk. The first two months of 1818 had been spent attending a hearing with the benchers, waiting, attending another hearing, waiting, filing an appeal to the judges, and even more waiting.

Ironically, it was while fighting for his professional life that Norman had felt more like a barrister than at any time in the seven years he'd spent studying and taking his suppers at Gray's Inn. He had prepared his case as he'd learned from his mentors, with much studying and diligence. As Norman had been prohibited from the Inn, he'd enlisted the aid of Human Torch—Robin Alderly, as he happened to be called—to smuggle out of the library volumes of the Inn's official histories. By sun and candlelight, accompanied by the constant roar of his young siblings' exuberance, Norman worked his way through generations of Keepers of the Records, searching their writings for cases similar to his own. As it happened, his situation was without precedent. No member of Gray's Inn had ever been called to task for bungling the Christmas revels to the point of arson. And so he'd focused on cases of expulsion and refusal to call to the bar. He'd orated brilliantly before the benchers—the same men who should have been calling him to the bar, rather than weighing whether to strike his name from the rolls of the Inn. Sadly, the judgment of the benchers had gone against him. Norman suspected politics at work; Mr. Turton had scowled and huffed throughout the hearings, his prejudice evident, and the other benchers had feared crossing him.

He'd been disappointed by the ruling, but not surprised, given Turton's determination to make an example of Norman. Already, he'd been drafting an appeal to the judges, which he had readied and dispatched within days of the benchers' ruling. His appeal had been a work both intellectually rigorous and emotionally appealing, a recounting of his own achievements, as well as the Inn's storied history as an institute not just of legal learning, but a center of culture. In centuries past, residents of the Inn had included poets, musicians, and theologians. The very bench tables threatened by the fire had been gifted to the Society by Queen Elizabeth as thanks for a banquet held in her honor, and for the "Certaine Devises and Shewes presented to her Majestie by the gentlemen of Grayes-Inn, at her Highnesse Court in Greenwich." The revels Norman had resurrected may have ended in misfortune, but it harkened back to a proud tradition, a time when the Inn had produced gentlemen of culture and distinction, not just advocates for the court.

The judges had acknowledged receipt of his appeal and then gone silent for three weeks. At last, this was it. Norman's fate was contained in this letter.

Abruptly, he stuffed it into the inner pocket of his coat and headed out the door, shutting behind him the sounds of his father's happy second family.

He strode down Tavistock Street, turned onto Southampton, and cut across the bustling Strand to reach the coffeehouse where he had scheduled to meet his friends. Norman was the first to arrive, and so he procured a table and ordered a pot of coffee and some refreshments. At other tables, men debated politics, the economy, and other topics of the day. In a corner, a thin fellow with a literary air about him bent over a sheaf of paper, pen scribbling madly.

The letter in his pocket seemed to weigh a stone. He was aware of it cocooned in his clothing, scant inches from his heart. He pulled it out and turned it in his hands, as if the wax seal might offer a clue as to the contents.

If the ruling against him was upheld, Norman didn't know what he'd do.

His father who, as a younger son, did not have a considerable fortune, had nevertheless financed Norman's education and housing for seven years, so proud was he when his eldest had been accepted at Gray's. Though the elder Wynford-Scott had never breathed a word of repayment, Norman had always intended to reimburse his father once he was a barrister. All of that investment would be for nothing, money lost, never to return.

Asking his father and stepmother to make room for him in their home, having to explain why, had already been a lesson in humility. His father had expressed confidence in Norman's ability to clear his name. But if he did not? If he was never to be called to the bar? The thought of becoming a disappointment in his father's eyes tormented Norman.

"What have you there? The lost Gospel of Saint Aloysius?"

Norman glanced up to see Sheridan Zouche regarding him through his quizzing glass from across the table.

"I've been standing here, watching you brood over that missive as if it held the Word of God for four minutes, and you never even noticed I was here."

"Why not make it a full five?" Norman asked.

"I was going to," Sheri mused, pulling out a chair and taking the seat opposite Norman's, "but then I realized that I was the one who looked odd standing here staring dumbly, not you, and this insight compelled me to bring my public idiocy to an end ahead of schedule. A very efficient process, you see."

Shaking his head, Norman chuckled. "You're daft, Zouche."

Sheri poured himself a cup of coffee and slanted a wry smile. "Daft enough to gape at you like a lovelorn idiot for four minutes, but not daft enough to do it for five. So, what is that, anyway?"

Norman nodded a greeting at Henry De Vere and Brandon Dewhurst who had just entered, and waited for them to reach the table before answering. "This is the final judgment on my appeal. It arrived just before I left, so I thought ..."

He glanced around the table at the faces of the three men. Along with Harrison Dyer, absent for reason of being at sea, these were Norman's closest friends in the world. Their bond had been forged in adolescence, but as men, they continued to stand together against whatever challenges life threw at them. If one man were in need, the others would be there for him; it went without saying. Theirs was a brotherhood of sorts, and though Norman now had several young half brothers, The Honorables were the brothers of his heart.

Brandon, seated beside him, clapped Norman's shoulder in wordless support.

"Whatever comes, big man," said Henry. His golden hair caught a band of light when he gave a firm nod.

"Naturally," Sheri concluded.

Puffing an exhale, Norman cracked the seal and opened the letter.

Sir,

The Twelve Judges, having fully investigated the charges preferred against N. Q. Wynford-Scott, Esq.,

His eyes, jittery with nerves, would not follow the text, instead skipping down several lines and hopping from word to word. *Unprofessional ... his defence ... two years ... deserving ... severe ...*

"Well, what does it say?" Henry's golden head was tilted in anticipation.

Norman gulped hard. Cleared his throat. Forced himself to read again, careful and slow.

Having done so, he blew out a long breath. "I've been screened."

"Screened?" Sheri tapped the table with his quizzing glass. "What the devil is that?"

"Severely censured," Norman explained. "Excluded from the Hall for two years."

"What's that to do with a screen?" Brandon inquired.

Norman chuffed a humorless laugh. "This order is to be affixed to the screen in the Hall for the duration of my exclusion, so all may see my name and punishment."

Sheri sucked air between his teeth. "*Oooo.* Puts my four minutes of public humiliation in perspective, though, doesn't it?"

"But that's good, though, isn't it?" Henry contributed. "You haven't been expelled. You can still be called to the bar."

"Two years from now!" Norman exclaimed, striking the table with his fist. "What am I—" At the startled looks from the other patrons in the coffeehouse, he covered his mouth, then continued at a lower volume. "What am I supposed to do for the next two years?"

"Practice as a solicitor? Your degree in civil law from Oxford gives you that much," Brandon suggested, but Norman was already shaking his head before the words were fully out of his friend's mouth.

"To do that, I'd have to resign from Gray's Inn, abandon any hope of ever being called to the bar. Then, I'd have to apply to practice as an attorney, an application that may or may not be approved, given this disciplinary action from Gray's Inn. This is limbo." He flung his arm, gestured widely with a hand. "Neither here nor there."

A long silence followed. Norman slouched, heavy with despair, and the other three stared into their coffee cups as if a solution would arise from the depths of the dark brew.

"You could work for me," Henry ventured uncertainly. He spun his cup on the table, hooked a finger into the handle, half raised the cup, put it down again. "You could ... help with the books, or, you know, actually," he picked up speed, his voice more animated, "we need a new foreman in the warehouse, someone we can trust. I caught the last bloke skimming goods to sell on the side."

Henry and his brother owned a shipping company, De Vere and Sons. To the best of Norman's knowledge, the young venture had yet to turn a profit. Henry'd already taken on their friend Harrison Dyer, who even now sailed eastward on a ship loaded with all of Henry's hopes for the future.

"Thanks, Henry, but I'd only be a charity case. I've no skills to offer. Would probably wind up losing you money."

Brandon's shoulders rose. "Maybe—"

"Thanks, but I'll figure it out." The other men regarded Norman uncertainly. "Really, gents, it'll all work out in the end."

He put on a smile, conveying confidence he didn't feel.

The others let the matter drop and moved on to other topics. Norman listened with half an ear. He swallowed coffee without tasting it; it felt like acid in his stomach. Continuing to live off his father was out of the question. Norman was twenty-nine years old, strong of body and mind, and fully capable of supporting himself. Yet the sad truth was this: He was overeducated and suited for no vocation whatsoever.

Manual labor of some nature might be in his future. Or tutoring. He pictured himself in the schoolroom of some nobleman's nursery. The memory of his siblings' weeping governess echoed in his mind. He suppressed a shudder.

Sheri said something, a name, that snapped Norman's attention to the conversation. "Repeat that, please?"

"I had a letter from Lady Fay."

Brandon raised a brow. "And how does she get on?"

Norman clasped his hands around his cup of coffee and feigned disinterest in Sheri's answer.

Besides the pressing matter of his status at Gray's Inn, Norman's thoughts had been consumed with Elsa—often the two were muddled together. Never before had he experienced such a turmoil of emotion over a woman. Though, to be honest, he'd never experienced any strong emotions relating to a woman. He had admired some, certainly; when he was twenty, he'd even fancied himself in love with Miss Grafton, the daughter of a local squire he'd met while summering at his uncle's estate in Dorset. For the bulk of his adult life, he'd been focused on his studies, first at Oxford, and then at Gray's Inn, neither of which institutions provided many opportunities to mingle with the gentler sex. And while Norman was the grandson (and now nephew) of an earl, his father's *mésalliance* with a dairymaid had resulted in his branch of the family being cut from the guest lists of the highest of Society's sticklers. In brief, Norman simply had not been around women enough to develop a strong attachment to one.

"She says she is doing well." Sheri said. "I have written Foster and shall withhold judgment on the matter until I hear from her."

Henry tipped his cup toward Sheri. "Do you not trust Lady Fay's own word?"

Sheri shifted in his seat. His eyes clouded with uncertainty. "I want to believe Elsa. But if you had seen her that last day, Henry ... She was like a different person. My friend of so long just wasn't there." Beside Norman, the surgeon sighed. "Unfortunately, Sheri, you're right to mistrust Lady Fay's report. Individuals with heavily entrenched habits often lie to conceal the extent of their use." Brandon tapped a calloused finger on the table. "Hopefully her ladyship is telling the truth. She's strong at her core, and she has trusted servants around her to help."

Help. That's all he'd wanted to do on that trip to Berrybrook. Including Elsa in the revels hadn't benefited either of them, but like a dolt, he had grasped at another chance to spend time with the beautiful, troubled widow, to shelter and protect her.

Everything had gone well until that last night. Arrogantly, he'd credited his own efforts at keeping her from alcohol with the relative ease of the trip. How foolish he'd been; how little he knew. Witnessing Elsa trapped in the snare of her cravings had shaken him. Hearing her anguish as she paced and cried had made him feel helpless, desperate to ease her suffering. Her body had demanded physical deliverance, and his own had innately responded to her call. How could it not? Elsa was gorgeous, sensual—and, finally, had turned to him. And she'd been so kind, in her way, about his inexperience, had matter-of-factly showed him the way of it, made him feel like a king when she'd come undone at his touch. In that instant, his heart had opened to her. There was nothing he'd not do to protect and comfort this woman.

But when it was done, as he held her while she slept and his raging erection slowly subsided, Norman began to feel guilty. Worried he'd taken advantage. But she'd been so cold with him the next morning, had spoken of their time together so callously, he'd felt rather poorly done by. She'd used him for her own purposes. He had participated willingly, of course, gladly; but his heart had been engaged while hers had not. He'd done everything in his power to assist and defend Elsa from her own destructive impulses, and in return, she'd crushed his hopes like a cockroach beneath her dainty heel.

Brandon had compared Elsa's habitual drunkenness to a sickness, and Norman, too, had sensed that she'd had little control of her own actions, especially the night of the revels.

But ... well ... he couldn't ignore, or forget, that her reckless behavior and her rash actions had led to the spread of the fire in the hall and now, finally, had culminated in the course of Norman's life being thwarted for two years.

He would be one-and-thirty years old when he'd be eligible for consideration for the bar, but would this blight on his record not tarnish it, taint his reputation as a barrister before he'd even begun advocating in court? Would he ever recover from this?

And who was to blame? Elsa Bloody Fay was who. Norman may have been the fool who brought her into Gray's Inn, but all the rest was her doing, and he'd taken the fall for it.

Since the day he'd left her at the door of Berrybrook Cottage, he'd not had a single word from Elsa. No note of thanks for his escort, no syllable of apology for the wreck she'd made of the revels and his prospects. Her persistent silence confirmed that their interlude really had meant nothing to her, that he'd been no more than a diversion to stop herself from turning to drink that night.

"To news of a more reliable sort," said Sheri, yanking Norman from his gloomy ruminations, "Elsa says one of the MPs of her borough there in Fleck recently died. Old Ben Jonson—you remember him, don't you, Henry? We met him down at Elsa's place that once. Jolly fellow, had a mince to his step, but Elsa was always fond of him. Died in a boathouse. Delightfully tawdry, Elsa says, just the way the old chap would want to go. Now there's to be a by-election to fill the seat, so she's campaigning on behalf of her husband's cousin. She's in alt to be back at the politicking, but the Fays have always held sway in that district, so it won't be anything like a challenge. The Whigs never even bother to run a candidate, since the Fays are Tories. Whoever Elsa tells people to vote for, they will."

"But it keeps her busy. Just what she needs," Brandon said, nodding his approval.

Henry's hand hovered above a plate of sweetmeats before he selected a sugared almond. "I'm glad for her," he added, popping it into his mouth.

"And I," Sheri contributed. "Things are looking up for her." He leveled a sharp look on Norman. "Nothing to say, counselor? You're usually the moral pillar of our little society, chirping on about moderate living and civic duty. Lady Fay's new lease on life must cheer you to no end."

Norman swallowed on a dry throat. What was there to say? He glowered. "Oh, believe me, Zouche, I'm cheered," he drawled. "Endlessly." While Elsa's life might be on the way up, Norman's had tumbled around his ears. And it was all her doing.

It seemed grossly unjust that Elsa could so easily walk away from the mess she'd made. While Norman was trying to salvage the remains of his prospects, Elsa was helping another man advance his. The more he thought about it, the angrier he became. An empty seat in Commons should go to a truly deserving candidate, not be bestowed upon Elsa's cousin-in-law at her say-so. Why should she have her way in this, when Norman's choices had been taken away? Why, he should—

The sound of Sheri's quizzing glass tapping the table brought Norman's eyes to his friend's. As if reading the train of Norman's thoughts, Sheri quirked a brow and said, "Ever considered a seat in Commons?"

Not until this very instant, and his reasons for even thinking of it were best left unsaid. He shook his head. "I've only ever wanted to be a barrister."

Sheri crunched a walnut. "Yes, well, you can't have that." His urbane voice carried an undertone of ruthlessness. "It's time for a new plan. You could do this."

"You'd be brilliant, Norm." Henry offered an encouraging smile. "Can you imagine having Parliament staffed with men actually educated in the law, instead of the shiftless gadabouts we're usually inflicted with?"

Brandon's dark head tilted thoughtfully. "It's a solid alternative to advocating, Norman, at least for the time being. I think you should consider it."

Norman promised to do so. Hours later, sleepless in bed, he stared sightlessly at the ceiling, attempting to ignore what sounded like a bread riot in the nursery upstairs, while turning the notion over in his mind.

Once he'd had some time to really consider the matter of standing for Fleck's vacant Commons seat, Norman had readily envisioned himself arguing a bill on the floor. It wouldn't be very different from arguing in court, with the notable exception being that he'd be advocating the best interest of all subjects of the Crown, not just an individual standing trial. Certainly, he had an abundance of ideas pertaining to the law—he'd been studying nothing but for the better part of a decade. He could work in Commons, might even be good at it, as his friends had asserted; it was just the small matter of getting elected that had him stymied.

His entire life to this point had been geared toward his ambition to become a barrister. What did he know of running for a seat in Parliament? *Not as much as Elsa Fay*, said an unwelcome thought. Norman punched up his pillow and flopped back with a scowl. Bother Elsa Fay. She wasn't a consideration here. Or shouldn't be, anyway. He had to think of his own livelihood, and consider whether he truly had something to offer as a member of Parliament. Heartless ruiners of careers could not factor into his decision. If Norman was going to do this ...

He *was* going to do this, he resolved. No matter he didn't know how to run a campaign. Other people knew, and he wasn't too proud to ask for help. He was going to stand for that seat and win. If, by happenstance, Elsa received some well-deserved comeuppance as a result of Norman snatching victory from her claws, he would be gracious enough not to enjoy it.

Too much.

Chapter Six

"Almost to 100," Elsa marveled after making the morning's mark in her journal. Ninety-seven days ago, Elsa didn't think she'd survive a week without alcohol, much less months. As recently as a month ago, her outlook had still been bleak. She'd been on the verge of collapse. In the past few weeks, though, she'd turned a corner. The morning ritual of tallying her progress no longer felt like tracking the days of a prison sentence, but rather had become one of her favorite moments of the day, an opportunity to recognize her progress and motivate herself to meet the challenge of another twenty-four hours without alcohol.

As she tucked the journal back into the drawer, Foster came in with the morning tea. "Will you wish to change, my lady?" Foster asked, nodding to indicate the blue dress Elsa had already donned.

"No need. I'm just running into the village for some ribbons later." She smiled at her maid, and her maid smiled back. Foster's pinched features had slowly softened in pace with the easing of Elsa's torments. For the first time in years, Elsa and her maid were comfortable with one another. Foster was no longer guarded; Elsa no longer defensive.

After taking her tea, Elsa donned half boots but impulsively declined to wear a bonnet, then set out the door. Once the weather had turned milder, Mr. Dewhurst's advice for taking daily exercise had become another behavior she relied upon to maintain her sobriety. Though the cravings weren't as bad as in the beginning, they were still present. She still experienced anxious energy that used to be her cue to have a drink. Now, she found she could curtail most of that energy by vigorous walking as she went about her visits or errands.

Elsa lifted her face to the sky, relishing the warm sunlight bathing her face. She couldn't remember when she'd last felt so well. She was almost a girl again, her blood coursing with vitality as she hummed along with birdsong and stopped to bend her nose to a pretty roadside weed. Those dark times—especially her last days in London—were behind her.

As she entered the village proper, Elsa slowed to a stroll, exchanging greetings with several people as she made her way to the mercantile.

She glanced toward the new hustings on the village green at the center of town, before which a small group was gathered. Erected in anticipation of the upcoming election that would send her cousin-by-marriage, Mr. Oliver Fay, to Commons, the hustings' boards were straight and bright, and the pleasantly sharp aroma of fresh wood hung in the air.

Upon the raised platform stood a man addressing the assembly. Elsa's breath caught in her throat. She would know that larger-than-life figure anywhere.

Her first response was delight. She'd missed his strong, steady presence and his sweet, secret smiles.

But that brief joy quickly gave way to confusion. What was Norman doing here, in Fleck? Bemused, Elsa's feet carried her forward to join the group.

"... time is right to address the concerns you have not just for Fleck, but for the nation," he was saying. Norman's gestures were stilted, as if he were unused to talking before a crowd, but his deep voice carried easily. "As an inhabitant borough, Fleck has the opportunity to send a strong message with her ballot. Your voices are not just those of freemen. *All* householders in Fleck have the franchise, and with it, you will tell Parliament that the people are ready for change."

"'Ere now, I don't care 'bout Parliament," called Freddy Thomson, the baker. "I'm up making bread before those toffs in London have gone to bed for the night."

A rumble of agreement passed through the crowd.

"And how much are you paying for wheat?" Norman asked. "And the rest of you, how much do you pay for the day's bread?"

"Too much," said another man. "Freddy charges dear."

"Got no choice!" the baker replied hotly. "The cost of wheat's through the bloody roof. I barely cover my own expenses. You see me prancing around in a high wig?"

An odd example of prosperity, but it gave the grumblers pause.

"You see?" Norman raised a finger. "But a relief bill passed through Parliament could lower the cost of your corn, Mr. Thomson, thereby reducing the price of bread for the rest of you." He paused while the throng mulled over this line of reasoning, then added, "But you gentlemen already know all this. I trust Mr. Fay has put forth his suggestions for making Parliament work for you."

A sort of stunned silence muted the crowd. Mr. Oliver Fay had done no such thing—he'd not once addressed the citizens of the borough of Fleck in any terms but social. The good villagers cast puzzled glances to one another. Elsa could sense their dawning dissatisfaction; an answering unease pulsed through her middle.

Norman's eyes found Elsa. He lifted a brow, his knowing gaze sardonic, and bent his head in the slightest gesture of acknowledgment. Heat flashed through her cheeks.

Beside the hustings, at the foot of the platform stairs, were Elsa's friend, Lady Laura Beaufort, and her husband, Sir Seymour Beaufort. When Norman began speaking again, Elsa skirted the crowd and made her way to Laura's side.

"Good morning, Lady Fay." Sir Seymour tipped his hat and bowed. He straightened and gave her a shrewd look. "Delighted to see you here, ma'am, though I'd rather hoped to see your cousin, as well." He leaned as though looking behind her. "No? He could not join you? Ah, well."

"Good morning, Sir Seymour," Elsa answered. She cast a questioning look at her friend and was startled to spot a blue-and-buff rosette on Laura's bonnet. "Lady Beaufort, a word, if you will?" She pulled her friend to the side and hissed, "What is this?"

"That's Mr. Wynford-Scott, from London. He's standing for the Whigs, for poor Mr. Jonson's vacated seat. Sir Seymour thinks the Whigs finally have a good chance of taking one of Fleck's seats. He predicts Mr. Wynford-Scott will be a great credit to us in Parliament and might even swing this borough for the Blues in the next general election!" She was flushed and a little breathless by the end of her recitation, her eyes twinkling with the excitement of involvement. Elsa knew the symptoms well, for she'd experienced the same during her heyday of political hostessing. Even her cousin's unchallenged—*previously* unchallenged—campaign to become Fleck's junior MP had stirred up those old feelings.

"But ... but ..." Elsa sputtered. She pointed an accusing finger at the Whig-colors ribbon Laura sported. "You promised to help me with Oliver's victory celebration. I was just on my way to order *orange* buntings from Mr. Goff." She placed meaningful emphasis on the Tory party's color.

Laura's eyes clouded. "I know!" she cried, clasping Elsa's hand. "And I'm ever so sorry, Elsa, dear. When you and I spoke of the celebration last week, I'd no idea that Seymour was in communication with Mr. Wynford-Scott and already planning to sponsor his candidacy. And ever since he arrived here three days past, well, it's just been a whirlwind of preparations. I haven't had a chance to—"

"Three days?" Elsa dropped her friend's hand, taking a step back. "Mr. Wynford-Scott has been in the neighborhood for three days?" Why hadn't he called on her? He should have done. Unless he didn't *want* to see her. Unless his sudden departure from her doorstep had been an abandonment in truth, and he wanted nothing more to do with her.

Why, then, would he come here, seeking a seat in Parliament from Fleck, standing against Elsa's cousin? Had he come to torment her? To punish her for the things she'd said that last morning?

Just then, Norman finished his speech to rousing applause. He descended the steps, his gaze fastened on Elsa, appraising. With every step he took, her heartbeat quickened.

Sir Seymour stepped in front of Norman and pumped his hand. "Marvelous start, sir! Really got their attention. Fleckers aren't used to being spoken to about political issues. Once they're accustomed to the idea, I daresay it'll catch like wildfire. You'll win in a landslide."

"Thank you for your vote of confidence, Sir Seymour. Your support is instrumental to my campaign." He clapped the man's shoulder, stepping around him. "And thanks to you as well, Lady Beaufort." He executed an elegant bow, nothing like the endearingly unpracticed gallantries Elsa was used to from him. "Your hospitality has given me a warm and gracious welcome to Fleck. I might relocate to the inn here in the village, though, as my associate Mr. Alderly is expected this very day and we wouldn't want to inconvenience—"

"Here I am, Wyn!" A young gentleman broke through the crowd, which had migrated closer to Norman—hands extended to press flesh with the man of the hour—and straightened the lapels of his coat. He was dressed to the height of dandy fashion, clothes tailored to within an inch of their life and lethally sharp collar points that rose alarmingly close to his vulnerable eyeballs, a total contrast to Norman's nice-but-not-worth-mentioning style.

There was something familiar about Alderly's face, but Elsa could not place him.

Then he spotted her and flashed an insolent grin. "Lady Fay! What a charming surprise. Don't suppose you've any of your uncle's finest to hand, do you? Can't imagine there's much to do 'round these parts in the evening. A bottle of that'd be just the thing to alleviate the boredom."

Uncle Seamus's whiskey. The revels. He was one of the young bucks dressed as minstrels—the very one who'd caught fire, if she could trust her hazy recollection of that night.

Her eyes cut from Mr. Alderly to Norman.

That night. That horrible, shameful night. Laughing and dancing and spinning so dizzy; Norman telling her to stop, his face that delicious anguished blend of wanting her to stop and *wanting*; hands on her now, two men's worth, she was shocking them all and she was glad for it, glad to ruin herself so flagrantly; fire fire *My God, a fire!* help Norman have to help *my duty* water will quench that fire; time coming undone after that, strands unraveling in little flashes of kissing and cursing but the pattern is gone, gone, gone.

Suddenly, she was trembling. The giant broke away from his friend, took a determined step toward her. His eyes, soft and kind, had seen the very worst of her, knew the squalid underbelly of her soul, had borne witness to her shame. Shame. And Guilt. Voices she'd not heard in weeks now rang in her inner ears: *RUN.*

He reached for her. Elsa stumbled back, arms wheeling. Laura caught her hand.

"Lady Fay?" Norman said. Asked. *Are you sober, or reeling drunk?* was the unspoken question.

Elsa didn't have to answer. Not to him, who had abandoned her when she needed him most.

RUN repeated the twins.

And so she did.

Chapter Seven

Elsa went; Norman followed—or tried to, in any event. Sir Seymour placed a staying hand on his elbow. "Allow me to introduce you to some of my neighbors, Mr. Wynford-Scott. Here is Mr. Martin, our cabinetmaker. Mr. Thomson you've met already. Hello again, Freddy, good of you to come out. Thank you for contributing to the conversation. Nigel, come and say hello to Mr. Wynford-Scott. Now, Nigel here, Mr. Steedmond, that is, is a first-rate thatcher. You'd think thatched roofs would be a thing of the past these days, but not so, not when you've a craftsman like Mr. Steedmond in the neighborhood."

Norman shook hands and said hello and desperately tried to commit to memory the name of each person he met. It was a lost cause, for his mind kept returning to Elsa, how she'd appeared at the back of the crowd like a fairy queen, raven hair loose down her back but for a dainty ribbon woven through the sides. His heart had leaped into his throat at the sight of her, and he'd forgotten his place in his remarks. The baker's interjection had saved Norman from wrecking his inaugural campaign speech.

"Mr. Mattingly," he repeated after Sir Seymour, pumping yet another hand. "Pleasure to meet you, sir. This must be your wife? Mrs. Mattingly. My pleasure, madam. How do you do?" He inclined his head in the way Sheri had shown him, slowly, allowing the recipient to feel the full presence of his attention for a moment.

After several minutes more, Robin Alderly sidled up and reached high to clap Norman's shoulder. "Wasn't that a fine speech?" Alderly said to the man shaking Norman's hand. "Excuse us, sir, I need a word with Fleck's next member of Parliament."

Alderly jerked his head, leading Norman across the square to a tavern housed in a two-story building with stone on the first story and stucco on the second. Old wooden buckets and a ramshackle wheelbarrow had been repurposed as planters arranged near the entrance, their abundant floral display giving a very untavern-like perfume to the air. Above the lintel, a carved sign bore the name Rabbit's Glen, and a shingle beside the door was painted with the image of a fluffy, large-eyed bunny surrounded by green grass.

"Good lord, even the tavern is picturesque," Norman commented. Fleck was like a child's idyllic vision of a village, where the craftsmen were second to none, the houses were all quaint and in good repair, and the flowers never stopped blooming.

"Dastardly, ain't it?" Alderly drawled. "Give me a dank drinking hole and grimy pavement beneath my feet. I can't wait to get back to Town."

Norman scowled. "You're free to go whenever you'd like, Alderly."

"Pfft. If only. I'm as exiled as you, so we might as well make the best of it."

Norman swung open the tavern door to find an interior as neat and charming as the exterior. Lace curtains fluttered around sparkling windows, and the ten or so tables all had the warm, satin gleam of a fresh polishing. At one, two old-timers sat with tankards at their elbows and a backgammon board between them. A serving girl polished spoons behind the counter, a white mobcap topping golden curls. Her round face broke into a smile when Norman and Alderly entered.

"Afternoon, gents. You was just out there on the hustings, yeah?" she nodded to the open window that afforded a clear view of the village green and the platform. "I listened a little—hope you don't mind." She clutched a spoon and rag to her middle.

"Not in the least, Miss ...?"

"Dove, sir. You spoke real well. I liked what you said about the wheat and such. Freddy Thomson's my brother-in-law, and don't we all hear him bellyachin' about the cost of corn! Don't know how you do that, sir, get up there so brave. I'd never have the courage to talk in front of a crowd. Cor, my knees are knockin' right now just thinking about it!"

"Bigger chance you'd never *stop* talking, Dove," came a gruff voice as a door behind the barmaid swung open. "Have you so much as offered these gentlemen refreshment?"

Dove's mouth popped open in an *O*. "Sorry, Mr. Denny." She hustled out from behind the counter. Mr. Denny caught Norman's eye and rolled his gaze skyward in silent, male communication. *Women!*

As they took their seats at the corner table, Sir Seymour entered the tavern and called a greeting to Denny before joining Norman and Alderly.

The squire clapped his hands and rubbed them together in an excited fashion. "That went superbly, Wynford-Scott, it really did. I admit to some trepidation beforehand, but you pulled it off with aplomb."

Dove brought a pitcher of ale and mugs. Alderly did the honors. "I only just caught the end, but I could hear you clear at the back of the green. Guess everything we learned at Gray's wasn't a total waste, eh?" he asked with a rueful smile as he handed over Norman's drink.

Norman had not been the only Fellow censured as a result of the catastrophic Christmas revels. Robin Alderly and his medieval-dressed mates had been found culpable for the fire to a lesser degree. Alderly, the literal torch that sparked the conflagration, had been screened for a period of one year, while the other men were out for two terms—though none were banned from the Inn's premises as Norman had been.

When Alderly had come to retrieve the Inn's record books from Norman, he'd inquired about Norman's immediate plans, seeing as he too had been cut loose and was looking for inspiration. Norman told him about the Commons seat he intended to stand for, and Alderly jumped upon the idea and offered to coordinate Norman's campaign. He'd had such a desperate expression, Norman hadn't had the heart to turn him down; and frankly, he needed all the help he could get.

Fortunately, Sheri had known just who else to contact on Norman's behalf, Sir Seymour Beaufort, a neighbor of Elsa's and a man who had kept mum about his progressive leanings owing to the Fay family's influence in local elections. The Fays always threw their weight behind Tories, and their favored candidates had been unopposed in every election going back fifty years. Like Alderly, Sir Seymour had eagerly latched on to Norman's proposed candidacy, and the men had exchanged letters at a furious pace, hammering out the finer points of Norman's stance on various issues and the whens and hows of his introduction to Fleck's electors.

Sir Seymour took a pull of his beer, then gestured with his mug. "A bit stiff on the meeting and greeting after the speech, but I daresay that'll come easier with practice."

"With your assistance of course, Sir Seymour," Norman smoothly replied. "I'd have been lost without your introductions."

He did not add that the largest factor contributing to his unease was how rattled he'd been by Elsa's appearance and abrupt departure. Encountering her was inevitable, and he'd imagined their reunion a hundred different ways, but still had been unprepared for the electric shock that had snapped through his body and turned his brain to mush the instant he laid eyes upon her. How could it be that after only one intimate encounter months ago, his body thrummed with desire at just a glimpse of her tumbled hair? How could it be that after she'd made it abundantly clear he meant nothing to her, his heart still kicked faster in her presence?

Uneasily, he reconsidered the wisdom in coming here, in pitting his ambitions against hers. Now that he'd seen her, he couldn't deny the frisson of attraction that hummed through his bones. Ruthlessly, he squelched those wayward impulses. This was the woman who had carelessly upended his life. He had to forget her, couldn't allow this infatuation to once again spell his ruin.

More men trickled into the tavern for a midday pint and a bite to eat. Norman tipped back the remainder of his beer and plunked the mug onto the table. "Could you introduce me around the room, Sir Seymour?"

The squire smiled shrewdly. "I think I can do better than that."

Together, the three men made a round of the tavern. Norman recognized one of the men he'd met at the hustings. "Mr. Mattingly, sir, pleased to see you again." The man brightened at Norman's recollection of his name. "But where is your wife?"

"Shopping for bits and baubles at the mercantile," answered Mattingly.

"No business for a man to involve himself in, eh?" Alderly ribbed.

"Just so, sir," Mattingly agreed.

"How about a pint for Mr. Mattingly?" Sir Seymour called to Mr. Denny at the bar. "Put it on my bill."

Norman's smile froze in place. He grabbed the squire's arm and quickly turned so their backs were to the room. "I can't do that," he whispered in a rush. "I won't win this election by buying votes with food and drink."

"Of course not!" Sir Seymour answered, affronted. "I am buying the beer, Wynford, not you. Your nose remains perfectly clean. But the electors do expect to be courted."

Norman frowned, uncertain. Did Sir Seymour's reasoning pass muster? Before he had a chance to collect his thoughts, Alderly called Norman to the bar to meet a laborer slouched on a stool. Soon every hand in the tavern clutched a pint compliments of Sir Seymour, but only after Norman had shaken them.

"... an' that's why I never come to the hustings," declared a Mr. Jonas, cordwainer by trade and politically apathetic by inclination.

Word must have gotten out that there was free beer to be had, for men, and quite a few women, were pouring into the Rabbit's Glen all the time. According to the borough's electoral registry, there were 437 men eligible to vote in the upcoming by-election; by Norman's estimation, all of them were stuffed into Mr. Denny's taproom.

"You make a fair point." Norman raised his voice over the clamor of thirsty patrons. "But consider, Mr. Jonas, how fortunate you are—how bloody lucky—to have the franchise at all. In much of the world, power still rests solely in the hands of those born to it. It's your civic duty to exercise your franchise, to make your voice heard!" he ended on a shout of necessity, rather than oratorical theatrics.

"Why bother?" piped in another man. "The Fays pick our MPs, and the rest of us are s'posed to just line up and do what they say, like good little bootlickers? And feel honored to do it?"

"At least his late lordship was around a good bit, God rest his soul," said Mr. Jonas. "Y'always knew he was interested in the community, like. And Lady Fay, the dowager, she's been good to every one of us. Heart of gold in that one."

"But where's our present viscount?" returned the second man. "Not cut from the same cloth as the last one. He's kicking up his heels on the Continent, has been for more'n a year, and it's his bloody brother Lady Fay wants us to vote for."

Mr. Denny shouldered through the press to collect empty tankards. "Enough, you bellyachers. Mr. Wynford-Scott's going to think Fleckers do nothing but complain."

Determining there was no more complimentary ale to be had, a number of men wandered out, granting Norman a little bubble of breathing room. Across the way, Alderly was tickling Dove beneath her plump chin. Sir Seymour stood at the door calling farewells to some and inviting others to come in for a drink, his treat, and *oh, while you're here, have you met Mr. Wynford-Scott?*

A pair of men—gentlemen, judging by their dress—replaced the working-class grousers. "Tell us a bit about yourself, sir," said one of them. "Your friend, Mr. Alderly, mentioned you studied at the Inns?"

Apprehension writhed in Norman's gut. He gathered his wits, recalling Sir Seymour's advice on handling this particular question. "Correct, sir. I studied at Gray's Inn for seven years and also took a degree in civil law from Oxford. The law is a particular passion of mine, which is why I'd appreciate speaking with you about my ideas for reforming—"

"You're a barrister, then?" interrupted the second gentleman.

"Well," Norman prevaricated, "I wish to look to the future and help create a more just England. Would you be so kind, gentlemen, as to name for me several social or economic challenges that plague the good people of Fleck?"

His question was answered with expressions of bewilderment. Norman shifted his weight from one foot to the other.

"Now, now, Mr. Wynford-Scott," said Alderly, sauntering over. "I heard you dodge the gentleman's question." Cupping a hand to the side of his mouth, he told the two men *sotto voce*, "He hates talking about himself. Makes his ears go red." The men chuckled. Alderly rocked back on his heels, thumbs hooked in his waistcoat pockets. "You asked if Mr. Wynford-Scott is a barrister? Well, here's the truth."

Norman's eyes widened. *What are you doing?* he silently demanded. Alderly flashed an easy grin. "The truth, my good sirs, is that Mr. Norman Wynford-Scott has not been called to the bar. So moved was he by his firsthand experience with the Crown's justice system, that he decided— Well, these were his very words. He told me himself, he said, 'Alderly, The People need an advocate.' Just like that, sirs, humble as your mother's Sunday roast. And I told him"—Alderly clapped Norman's shoulder in that too-far reach again and gave him a fond smile—"I told him *he* was the advocate The People need in Parliament, and that I'd dedicate my all to get him there. And so we both of us took leave from our studies at Gray's Inn to pursue this noble undertaking."

The gentlemen made sounds of admiration. Norman's thanks tasted like ashes in his mouth. He understood the necessity of saying he'd temporarily stepped away from Gray's Inn to pursue a seat in Commons. It was the truth ... of a sort ... and the most prudent explanation of his leave of absence without dredging up the matter of his screening.

"Well, you certainly have my attention, young man," said one of the fellows. "You're a credit to the opposition party, and I, for one, believe it would be Fleck's privilege to send you to Parliament. This country needs more men with a mind for public service."

"I couldn't agree more." Norman shook the man's hand. "Thank you for your support."

When they'd left, he turned his head and leveled a glower on Alderly. "What?" said the younger man. "You were drowning out there. I threw you a lifeline. You're welcome."

"We agreed a straightforward taking-a-leave-of-absence story would be best. I don't need embellishments like these. You lied to those men."

Alderly barked a laugh.

Norman sighed and ran a hand down his cheek. "I don't like it, is all. It feels wrong."

"Maybe it is." Alderly shrugged. "I'll leave that to the philosophers. Think of it this way: These little untruths are only temporary, just until the election. Once you've taken your seat, you will take Parliament by storm and dazzle this sleepy little borough, and they'll return you as often as you like on the basis of your work in Commons. The topic of Gray's Inn will never arise again."

Norman considered his toes, some six-and-a-half feet below. "I suppose you're right."

"Mrs. Mattingly!" Sir Seymour called out the door. "Looking for your husband? Here he is, keeping us rascals company. Won't you join us, madam? And you as well, Lady Fay."

Norman's eyes flew to the entrance just as Elsa stepped into the rectangle of light delineated by the doorframe. Their gazes locked, and time seemed to stop. Her indigo eyes were clear, her complexion graced with a kiss of healthful color. The temptation of her body was like a magnetic force drawing his eyes down. *Exquisite.* Even in a prim muslin frock, her curves called to him, made his hands hunger to touch. His eyes returned to her face. She was watching him look at her. Elsa's plump lips parted slightly, the roses in her cheeks a little redder. Norman's body responded to her unspoken cues, hardening, preparing to lay claim—

"Come in, my lady, have a drink, won't you? With my compliments."

Sir Seymour's question shattered the moment. Elsa paled; her mouth snapped shut. "No, thank you." She shot Norman a look of hurt. "It would be unseemly to fraternize with the enemy." Her tone was teasing, but she bared her teeth in almost a snarl. "Gentlemen." With a curt nod, she was off.

Enemy? Norman internally reeled at the word. Was that how she saw him?

Grimly, he set his jaw. If Elsa Fay was determined to have a battle, then Norman would give her just that.

Chapter Eight

"You said it would be uncontested!" Oliver Fay fumed. He paced the length of the solarium she'd had added to the rear of the cottage, paused to watch a hedgehog, atypically out in the daytime, waddle across a stretch of grass and seek shelter beneath an azalea. He rounded, jabbing an accusing finger in her direction. "You assured me I had only stand for the seat and it would be mine."

Elsa maintained her composure, careful not to show any of her own turmoil. Idly, she plucked a loose hair from her ivory skirt. "In my defense, Cousin Oliver, Fleck's elections *have* been uncontested for half a century. This is rather an exceptional circumstance. Still, I don't believe you have reason for concern. Mr. Wynford-Scott is an outsider, while you have roots here."

"*Pah!*" Oliver swiped his hand through the air. "My parents are long gone, and my brother has scarcely been in residence since inheriting Cousin Harvey's title. It's just you and me now, Elsa, and you're only a Fay by marriage." The heels of his shoes tapped a rapid tattoo against the tile floor; he looked like he was running in place. His small brown eyes narrowed. "Perhaps our influence is no longer as great as it once was."

Elsa harbored similar misgivings, but it was her job to inspire confidence in her candidate, not undermine it. "Nonsense. The Fays of Beeswick Hall have provided patronage and guidance to the people of Fleck for more than a century."

The family seat, Beeswick Hall, lay but two miles from Berrybrook Cottage, but Elsa had not stepped foot in the place since a month after Harvey's death. As soon as she'd been able to secure the funds of her inheritance, she had purchased her little home here and her townhouse in London and walked away from the houses that had seen some of the darkest moments of her life.

Oliver collapsed into the chair beside Elsa's in a dejected slump. "But the Hall is shut up, and that underhanded Sir Seymour has come out in support of this Wynford-Smith—"

"Scott."

"—and he's far more educated in the law than I, and he's giving speeches about issues. *Issues*, for God's sake!" With a growl of frustration, he pressed his hands to the silver wings frosting his close-cropped dark hair. Instinctively, Elsa dropped her gaze to her hands, now twisted together in her lap. Her stomach quavered. Oliver did not look much like Harvey, but his voice was similar, and when his temper began to rise ...

The desire for a drink speared her throat. She drew several slow, deep breaths. *I am safe*, she reminded herself. *Harvey is gone.* When the flutter of fear subsided, she addressed her craving. *I have not had a drink in ninety-seven days, and this will not be the day that breaks me.*

"Tell me about my rival."

In her mind's eye, Elsa saw Norman standing up there on the hustings, a veritable fortress of a man, stilted in manner but eloquent in speech as he addressed Fleck's electors intelligently, but in a way that was accessible to them and their concerns. Were he not campaigning against Oliver, Elsa would have cheered and applauded him. He was a gifted orator and would make a formidable member of Parliament.

But he *was* standing against Oliver. And more to the point, she was convinced that he was really here to stand against *her*. At the Rabbit's Glen, when Sir Seymour offered her a drink, Elsa caught a sardonic tone to his voice, a wry slant to his smile. If he knew about her habitual drunkenness, he must have learned of it from Norman.

The idea of such a betrayal sent a stab of pain through her chest. After Harvey died and Elsa began taking lovers, she had always conducted her affairs in London, where it was easier for her activities to go overlooked. The jaded *ton* didn't much care what she did as long as she was discreet. Fleck was her safe haven, but if word of her drunkenness and bedroom activities got out, it would not be much longer. She would no longer be a respected pillar of the community, but a moral bankrupt, a persona non grata.

Norman, for all his kind eyes and careful manners, posed a danger. She would do well to remember it.

"Mr. Wynford-Scott is highly intelligent. As you say, he knows more about the law than you ever will."

Oliver scowled. "If that's supposed to make me feel better ..."

Just then, the footman announced two visitors, Mrs. Cecily Easton and Mrs. Amelia Hewett.

"Well!" the young and exuberant Mrs. Easton exclaimed. "Hasn't our quiet little by-election turned into quite the intrigue!"

"Hardly," drawled the older Mrs. Hewett. She looked pointedly down her beakish nose at Oliver. "Mr. Wynford-Scott is the only candidate who seems to be doing anything."

"And that's why I asked you here," Elsa said. "You were both kind enough to offer your assistance with Mr. Fay's events. With this unforeseen addition of a rival candidate, our efforts will have to be a little more vigorous than previously anticipated. I was just telling Mr. Fay about Mr. Wynford-Scott. I am personally acquainted with the gentleman, as we have mutual friends in London."

The footman returned with the refreshments Elsa had ordered. She poured beverages into crystal tumblers that had been, in their former life, her scotch glasses.

Mrs. Hewett held her glass aloft, appraising the contents with a gimlet eye. Then she brought it to her nose for a cautious sniff. "What is this?"

"Chilled tea, with muddled strawberries and a dash of cream," Elsa replied. "A recipe of my own devising." Without the diversion of intoxicating beverages, Elsa had tired of pot after endless pot of tea and, lately, had taken to concocting new drinks to entertain her palate.

Cecily took a sip, let out an appreciative "*Mmmmm*," then smacked her lips. "Delicious, Elsa! Please give me the recipe. This would be perfect for my summer lawn party."

"Of course, dear. Just now, though, we really must put our heads together about the campaign." Returning to her own seat, the familiar weight of the tumbler in her palm, Elsa leaned forward. "Now, Mr. Wynford-Scott is intelligent, and he knows the law inside and out. We'll never defeat him if we try to campaign on bills and exploratory committees and all that dry stuff. No offense, Cousin Oliver, but he will run roughshod over you if you try to approach on that front."

"None taken." Oliver sipped his chilled tea, wrinkled his nose. "Have any brandy to hand, Elsa? This could use a dash."

"No. Mr. Wynford-Scott has two weaknesses we can use to our advantage: He is not familiar with Fleck as we are, and he is socially reserved. Since we cannot woo voters on legal matters, we will have to entice them to come to the hustings for us in other ways."

Cecily's face creased in confusion, but Mrs. Hewett's eyes narrowed in shrewd understanding. "A charm offensive." Elsa nodded. The old lady cracked a laugh. "Marvelous! My sisters and I used to assist our mother when she went to every house in town, delivering cakes and jams and soaps and little sweets for the children on our father's behalf. He was returned to Commons every election, until he retired," she said, her voice ringing with pride.

"Just the sort of thing I had in mind," Elsa said. "Also, ribbons, banners, and buntings in Tory orange. We must get visual markers out there," she said, recalling Laura's Whig blue ribbon at Norman's speech. "Cecily, can you see about organizing some women to make and distribute those things? And Mrs. Hewett, since you have experience with it, can you take charge of the door-to-door gifts?"

Mrs. Hewett's spine straightened. "Leave it to me, Lady Fay."

"Excellent. Now, Oliver, if you do not yet have one, I need you to order an orange waistcoat and cravats. You wouldn't wear the waistcoat and cravats together, of course, but use them to add a dash of orange to your ensembles. Oh, and perhaps a hat?" She tapped her lip. "I wonder if I've time to get an order in to Mr. Milton in London. He did the most ingenious—"

"Elsa!" Oliver blurted.

She startled, nearly dropping her glass. "What?"

"In all of your schemes, am I anything but a doll for you to dress up and pose? Ribbons and jams and hats—my God! I do not want a petticoat campaign—begging your pardon, ladies," he hastily added, nodding to the others. "But you seem to have planned this whole thing around women. Need I remind you who does the voting?"

Mrs. Hewett snorted into her drink. Cecily's mouth carved a sly smile. Elsa clucked her tongue. "Oh, Oliver. You really should have married. Had you done so, you would know that while it might be a man on the hustings stating how he votes, that vote is the communal property of everyone in his household. You can be certain each and every elector will have heard plenty from his wife and children, and that there may even be grief if he casts that vote against their wishes. Men want harmony at home. They listen to their wives." She tilted her head and pinned him in a sharp stare. "Mr. Wynford-Scott is going for the intellect, economics, this and that reform. He's good at that, very good, but he lacks the emotional connection that will sway the hearts of Fleck. If you want to win, dear cousin, you would be wise to begin with the women."

Oliver pursed his mouth thoughtfully. Elsa straightened and smiled sweetly. "Or, if you do not care for my advice, you're welcome to try to find someone else who knows how to win an election."

• • •

The following morning, Elsa met Lady Laura Beaufort in front of the village's little chapel as throaty clangs reverberating from the squat bell tower sounded ten o'clock.

"Meeting like this feels clandestine almost," Laura said with a note of delight.

"Well, neither of us can come to the other's home until the election is over, or risk our assorted menfolk accusing us of duplicity," Elsa pointed out. "The village is neutral territory. Speaking of duplicity, what can you tell me about Fleck's favorite Whig?"

Elsa had kept an eye on her drive, expecting Norman to appear, not sure whether she hoped for the visit or dreaded it. Thus far, it had been a moot point, for he had not come.

Laura twirled her parasol between her fingertips. "Well, you didn't hear it from me, of course, but last night, Sir Seymour told Mr. Wynford-Scott that they would spend today visiting the mills and some of the outlying farms. Mr. Wynford-Scott is most eager to prove himself a friend to the common man. He said something about farmers being like mothers to us all. Mr. Alderly laughed, but you know, I think Mr. Wynford-Scott really meant it."

He would have, Elsa thought. Norman had a way of seeing the good in others—or the potential for it. Even her, she realized. Though she'd shamed herself with drunkenness in front of Norman numerous times, he'd still asked her help with his Christmas revels.

For the first time, she wondered why. She'd been a mess back then, starting her day with gin in her tea and continuing to imbibe until she passed out at night. As she'd pointed out to whoever would listen, Norman was an intelligent man. Inexperienced with women, perhaps, but he was well aware of her predilection for drink. Hell, on more than one occasion, he'd had to see her home when she was too far gone to take care of herself.

And yet, knowing what he knew about her, he had asked her to assist him in staging what would be an incredible feat for him at Gray's Inn. He'd trusted her. Believed in her.

Misplaced trust, said the little voices.

She'd spoiled his important night; it was true. But that didn't give him leave to come here and torment her, to stir Guilt and Shame back to life when she'd being doing so well to forget the muck she'd made of everything in London.

Unaware of her companion's dour musings, Laura went on, "And then tomorrow, Mr. Wynford-Scott is going canvassing here in the village. Oh, there's Mrs. Keane," Laura interrupted herself to wave at the barber's wife stepping out of the vicarage, cradling her infant son.

Laura and Elsa bent over baby Jacob and lavished him with compliments. As Mrs. Keane went on her way, Elsa felt a pang of longing in her heart. Politics were a cold replacement for a child, but she would find a different sort of fulfillment as Oliver's political hostess.

"When I came down this morning," Laura said, her eyes also following the young mother, "Sir Seymour and Mr. Wynford-Scott were already gone from the house. I was glad to have our meeting to look forward to, for I don't care to be left alone with Mr. Alderly."

Elsa raised her brows. "What's he done?"

"Nothing, he's just too … oh, I don't know. Too polished, I suppose. Too witty. Too charming. Too well dressed. He's perfectly polite, but I can't help but think there's a hidden meanness beneath all that civility."

Elsa suppressed a shiver. Her friend's words reminded her of her late husband. Her gaze moved down the lane where she saw an enormous horse plodding their way, a smallish figure on his back, and a tall man striding alongside. When they came a bit closer, Elsa could see that it was Sir Seymour astride Apple. The squire's face was pale, his lips pulled tight.

"Sir Seymour!" Laura ran to intercept them. "Husband, what's happened?"

Norman caught Elsa's eye. A shadow of worry creased his brow, but he nodded at her in greeting.

Sir Seymour made a bow from the saddle, which drew a wince. "Good morning, my dear. Lady Fay. Nothing to worry about, darling. Just wrenched my knee, is all."

"Where is your horse?"

"Left him at Olstead's place. Made a damned fool of myself bragging to Mr. Wynford-Scott here how Jasper and I could take the millstream. Cleared it just fine, but the horse landed hard and stumbled. Pulled his shoulder, I think, and down I went."

"You made a fine showing," Norman assured the squire. "Lady Beaufort, you'd have been proud. Your husband threw himself clear of the horse and rolled, nimble as an acrobat. If it hadn't been for catching his foot on a root, he'd not have a scratch on him."

"Generous assessment," Sir Seymour grumbled. "If you don't mind, I think I'll hobble from here. The surgery's just there," he said, pointing, "and sitting on this confounded broad beast of yours has made me numb in places I'd rather not mention in front of the ladies."

Norman assisted Sir Seymour down. The squire put his arm across his wife's shoulders, and together, they staggered to the surgeon's house just down the way.

After the couple disappeared through the door, an awkward silence fell between Elsa and Norman. They looked at one another, the air thick with things better left unsaid.

"I'd best be on my way, then." She nodded before adding, "Good morning, Mister—"

His hand shot out, clasped her shoulder. "Elsa, don't go. Please. I don't like this coldness between us."

"How novel, to hear you pleading with me to stay, as I so clearly recall begging the same from you, when I was in need. A request you flatly refused." She widened her eyes as if an epiphany had just come to her. "Perhaps *that's* the reason for this coldness between us."

Lifting his hat from his head, Norman swiped the back of his wrist across his brow. His face was smudged with dirt. "That's not how it was, Elsa. You'd made it clear you didn't want anything more from me after ... Well, after." Elsa's eyes narrowed dangerously, and he hastily went on, "Besides, you needed to do things on your own, didn't you? Fight your habit. Stand on your feet and face it down yourself." He smiled, that shy, lopsided, boyish smile that made the corners of his eyes crinkle and her stomach flip. "You did it, didn't you? I knew you would. And you look wonderful now, Elsa, healthy and well and beautiful and—"

"So why are you here?" she blurted, tamping down the little spurt of pleasure at his compliment. "Why have you come now, if I need to stand on my own? Because you *are* here on my account, aren't you?"

"Elsa ..." he said cautiously. "It isn't so simple."

"Aren't you?" she insisted. He said nothing, just stood there looking so torn, like she was the one hurting him, instead of the other way around. "I don't understand you, Norman. You abandoned me months ago. And yes, I did find my way through it, but it was hell, Norman. It was hell. I really could have used a friend."

He flinched. "Are you saying I should have spent the winter living in your house?"

"Of course not, you great lummox, but you could have written. You could have asked how I was getting on. Instead, I only had the occasional note from Sheri, and those have become nothing but bland niceties since he married. As it should be," she added primly, "but it didn't leave me with much in the way of contact with the outside world."

A muscle in Norman's jaw ticked. "Perhaps I should have written," he conceded, crossing his arms over his chest. "But I didn't know whether my correspondence would be welcomed. And there were matters demanding my attention."

Something in his tone raised the hairs on the nape of his neck. "What matters?"

"Nothing. It doesn't signify." Apple bent his neck and lipped Norman's pocket.

"Are you carrying sugar around? He'll burst his buckle, if you aren't careful."

"He likes it," Norman answered defensively, fishing out a treat for the greedy equine. "I feel badly that he has to carry gigantic me around. The occasional lump of sugar seems fair compensation for services rendered."

Elsa couldn't resist softening at the sight of the large man feeding his horse a sweet, his pale face streaked brown. "Why are you dirty?"

"Mr. Olstead's plow had flipped into a ditch. The way it was laying, it was too much for his horse to drag out on its own."

"So ... *you* teamed up with the horse to pull out the plow? Why didn't you have Apple do it?" At Norman's scandalized expression, she rolled her eyes. "Oh, yes, how forgetful of me. Poor, overworked Apple. Wouldn't like to make the draught horse pull anything. Heaven forfend."

He laughed at her teasing, a wonderful, open-throated sound that made her close her eyes in pleasure. Her blood quickened, and needy sensations darted across her skin. She never took a lover while she was in Fleck, but it had been a long time since she'd had an assignation. Months and months. The sample she'd had of Norman's lovemaking that fateful night in the inn now seemed a stingy morsel. She wanted to go to bed with him. Badly. But it couldn't happen. Not in Fleck. Perhaps nowhere. Not when he stood in the way of her regaining her place in London political circles, the one place she knew she could live a fulfilling, sober life.

"Go back to Gray's, Norman," she said quietly when his laughter subsided. "Surely you're due to be called to the bar this term. Withdraw from this campaign. Please."

He took a step closer. And another. Elsa's stomach fluttered. One of his hands cupped her nape, the other slipped to the small of her back, and he pulled her close. She'd missed them, those hands that had brought her such exquisite pleasure. To have them upon her again was bliss. He was warm and smelled of dirt and horse and fresh air and still that steady, sure aroma that was pure Norman. Her breasts plumped, her nipples taut with anticipation.

He brought his head alongside hers, touched his nose behind her ear. Elsa felt the hairs of her temple caught on his mouth. Was he going to kiss her? Was he going to—

"I cannot go back to Gray's," he murmured, "and I will not withdraw from this contest. I want that seat, Elsa, and I will win it."

Turning her head sharply to meet his eyes, Elsa's heart caught in her throat. The soft green of his eyes gleamed with warmth and wanting, and she had the oddest suspicion that when he spoke of winning the seat, he wasn't talking about Parliament, at all.

Chapter Nine

The following morning found Norman looking down the length of Weatherhill Lane. Located on the eastern edge of Fleck, the stone-paved street was lined on one side with houses, while the land dropped away on the other side of the road to overlook a dell, through which ran the millstream where Sir Seymour had suffered his accident the previous day.

Each house on Weatherhill Lane had only a scrap of garden, but the residents had made the most of their little portions of earth. He unlatched the gate of the first house and stooped to pass beneath an arbor draped with wisteria vines. A middle-aged woman in a plain brown dress with a white apron tied about her waist answered his knock with a white apron tied about her waist.

"Can I help you, sir?"

"Good morning, madam," Norman said, touching the brim of his hat. "My name is Norman Wynford-Scott, and I am standing for the vacant Commons seat here in Fleck."

"Are you now? *Hmm.*" She gave a nod of approval. "I've lived in Fleck all my life, and no one standing for Parliament has ever bothered coming to my door. Would you like to come in?"

"Jess, who's there?" called a man's voice.

"Mr. Wynford-Scott," the woman returned over her shoulder. "Standing for Ben Jonson's seat, he says."

"*What?*" There was a clatter of crockery, and then the man of the house appeared, wiping his palms down the front of his waistcoat. "The Whig, are you, young man?"

"Yes, sir." Norman extended his hand. "Norman Wynford-Scott, at your service, sir."

"John Gregory, at yours. My word, that's quite a grip you've got there, young man. I suppose you're here to persuade me to vote for you."

Norman chuckled. "I would be honored to have your vote if you feel I've earned it. Mostly, however, I wanted to introduce myself and ask what issues are on your mind and discuss what the government can do to help address those problems."

Husband and wife exchanged an impressed look. Gregory placed a hand on his chest and mummed a chest pain. "The Lord might as well take me now, for I've seen it all. A politician asking what he can do for me!"

They passed a lively ten minutes discussing matters ranging from taxation to refuse disposal. Mr. Gregory shook Norman's hand again before he departed and pledged his vote. Norman was smiling wide as he knocked on the next door. Robin Alderly had offered to come along with the registry of electors so Norman would know ahead of time who dwelt in each house, but Norman preferred to do things this way, learning about Fleck's constituents from the people themselves, rather than from a ledger.

In the next house dwelt two spinster sisters. There was no vote there for Norman to earn, but that did not stop them from voicing their opinions on civic matters large and small. "Agatha, what was it you said about the window tax? Do you remember? Oh, a year or so ago, I suppose. No, I didn't think to mark the date! It was so clever, Mr. Wynford-Scott could surely benefit from hearing it. What was that? You'll have to speak up, dear."

Norman, too, had trouble hearing the lady, for a clamor had started up at the opposite end of Weatherhill Lane. Glancing toward the hubbub, he saw a group of about a dozen people waving orange pennants and streamers. A fiddler and flutist playing lively tunes gave the procession a carnivalesque air. Two persons broke away from the front, a man and a woman. Though separated by the distance of ten houses, Norman immediately recognized Elsa, her black hair tied up in a crown woven with orange ribbons and her dress likewise festooned with Tory-orange trimmings. The man beside her he presumed to be her cousin, Mr. Oliver Fay. The gentleman wore an orange hat and gloves with his otherwise subdued ensemble. Buoyed by the cheers of their supporters, Elsa and Mr. Fay approached the door of the first house on that end of the street.

What were the odds that on the very day Norman came canvassing Weatherhill Lane—the first time in living memory any candidate had done so, according to the residents—the Fay campaign would show up on the very same street for the very same purpose? "Unbelievable!" he bellowed.

"That's what I said, when Agatha put it to me that way!" agreed the old spinster. "A tax on air and light—gifts to us from God Himself. By what right does Parliament justify such a taxation?"

Norman thanked the sisters for their time and strode down the brief walk, his eyes narrowing on Elsa's little parade as he approached the next house. If she thought he would be outdone by gaudy showmanship, she would soon discover the error of her assumptions.

Jaw clenched, Norman raised his fist and pounded on the door.

• • •

"And who is this?" Elsa stooped to smile at the girl peeking around her mother's skirts.

The mother, clutching the candles and soaps Elsa had produced from her basket of canvassing goodies, stroked the child's head with her free hand. The woman's husband and Oliver stood off to the side, their heads bent in conversation. "This is our Mary."

"Hello, Mary," Elsa said. "How old are you?"

"I have a brother!" Mary yelled in reply.

Elsa widened her eyes. "Do you? Is he here? I have treats for the both of you."

"Sammy!" The girl spun and ran, yelling for her sibling. A moment later, she returned with an even younger tot in tow, his pudgy hand clasped in hers.

"For you, Mary." Elsa reached into the basket and produced a length of orange ribbon. "For your lovely hair. And for you, Sammy, look!" With a flourish, she produced a wooden soldier painted the requisite orange. The little boy squealed with delight and immediately stuffed the doll's head into his mouth.

"I want a soldier, too!" Mary wailed. "Here Sammy, I'll trade you my ribbon for the solider." The baby, uninterested in the finer points of the barter system, yowled in protest when his sister tried to pry the toy from him.

"That's quite all right," Elsa said with a laugh. "You may have the ribbon and a soldier of your own, too, Mary. I should have asked which you'd prefer."

On the street, the musicians struck up the music Elsa had instructed them to play after she and Oliver had spent ten minutes at each house. She rose and took the mother's hand. "They're absolute darlings."

"Thank you, Lady Fay," the woman answered. "And thank you so much for the lovely gifts. Mary, what do you say to Lady Fay?"

"Fank you," Mary intoned then scampered back into the house.

Oliver was taking his leave of the husband. Elsa took the man's hand when Oliver released it. "Thank you for your time," she said. "You have a beautiful family. I hope we can count on your vote." Then she planted a kiss on his cheek, prompting cheers from the onlookers.

Their merry little troupe moved on to the next house. As Elsa swept through the front gate, she glanced down the lane and saw Norman speaking with the householder several doors down. The householder, however, kept glancing down the lane at Elsa's canvassing party, leaving Norman struggling to hold the man's attention. A satisfied smile curved her mouth. This was her one-hundredth day without drink, and she felt like celebrating. How better than to spread music and gifts to her neighbors—especially if doing so could detract from the man who was trying to rob her of this victory? Thanks to Laura, she'd known ahead of time where Norman would be this morning. Her political activity was the one thing she had ever done successfully. She needed this, needed to prove to both herself and Norman that she was good at this—better than him.

More doors knocked upon, more gifts given, more children admired, more cheeks kissed. One enterprising oldster told Elsa she'd have the promise of his vote for Mr. Fay if she bussed him on the mouth. Elsa feigned uncertainty until the crowd cheered her on; then she kissed the fellow's lips with a loud *smack.*

"I have your word, then," Elsa laughed as they turned to leave, "and I'll hold you to it!"

One of the women swapped Elsa's empty gift basket for a full one. The lads playing the flute and violin marched in a circle, showing off the banners they wore like capes, painted with the words: A VOTE FOR FAY IS A VOTE FOR FLECK! "Onward!" called one of the men. Oliver gave Elsa his arm, and they turned to the next gate ...

Just as Norman reached it.

• • •

Oh, wasn't this just rich. Norman stepped to the gate just as Elsa and her cousin reached it from the other direction. Why couldn't they wait a few minutes for Norman to speak to the residents first? Or skip this house and come back later? Elsa's grin was more a baring of teeth, and her cousin likewise had peeled his lips back in something cordial-adjacent.

"Good morning, Lady Fay," Norman said, tipping his hat. "What a pleasant surprise."

"The pleasantest," Elsa agreed, her convivial tone belied by the flash of ire in her eyes. "Lovely weather we're enjoying today." Behind her, the Tory supporters were falling quiet. The violinist, oblivious to the import of the confrontation, kept sawing his bow across the strings; the other musician bopped his head with the flute.

"Capital. And may I say, Lady Fay, you are looking especially lovely this morning." Her hairstyle was expertly done, but the simple concept put him in mind of a miss on her way to a country fair. Her dress was an intriguing juxtaposition, an elegant ensemble fit for Town. She wore a spencer of pale yellow velvet over a silk dress of butternut orange—a much kinder take on the Tory hue than the eye-searing shade of the pennants and whatnot the others were bandying about.

"You look like a night sky," he said abruptly. "Sunset and darkness"—his gaze swept over her gown and cut to her hair—"and the moonlight of your skin. And your eyes are the deepest blue of the midnight heavens, crystalline and perfect, cradling the cosmos in their depths."

Elsa's hard smile faltered, fell. A question passed through those indigo irises.

Suddenly aware of their audience, Norman hastily added, "Of course, you'd look better in blue than that abominable shade." He extended his hand to Elsa's companion, ignoring the daggers shooting from the lady's gaze. "You must be Mr. Fay. Norman Wynford-Scott."

"An honor, Mr. Wynford-Scott," Fay answered. "Your presence here has certainly invigorated our local political discourse."

"Thank you. Shall we?" Norman swung open the gate and swept his hand for the Fays to precede him.

Elsa arched one black, winged brow. "Together?"

"Why not?" Norman lifted a brow in return. "It may be illuminating for all involved."

Norman stood just behind the Fays on the stoop while Elsa knocked. The door sprung open at once, revealing a couple that had clearly been watching the goings-on from their front window. Both husband and wife sported eager smiles. The husband's face looked freshly scrubbed; his hair bore the furrows of a recent combing.

"Lady Fay!" the woman declared. "And Mr. Fay. And Mr. Wynford-Scott, too, isn't it? How nice to see you all. *What can we do for you?*" she asked in a wry tone, punctuated by a wink.

"Hello, Mrs. Talwin, Mr. Talwin. How are you today?" Elsa began. "Mr. Fay and I are taking advantage of this beautiful morning to greet our neighbors and offer small tokens of our esteem. Have you tried this new jam Mrs. Duff created? Melon with basil. The most delicious spread ever to touch a scone, I declare."

Elsa fished a jar out of her basket and pressed it into Mrs. Talwin's hands. The woman made an appropriately impressed sound. "*Oooo*, delightful! Thank you, my lady. Mr. Fay." Mrs. Talwin turned expectant eyes on Norman.

Elsa twisted about to give him an amused look. *Beat that*, she seemed to say.

Norman cleared his throat. He might not have baubles and trinkets with which to buy votes, but he did have ideas. Lots of them. "Mrs. Talwin, if you wished to purchase a jar of that jam from Mrs. Duff, how would you reach her?"

The older woman screwed up her nose and looked at her husband, as if wondering whether Norman was trying to fun her. "She lives just over the way," Mrs. Talwin answered, nodding across the valley. "I'd take the millstream road, cross the bridge, and—"

"And if there's been a heavy rain?" he interrupted.

"Oh, no, in that case the road would be a mess. The bridge might be under water. I'd have to wait for another day to get my jam." She hoisted her gift. "Good thing I've this one to tide me over!"

"What if I told you," Norman said, "that the government could send an engineer to survey the millstream road and build a drainage system to divert water away from the road? How about a raised bridge that wouldn't be washed over with every rain?"

The woman's eyes were agog. "You could do that?" She elbowed her husband. "Hear that, Mr. Talwin? Mr. Wynford-Scott says the government can fix up our roads! Why haven't they done it before now?" she asked, turning a befuddled look to the Fays.

Oliver's lips moved silently. Elsa jumped in with a reply. "The government in London can only respond where it knows there is a need, Mrs. Talwin. Our esteemed opponent has taken note of our admittedly ... adventuresome roads here in Fleck, the same as any passerby could do. But it takes someone with a lifetime's experience in the community to know what this borough most needs. What Mr. Wynford-Scott suggests is a public roads improvement project that would necessitate a considerable amount of tax revenue to fund. How do you feel about an outsider coming to Fleck and raising your taxes, Mr. Talwin?"

The man shot Norman a dirty look. "Not very well!" His wife shook her head at Norman, as though he'd been caught pilfering from the collection plate.

Norman's startled gaze flew to Elsa. Her full lips quirked. In spite of himself, he admired her quick reply and the acuity with which she'd countered his proposal. The woman knew her way around a government project. Who would have thought a man could find such an attribute arousing? Yet here he stood, fighting to squelch the physical symptoms stirred by her political savvy.

"The Fays have always looked after Fleck," Oliver offered, his smooth voice a balm to the alarming fright of taxation. "With my brother, Lord Rollo Fay, in Lords and myself in Commons, Fleck will have twice as many Fays championing this district in Parliament."

"Will it?" Norman interjected. "Where is Lord Fay?" He spread his hands and gestured to the open countryside. "Here? Is he sitting his seat in the Lords?" Elsa's expression soured; she turned her face away. "It's my understanding that the viscount is traveling the Continent and has been for some time, neglecting his responsibilities to the very people whose rents make possible his luxurious life. Are you sure the Fays are still the best family to speak on behalf of this community?"

There was a strained silence, which Oliver finally broke. "In answer to Mr. Wynford-Scott's allegations, I assure you, Mr. and Mrs. Talwin, that I shall execute my duty as a member of Parliament to the best of my ability. And I thank you, Mr. Wynford-Scott," he added, turning to Norman, "for highlighting a point of concern. I shall think over what you have said, as should we all." He touched the brim of his hat and briskly strode back up the walk.

With her cousin's departure, Elsa returned her focus to the stoop. She regarded Norman thoughtfully, her brow pleated and lips pursed.

"Well, kiss him already," Mrs. Talwin told Elsa. "He's been bouncing around like a schoolboy this past half hour, waiting his turn for a kiss from the lovely lady."

At once, Elsa brightened, beaming a smile to the older couple. She circled her arms around Mr. Talwin's shoulders and kissed his weathered cheek. Mr. Talwin clapped a hand over his face as if to cherish the caress forever.

"I hope Mr. Fay can count on your vote." Elsa pinned an orange ribbon to Mr. Talwin's lapel, then added another kiss for good measure.

"I'm happy to kiss you, as well, sir," Norman deadpanned, "if that will win your vote for myself."

Mr. Talwin's face flared a screaming red. His wife hooted with laughter, as did the Fay supporters assembled in the street.

"Get on with you," Mr. Talwin said gruffly, waving his hand. Then to Elsa, "You should kiss *that* one. He'd pledge for your cousin on the spot."

Hoots of encouragement sounded from the parade. The flutist trilled. Elsa looked at Norman, raised her brows, and shrugged. She stepped forward, her eyes on his mouth.

Norman bent, catching her around the waist and meeting her lips with his own. The contact thudded through his entire being like a nail driven home. Her mouth was soft, yielding. Her hands splayed over his chest. The exotic fragrance of her perfume filled his nose and wrapped around his brain, driving away every thought but her. Holding her so briefly the day before and brushing his nose over her hair had been a tease, a torment. He wanted her again, wanted to possess her fully.

A muffled sound rose in her throat. Norman lifted his head, met her look of wide-eyed wonder.

"If that don't turn him Tory," crowed Mrs. Talwin, "nothing will!"

They said their farewells to the couple, then made their egress down the walk. Of habit, Norman gave Elsa his arm. She tugged on his sleeve and gestured him to bend close. She whispered, "Today is 100 days."

One hundred days? He frowned quizzically, but she just smiled and kept walking. They were met with such cheers from the crowd as they reached the gate, Norman was put in mind of a newlywed couple emerging from church.

"Well, Mr. Wynford-Scott," Elsa said, color high on her cheekbones, "you were correct. That was most illuminating. Good day, sir."

"Good day, Lady Fay." Norman bowed; upon straightening, he met Elsa's gaze one last time. She gave him a tiny smile, then proceeded onward to the next house.

In his turn, Norman resumed his solitary canvassing of Weatherhill Lane, this time knocking at the homes Elsa had already visited. When he introduced himself at the next door, the homeowner laughed and pointed at Norman's coat. Glancing down, he discovered that Elsa had pinned an orange ribbon to his lapel while distracting him with her kiss.

Nimble-fingered, quick-witted, politically shrewd, and dangerously seductive—a combination lethal to any man's senses. Norman couldn't afford to lose his head here. Elsa was savvy, playing to her popularity with the people of Fleck to entice them to vote for Mr. Fay, but Norman was a quick study. He refused to buy votes with jams and kisses, but he could show this village that he was a true friend and the representative they needed in Parliament.

Although, he thought ruefully as he unpinned the mocking orange ribbon from his lapel, kissing one's way to victory was a deuced clever plan.

Chapter Ten

The hustings was festooned with flowers and ribbons enough to make a maypole envious. Elsa stood on the platform beside Oliver, overlooking the picnic she and her brigade of lady volunteers had organized for the community. There were games and footraces, music and dancing, and plenty of prizes, food, and drink to go around. Some of Elsa's tame concoctions filled the punch bowls.

Oliver had protested that there must be beer, as well, and several of the women echoed his opinion. Elsa had relented at last, but ensured the beer table was behind the hustings, so she could avoid looking at it. Just knowing Mr. Denny from the Rabbit's Glen was right behind her, pulling pints for anyone with a thirst for it, made her throat dry.

"Come on," she said to her cousin, "you have to mingle."

He exhaled a weary sigh. "What's the use? I'll only be asked what I mean to do about excise taxes, or where I fall on land reform, or would I please make a statement regarding prisoners' rights. Did you ever hear such a thing, Elsa? Prisoners' rights!"

She gave him a nudge and led him to the stairs. Oliver plodded behind and continued grousing. "Everywhere I go, it's *issues* and *matters*. Wynford-Scott has gone and turned this contest bloody *political*."

Elsa ducked her head and smiled. Over the last weeks, Norman had proven himself a formidable opponent and a fine candidate. Not only was he well versed on the issues facing the nation at large, he had thrown himself into the task of getting to know Fleck and what needs faced the community. Nothing was too small for Norman. Besides retrieving the ditched plow, he had fetched eggs out from under Widow Gordon's ornery hen, dragged a heavy felled limb from the vicar's garden, and retrieved a toy—one of the Fay's wooden soldiers, no less—from the well where a boy had dropped it, earning Norman the hero worship of at least one seven-year-old constituent. Were Elsa not committed to her cousin and to the cause of regaining her own political life, she would have been proud to campaign on behalf of such an outstanding prospective member of Parliament.

And her opinion was in no way colored, she assured herself, by the kiss that plagued her dreams, even more so than her memories of that darkly passionate night they'd shared on the road. The way her blood sang in reply to his kiss on the Talwins' doorstep had been the response of her while completely sober and in full control of her faculties. She longed for him still, wished she could experience the pleasure of his touch without either the specter of her drunkenness or the obstacle of the election standing between them. Perhaps, when this was over ...

"Relax, Cousin," she admonished a grimacing Oliver, who was tugging at the stiff collar of his new orange waistcoat. "Enjoy yourself. There's only ten days remaining to the election, and then this will all be over and you'll have your seat."

The look he shot her silently begged to differ. "I've a feeling my troubles will only have just begun once we're in London. With you serving as my hostess, I'll never see the end of your managing."

Ignoring Oliver's complaints—men could be *such* grumblers— she smiled brightly to the man approaching her. "Mr. Gregory! How good of you to come. You remember Mr. Fay, of course?" Soon, the familiar pattern of hostessing took her mind from Oliver's doubts and soothed her anxiety over the alcohol so close to hand. There were men to charm and ladies to befriend, and Elsa did so with ease, moving from guest to guest as she had done in London for Harvey.

The sun was halfway toward the horizon when the festivities began to disperse. Elsa called good-bye to happy electors and their delighted families. Oliver was once more at her side, and at least put on a show of cheer, even if he did not feel it.

"Oh, such fun!" came a woman's voice from behind her. Elsa turned to find Laura casting a glum look around the remains of the picnic. "It's not fair that I had to miss out on such a lovely time, just because my husband supports the opposing candidate."

Elsa chuckled at Laura's pout. "As if you aren't having fun of your own? Or did I simply overlook my invitation to the dinner party you held on Mr. Wynford-Scott's behalf? By all accounts, it was a spectacular affair. Live fish in bowls of floating blossoms, I heard."

Laura slanted a wry smile. "Point made and taken. Still, I wish you could have been there, and most especially, I wish I could have consulted you on the menu. Oh, I agonized over it for hours!"

Oliver turned away from a departing guest and addressed the newcomer. "Lady Beaufort, good afternoon."

"Hello, Mr. Fay. Won't we all be happy when this season of election fever has passed? I declare, I've never been so exhausted in my life."

"Indeed," Oliver agreed, "there is a special fatigue that comes with campaigning for which I was entirely unprepared. Confound it!" he suddenly blurted. "What are they about? This is my damned picnic." Shooting a glower at Laura, Oliver took off at a brisk stride.

Spinning about, Elsa saw that Sir Seymour stood on the edge of the green, greeting villagers as they left. A small group waving blue flags stood behind him, and the church pianist was gathering up children and directing them in an impromptu sing-along of "God Save the King."

"Laura!" Elsa cried in dismay. "How could you?"

Her friend shrugged helplessly. "It wasn't my idea, Elsa, I swear. I only arranged for the music and ordered flowers for the nosegays."

Sure enough, two cherubic-faced little girls armed with baskets of flowers were handing out nosegays of blue flowers.

Norman stood on the edge of the gathering, back turned to the crowd, his head bent in conference with Mr. Alderly.

"Upstage my picnic, will you?" Elsa fumed. Lifting her skirts, she marched across the green, hot on her cousin's heels, determined to give that Whig scoundrel a piece of her mind. And not a nice piece, either.

Oliver already had Sir Seymour in hand. Though Elsa could not hear his words, Oliver's sharp gestures and flushed face indicated the direction of that conversation.

"Here miss!" One of the little girls stepped in front of Elsa, proffering a little bouquet of cornflowers and baby's breath tied up in a blue ribbon. "A gift for you from the party of reform," the child recited. "Please 'member to support Mister Wyn ..." Her nose screwed up in concentration. "Mister Wynford-Shlot."

"Close enough, darling. Thank you." Elsa took the flowers from the beaming child and clenched them in a tight fist, her eyes narrowed on the giant man's back. Clubbing him over the head with the flowers wouldn't do any harm, but it would be *so* satisfying to watch them erupt all over his stupid, sneaky face.

She heard the low rumble of his voice, and he was making agitated gestures of his own, seemingly oblivious to the fracas erupting behind him.

Elsa stopped, practically standing on Norman's heels. The second he turned around, he'd have a face full of botanical ire.

"Calm down," Alderly said, placing a hand on Norman's arm. "No one knows about our screening. And as I've told you, as soon as the election is behind you, there's no reason to think it will ever come up."

Hissing sharply, Elsa staggered back as if struck. Directly into Oliver. "Steady on," her cousin said in a low voice, "just let me get my hands on—"

Panic surged in Elsa's middle. "No." She grasped Oliver's arm and pulled, suddenly desperate to be anywhere but here. "Leave it, Oliver, please."

A phlegmy sound of disgust rattled in his throat. "What? We cannot let them get away with this!"

Get away, her mind echoed. The thought had great appeal. Her nape crawled. Had Norman turned around and seen her? She couldn't look.

Screened.

"Do as you will," she said tightly. "I have to ... Mrs. Hewett needs help with the punch bowls. Excuse me."

Bunching her skirts in one fist, she hurried across the green, then darted down the street that would carry her home. Air rasped through her tight throat as Alderly's words whirled through her mind.

Screening. It was a form of punishment at the Inns of Court, she knew from her past political associations with barristers and judges. It was held in reserve for transgressions that warranted severe censure, but fell shy of expulsion or disbarment.

There was only one thing over which Norman could have possibly been screened: the Christmas revels. He'd been sent away from the Inn because of her, because of her stupid drunken shenanigans. A sobbing gasp tore from her chest, and hot tears splashed on her cheek.

Now she knew why he'd come to Fleck and why he wanted so badly to defeat her.

• • •

She was sitting on a stool by the door when the knock came. Though she'd expected it, the shuddering of the door in its frame startled her from the stupor in which she'd passed the late afternoon.

When Norman saw her, the smile slid from his face, to be replaced by an expression of concern. "Elsa? What's happened? I came as soon as I could. Your note didn't say ..."

His words faded, overcome by an expectant silence.

Elsa stepped back. "Thank you for coming, Norman. Please, come in."

He removed his hat and ducked his head to enter her house. *How often must he do that*, she mused, *bend to fit in a world not built for a man of his size?*

She led him into her parlor, where a pitcher of her chilled strawberry tea awaited. As she poured the drinks, she asked, "Do you mind being so tall? I imagine it must be a nuisance."

"It is, at times. Thank you," he said as he accepted his glass. He took a sip. "That's good!"

"Made it myself," she said, sitting beside him on the settee. "After I stopped drinking, I became creative with nonintoxicating liquids." Despite her distress from the day's revelation, she experienced a thrill at being able to speak so freely. To whom else would she have dared utter the words *after I stopped drinking* ...?

Looking down at the glass cupped between his palms, he smiled. "Good for you, Elsa. That's a brilliant idea."

She shrugged, uncomfortable with his praise. How could he speak so kindly when she'd wronged him so?

"The worst part about being my size," he said after a moment's pause, "is that I worry about inadvertently causing injury to others. Just before coming here, I nearly elbowed Sir Seymour's footman in the face when the poor man helped me into my coat."

A sad smile curved her lips. She was the one who had caused inadvertent harm. "I don't think you could hurt another person even if you wanted to, Norman. You're so considerate, always watching where you step—"

"Because I trampled countless toes when I had my growth spurt."

"... begging your pardon for no reason other than standing in the open air the same as everyone else. You even apologize to that spoiled beast you call a horse for having to carry you. Speaking of ..." She glanced out the window to the empty drive.

"I left Apple in Beaufort's stable," he said, chagrined. "It was only a mile and a half. But I'll have you know"—he wagged a finger—"I am capable of hurting someone when I want to. Struck a man for the first time not long ago."

"Really?" Leaning back, Elsa crossed her legs. "I am all astonishment. You must share the tale."

He lifted one shoulder in a shrug, the muscle rolling beneath the brown superfine of his coat. "It was some fool at Gray's. He, *um* ... he slandered a lady's honor." Norman did not meet her gaze, instead casting his eyes at the portrait of Elsa's deceased parents that hung above the mantel.

Her heart sank. "It was me, wasn't it?" she asked. "The night of the Christmas revels."

He nodded.

Elsa drew a shuddering breath. "Norman, were you punished for what transpired that night? Were you screened?"

He froze, his eyes wide. After a moment, his gaze dropped. He rolled his glass between his palms, his jaw clenched. When he glanced at her, his eyes were shuttered. "Yes."

"For how long?"

"Two years."

Elsa nodded slowly, absorbing this intelligence. Two years. His life had been arrested two years, because of her. He should have been called to the bar by now; instead of launching his career as an advocate, he'd been forced to find another living.

"I don't know ..." she started, but her voice was thick with unshed tears. She cleared her throat and tried again. "I don't know how to apologize for what I've done, Norman, but you can have those inadequate words: I'm sorry. I'm so, so sorry for what I did that night. You worked so hard to get to where you were, and I wrecked it. I ruined everything for you."

"Elsa ..." Norman took her glass and set both on a table. His knuckle slipped along her jaw and tipped up her chin. He regarded her with warmth and a bit of exasperation, but he said no more, simply reached for her hands. Her fingers were dwarfed by his; the comfort of his firm grip gave her the courage to go on.

"I will go to London straightaway and speak to the benchers." Her breath hitched on a cry. "They should know that none of what transpired was your fault. It was I who brought that flammable whiskey, and it was I who got so drunk on it that I became thoughtless and started the fire. Your only transgression was inviting me to participate."

Her lips quivered, and tears ran freely from her eyes. Elsa lowered her face, her eyes on where their hands were joined together, expecting every second that he would take his away.

But he didn't.

"Are you still trying to get me to abandon this contest?"

She breathed a watery laugh. "Of course. Is it working?"

"Elsa, why are you so sad?" he asked.

His voice held such compassion, she could scarcely stand it. Why could he not stomp about and yell and tell her what a wretch she was, as she so richly deserved? "Because, no ..." she gasped, "no matter what I do, that night keeps haunting me. The consequences of my abominable behavior never seem to end. Bad enough I nearly ruined my own health with my drinking, but I ruined your life, too. You! The gentlest, best soul there ever was. And I—I hate myself for it, Norman, I do. I had thought I'd put this all behind me, moved beyond that night, but I haven't. That was arrogance on my part, I suppose, to think I wouldn't have more to answer for."

His brows drew together in a sharp *V*. "Arrogance?" His eyes hardened. "You would call it *arrogance* to move past a painful moment in your life? Elsa ...” Norman pressed a hand to his mouth. Then he stood, rolled his shoulders back, and cracked his neck. He paced to the other side of the room, pivoted on the ball of his foot. His gaze found hers and held. And held. Firming his lips, he nodded, as if reaching a decision.

“At first, I did come here because of what happened, because of the screening. I was angry; I shan’t deny it.”

“Of course you were.”

His lips carved a humorless smile at her reassurance. Then he resumed his seat and scrubbed a hand through his hair, resulting in a rumple of brown waves. “I denied it to myself. Believed my primary interest was in the seat itself, not in thwarting you.”

A pang flashed behind her sternum. She rubbed the spot. “If I could take it all back, Norman ... You must believe I would.”

Soft green eyes followed the press of her fingers above her breasts. Slowly, he extended one of his own large hands and traced the almond shape of her fingernail with his blunt forefinger. “I know you would, Elsa,” he whispered, lightly dragging his finger down the back of her hand before enveloping it with his palm. Their entwined hands rested on her chest, heavy against the fullness of her breast. There was no way he did not feel her heart’s wild tempo.

His thumb described small circles on her skin, gentling her distress while stirring those desires she had struggled to hold at bay.

“But then I saw how well you were loved here,” he went on, “and I heard you speak. Do you know, Elsa Fay, you’re the sharpest politician I’ve ever met? No, it’s true!” he insisted at her sound of protest. “I’m glad it’s your cousin standing against me and not you, else I’d have no chance at all.”

She chuckled nervously, squeezed his hand. He returned the pressure, solid and comforting. “Do you forgive me?” she asked in a small voice.

Lifting his brow, he gave her an exasperated look. "Come here." With a tug, he pulled her into his lap. *Finally.* Elsa went willingly, gladly, knowing she was forgiven as he enveloped her in the shelter of his arms that felt like home and smelled so manly and good. His embrace was a physical relief, as if the sensation of his touch was the vital component her life had been lacking.

"You're forgiven, minx." One hand slid to the small of her back, holding her firm. The other cupped the side of her neck.

Elsa's arms slipped around his shoulders. She swung one foot idly, enjoying the novelty of being in the arms of a man who made her feel positively pocket-sized. Lifting her face, she grazed the underside of his jaw with her nose. Norman sighed his approval. "Will you continue, then? In the election, I mean. Since you aren't angry any longer ..."

Norman drew back, a small frown puckering his brow. "I mean to win that seat, Elsa."

"But you said—"

He brought a finger to her lips. Caught her eyes in a piercing gaze. Elsa's throat tightened painfully with the effort of not drawing his finger into her mouth. Vexing man. Infuriating man. Enormous, handsome, desirable man.

"I said my anger was part of the reason I chose to stand for election, yes, but that's not the whole of it. I cannot be called to the bar for at least two years, and it remains to be seen whether this little brouhaha will cast a pall over my future as an advocate. I need an alternative, and this is one I'm suited for."

A flurry of anxiety, like snowflakes, settled on her shoulders. It wasn't that she didn't understand Norman's reasons, it wasn't that she didn't sympathize, but him winning would mean her losing her chance at regaining the life in which she'd flourished. If she could not be Oscar's political hostess, what *would* she be? She'd be left floundering for an occupation that could help her keep her drinking habit in check. *Please, don't make me quill and knit and tat and spend an hour every Wednesday night with the Fleck Christian Ladies' Auxiliary.* The very thought of such a fate had her longing for a drink to numb the pain.

"Let's not talk about the election any longer," she pleaded, shying away from the unwelcome thoughts and burrowing into the strength of him. "Please." She couldn't bear to think about the ramifications of failure. Not tonight, when she wanted nothing more than to relish the sweetness of knowing she was forgiven and the simple joy of being a woman in the arms of a man. Clinging to his neck, she kissed his cheek. He shifted beneath her, restless.

"Last week," he said, his baritone voice the slightest bit strained, "last week when you said '100 days,' you meant 100 days since your last drink of alcohol, didn't you?"

She nodded against his temple. Kissed his cheekbone. Her fingers burrowed into the silk of his hair.

His breath came faster; his fingers clutched her waist. "It took me a couple hours, but I finally figured it out. At first, I thought you meant the days since we were in bed together, but the count was wrong. On the 100th day since your last drink, it had been ninety-eight days since I had you in my arms."

And with that, her joints went to jelly. Had he really been keeping a count of his own? Norman lifted his head, met her eyes with a melting half smile. As if in answer to her unspoken question, he said, "Ninety-eight days of wanting and missing you. Ninety-eight endless nights."

A cry escaped her. Elsa bought her hands to his cheeks and pulled his mouth to hers, poured months of longing and loneliness into her kiss. Norman slanted his mouth and parted his lips; Elsa opened hers in response, suckled his warm tongue into her hot mouth. She slid her tongue alongside his, back and forth, imagining it was her foot gliding up and down the length of his bare thigh while he lay atop her.

Norman's hands bracketed her hips, lifted and turned her so she straddled his lap. Elsa rocked against him, and he thrust upward, bumping his erection against her swollen mound through their clothes. She whimpered into his mouth; her nails nipped his shoulders. Allowing her head to drop back, she relished the sensation of his mouth working the column of her throat while one of his enormous hands enveloped her breast, massaging and claiming.

"Where's Foster?"

"Gone," she answered, kissing his cheekbone and brow and nose. "I sent all the servants away for the night." She clutched his cheeks and brought her forehead to rest on his. "Make love to me?"

"Yes," he growled. "God, yes."

He stood, easily supporting her weight with one arm, the other hand tweaking her nipple, driving her wild. There was something to be said for taking a giant for one's lover. She directed him to her bedchamber, where he deposited her gently onto the leaf-green counterpane. On her knees, Elsa loosened his cravat and then worked the buttons of his waistcoat.

"Wait ..." he breathed a laugh and shrugged out of his coat before shedding the waistcoat and cravat. His hands dived into her hair, and he kissed her deep, working loose the pins that had restrained her coif all day. He combed his fingers through her hair, untangling her locks and arranging them over her shoulders. Then he hung his head over her shoulder to see her back as he unfastened the line of buttons running down her dress.

When the muslin gaped, Elsa pulled it down her arms, pushed it to her hips, then flopped back onto her bum and held her legs out for Norman to finish the job. There was smiling and laughter as they undressed one another, playful tweaks and tickles as they revealed themselves to one another.

Finally, Norman shucked his breeches, and Elsa glimpsed his cock for the first time. It was commensurate with his height and then some, thick and heavily veined. The head, bulbous and ripe as a plum, oozed liquid from the slit at the tip; her mouth watered, her innards ached. It had been a long time since she'd lain with a man. She felt like she'd been waiting her whole life for this one. That he was hers and hers alone—

But was he? He was much bolder than he'd been the last time, more self-assured. "Have you been with someone? Since we were together?" She strove for a casual tone, but did not succeed in entirely suppressing the spurt of jealousy she felt at the notion that another woman may have claimed him.

He shook his head and stroked a hand down her breast. "No one, Elsa. There's no one but you."

Purring her approval, she wrapped a hand about his shaft and commenced stroking, base to tip.

Norman let out a guttural sound; his eyes rolled back in his head. "Sweet Jesus, Elsa." He bucked against her. She swiped a tongue over his tip, lapping up the glassy pearl and moaning at the salty-sweet flavor.

Beneath her fingers, she felt his blood fizzling in his cock, sensed his bollocks drawing up tight. She pulled the head into her mouth, laved her tongue around its spongy circumference.

Norman's hips jerked. When she glanced up, Elsa saw a sheen of perspiration on his brow. It wouldn't be long now. With a happy moan, she slid her eyes closed and she lowered her head to take more of him into her mouth.

"No, wait, please." His hand came to her shoulder, and he gently guided her back onto the pillows. "That's so good, what you were doing. Too good. I don't want to end that way."

"Come here." Elsa parted her knees wide and wider until he was comfortably nestled in the cradle of her hips. Norman's fingers parted her, sank into her silken heat. Elsa's head tipped back on a low moan. He found her clitoris with his thumb and rubbed little circles around the taut bud.

Elsa arched against him, her legs writhing.

"May I ...?" he panted.

"Yes, yes, go on."

Norman reared up over her and fitted himself at her entrance. As he notched the head into her welcoming heat, he leaned forward and grasped one of her hands with his, tangling their fingers together above her head, while the other fed his considerable length into her body. Elsa felt herself stretched to the limit to accommodate his width, a pleasurable burn that singed her nerves from head to toe.

When he stopped, her eyes fluttered open to find him staring at their joining, a look of consternation on his face. "I don't want to hurt you. You'll have to tell me if what I'm doing is ..." His voice faltered. "I want to be good for you," he confessed, his face a miracle of raw emotion.

Inside her heart, something golden and new began to grow. "More," she urged. "Give me your all. I can take it. I can take you."

With a groan of surrender, he sank his weight onto her and drove his cock home. Elsa bowed upward. Never had she experienced such a sensation. She was so full, she wasn't certain where Norman stopped and she began.

Then he started moving, and any semblance of two separate entities was utterly obliterated. Norman's body was Elsa's pleasure, his withdrawal and thrust were her own nerves coming to life, the slide of his sweat-slick belly against her sensitized nipples was her climax building and building.

Elsa brought her legs to his hips, urging him to ride her harder, to thrust ever deeper. It was beautiful madness, this absolute possession. Her fingers grappled at his back as she slipped into the abyss. "Norman," she cried, lost, but then he was there, his mouth on hers as she broke and fell to pieces around him in convulsions and tremors of pleasure.

And just as she drifted downward, Norman found his own release, calling her name as he came, the pulse of his heavy cock inside her triggering another orgasm. She came and came until her vision went black at the edges.

When she was sensible again, she was cradled in his arms, nestled against his chest. "Did I smother you?" he asked, fretful. "You were so dazed."

"I was dazed because of the back-to-back orgasms you gave me, you great lummox, not because you smothered me."

"Oh," he said. And then, cheerfully, "Oh."

His fingers combed her hair again, and Elsa hummed in satisfaction. When she felt sufficiently recovered, she rose and went to the washbasin, her hips swinging loose as she crossed the room to clean herself. She brought the flannel back and tenderly cleansed Norman's softened member, laying heavy against his thigh like a slumbering dragon.

"I hope your first time did not disappoint," she said, unaccountably nervous. It was a first time of sorts for her, too. Never had she shared her bed in Fleck with any man. Norman's opinion mattered a great deal—more than any other lover's ever had.

"That was beyond wonderful." His brown hair flopped onto his forehead, and he swiped it back with a large hand. "I would do that with you incessantly if you let me." He gave her an impish grin. "Will you?"

Laughing, she fell into his arms. She rode him that time, her thighs jouncing as she worked his cock, her breasts bouncing in time with the pace she set. Norman's hands enveloped her buttocks as he held fast to her as if clinging for his life, letting Elsa take him where she would, until they careened over the edge together.

Later, she stirred against his side. "What time is it?" she asked, her voice thick with sleep.

Norman sat up and found the clock on her mantel. "Almost midnight."

Elsa fished her journal and pen from the drawer of her bedside table and opened the book to the double pages that recorded her sobriety. With Norman looking on, she made the day's tick.

"One hundred and six full days of sobriety," she said.

Norman rested his chin on her shoulder as he ran a finger over her marks from the beginning to the most recent.

"I'm so proud of you, Elsa. Look at you. You're so strong. Look at what you've achieved."

That golden warmth in her chest unfurled a little more, and she leaned her head against his. "I'm no hero. It hasn't been easy."

"That's what makes you a hero," he countered. "If it was easy to stop, there would be no drunkards. But it isn't easy; it's bloody difficult. And you did it. You're doing it, every day." He was quiet for a time, then said haltingly, "I'm sorry I left you when I did, when we arrived here. You asked me to stay, and I should have."

Elsa shook her head. "No, you did exactly the right thing. It had to be that way. I did have to stand on my own." She turned to face him, brought a hand to his cheek. "But I'm so glad you're here now."

Chapter Eleven

A soft rain fell from low, gray clouds, preventing the morning from lightening beyond a twilit gloaming. Elsa couldn't have been happier.

Snug in her bed with Norman, with the low light and silver, watery windows blurring the garden, the rest of the world seemed a very distant concern. Her hands were stacked on his chest, and her chin on her hands. They spoke of inconsequential nothings, exchanging lovers' talk.

She ran her nails over his stomach while his fingers sifted through her hair. "It's so dark," he observed. "Like a spill of ink."

"Too bad you cannot employ the blotter on me."

"I would not undo you, even if I could." He glanced from where he'd been staring at his hand in her hair to meet her gaze. His jaw was rough with morning whiskers, russet spattered with gold, and his nut-brown hair a floppy jumble about his head. "You're perfect just the way you are."

She hid her smile against a rise of chest muscle. "You undo me with your sweet words."

"Then I'll say nothing more. I shouldn't like to be responsible for annulling your existence."

Instead of speaking, he reached down and pulled her up his length to lie on her side facing him. Their mouths found one another, and they kissed, slow and unhurried. Elsa's body warmed, her blood quickening in areas still pleasurably sore from last night's lovemaking.

Norman touched his brow to hers. They lay like that for a while, and for Elsa, it was such a luxury just to enjoy physical contact without the expectation of sex. In the past, though, she'd expected sex just as much as her partners had; she would not have wished to share intimacy of this sort with anyone she'd brought to bed.

"Are you sorry I was your first?" she asked, her voice small. "You should have had someone as untried as you, perhaps."

He snorted. "As if I could bed a virgin without causing serious injury to the poor woman. You saw what I'm working with here, did you not?"

A fit of giggles took her.

"I wasn't waiting for anyone or anything in particular," he said after a moment, "but now I think I must have been waiting for you."

There he went again, making her innards melt with his open, unaffected tenderness. A poignant pang went through her chest, taking her breath. Elsa closed her eyes against a prickling at the corners.

"Are you crying?" He sounded bewildered.

"No." She burrowed against his neck. "My feelings are just trying to leak from my face."

Sometime later—she must have dozed—Norman woke her with a kiss on her brow and her name rumbling through his massive chest. "Mmm?" she managed, reluctantly lifting her eyelids.

"When will your servants be home?"

"Noon." She scratched her nose with the back of her wrist. "I gave them yesterday evening and this morning off."

"It's ten now," he said, consulting a watch he must have retrieved from his waistcoat. "I should be well away before twelve, in case someone comes home early."

The reminder of the outside world and the troubles it held gave her a moment's regret. Once he was gone, they would no longer be simply Elsa and Norman, but opponents vying for the same prize, which only one of them could have.

"Are you hungry?" She squirmed her way to the headboard and sat up against the pillows. "You must be. Look at you. You probably fight Apple for rights to the trough. Between the two of you mammoths, you could eat your way through the entire county in a week."

He pulled a face at her, then swung his legs over the side of the bed, wiggling his long toes into the rug. "You stay here. I'll head to the stable and find a sack of feed for myself, then come back through the kitchen and scrounge together something for you."

Norman plucked his breeches from the floor, shook them out, and pulled them on. When he crossed the room to where his shirt had caught on a picture frame, he glanced out the window.

"There's a horse tied in front of your house. No rider."

Just then, a knock sounded on the front door.

Elsa sprang from the bed and ran to the window. A familiar palomino idly hoofed the gravel. "Oliver," she moaned. "What's he doing here?"

In a frenzy, she rushed into a chemise, pulled an old morning dress over her head, and grabbed a shawl before darting to the door. "Stay here," she whispered to Norman.

He blinked slowly. "That would probably be prudent," he drawled.

She rolled her eyes at his sarcastic tone, closed her bedchamber door, and pattered downstairs just as her cousin loosed another volley of rapping.

Elsa wrenched open the door. "Oliver!" Her voice sounded overbright to her own ears and her breathing labored from her mad rush from naked to presentable. "What brings you here so early? I trust all is well?"

His gaze took in the disarray of her hair, traveled down her slapdash ensemble, and came to rest on her bare feet. He lifted a brow. "Perhaps I should ask the same of you, dear cousin." He stepped past her into the house, his eyes swinging from one side to the other.

"Forgive my dishabille," Elsa said. "Foster has the morning off, and I'm simply hopeless without her. Return this afternoon and you shall find me neat as a pin."

"This cannot wait." Oliver strode to the parlor, leaving Elsa to hurry after him.

"Oliver, is something wrong?"

The man paused before the cold fireplace and turned. He slapped one of his riding gloves against his thigh. "Wynford-Scott."

A flurry of alarm scattered through her chest. *How does he know?* Light-headed with anxiety, she clutched her shawl in tight fists. "What of him?" she asked, carefully bland. He didn't know. He couldn't.

"Yesterday afternoon, I overheard Mr. Alderly make mention of a so-called *screening* pertaining to my opponents. You were standing there, as well. Did you hear that?"

Elsa's breaths came shallow and fast, as though she were tightly corseted. What was he getting at? "I ... I don't recall."

Deep grooves folded around Oliver's mouth as he smirked. "I wasn't familiar with the term, but last night I went into Ipswich to consult a barrister I know there. As it turns out, screening is a disciplinary procedure at the Inns of Court." His eyes lit with triumph.

Elsa shook her head, an ominous dread prickling at the back of her neck. "What are you saying?"

Abruptly, he crossed to where she stood and grabbed her arms. "Elsa, this is our chance to ensure my victory!" he said in an excited rush. "Once it's known that Wynford-Scott lied about his leave of absence from Gray's Inn, that he was really driven out in disgrace, he'll be finished."

A cry escaped her mouth before she could stop it. Elsa pulled out of his grip. "Oliver, you mustn't!"

"Why not?" he demanded hotly.

"You don't know anything for sure. This is hearsay, speculation. You were eavesdropping. You cannot purposely ruin him on such thin evidence!"

She thought of the man upstairs in her room, with his flop of hair and his kind eyes and his penchant for rescuing toy soldiers from wells. To see his name dragged through the gutter, his reputation in Fleck tarnished because of her actions ... she couldn't bear it. Elsa meant to see Oliver elected to the House of Commons, but they would win fairly. Hurting Norman again was not an option.

Her cousin ran a hand over his short, graying hair. "It's evidence enough. I might not know the particulars, but I know he's been sent down from Gray's, he and Alderly both, based on what that popinjay said. *Our screening*. That alone is a fact worth telling. Wynford-Scott's presented himself as some altruistic servant of The People, which is a far cry from the truth. All of his noble *issues*," Oliver sneered, "are simply camouflage for the fact that he cannot be called to the bar."

Elsa shook her head all throughout her cousin's speech. "No, Oliver. Do not do it. This is not how you want to win the—"

"I will not win otherwise!" he shouted. His nostrils pinched white, and his eyes bulged. A vein popped from his temple. "If the polling was held today, I would lose." He smacked a fist against his chest. "*That man*," he pointed wildly, incidentally landing in the approximate direction where Norman waited in her room, "has turned Fleck into a borough of Parliamentary scholars. Everyone has opinions now, some romantic delusion of *vox populi*."

"Maybe they should," she countered, her steps circumscribing an arc, forcing Oliver to turn to keep her in his sights. "Is it wrong for people to have thoughts about the way they are governed?"

"You promised me this seat," he hedged. "Said I was the obvious choice, that there would be no contest."

"But there *is* a contest," she snapped, bringing her hands to her waist, "and pouting about it won't change the fact. Now," she moderated her tone, "win or lose, you must conduct yourself like the gentleman you are, Oliver. Do not dishonor yourself by engaging in dirty politics."

Eyes downcast, his tense jaw worked side to side. He huffed a breath, nodded. "Thank you, Elsa. You know I value your advice. I appreciate all you've done for me. Without you, I wouldn't have stood a chance against Wynford-Scott at all."

Relief bathed Elsa's nerves; a knot between her shoulders released. "You've conducted a strong campaign, Oliver. I'm proud to stand beside you."

With a brotherly kiss on her cheek, he took his leave. Elsa watched from the front step as he donned his hat and turned his collar against the drizzling rain before swinging up into his saddle. He lifted his hand in salute; she waved in return.

Back inside the house, Elsa leaned against the shut door and exhaled deeply, feeling as if she'd just missed colliding with a runaway mail coach. She gave herself a few moments to allow her alarmed heart rate to return to normal. A soft pattering sound drew her eyes to the stairs; she saw Norman's feet on the landing above.

She came to the bottom of the stair and lifted her eyes.

He'd donned his breeches, shirt, and waistcoat. His cuffs were still loose, and his feet as bare as hers. There was no nervousness in seeing him this way, other than the flutter in her stomach at the sensual appeal of his rumpled, unshaved appearance. Neither did she feel self-conscious over him seeing her half-dressed, her face as yet unwashed and hair a tangle. Before, she'd never have allowed a lover to see her looking anything but her fashionable best.

But that was before.

Norman rested one hand on the wall; the other gripped the top of the bannister in a tight fist. "Is everything all right? I saw Mr. Fay leave, but you didn't return."

She stepped onto the bottom riser. He took one step down. "Oliver was just confirming the details of this evening's campaign event."

Her gut twisted even as the untruth slid past her lips, but there was no reason to alarm him with Oliver's threat of revealing Norman's secret, not when Elsa had put a stop to it before it amounted to anything.

His sigh echoed through the stairwell. "Back to the campaign, are we? Not thinking about it for a night was a blessed respite." He took another step. So did she, feeling as she did that she was approaching her fate.

His sudden smile put an appealing dent in his cheek. "Although, I'd wager that through our combined efforts, we can contrive to ignore politics for another thirty minutes or so." They met in the middle of the stairs. Norman lifted her by the waist and swung her around, placing her several steps above him so their eyes were almost level.

Elsa cupped his jaw and swept the pad of her thumb over his stubble, while his hands remained on her waist. She touched the corner of his mouth and stared at his lips. A memory filtered down from her inebriated past. "I've always loved your lips," she confessed. "I used to think what a shame it was they were put to such a dull purpose like advocating, when it was so patently clear that their true vocation is kissing."

Heat flared in his eyes as his gaze moved to Elsa's mouth and then lower. "Then I must use my gifts as God intended." Norman grasped the loose neck of her dress and yanked it down, exposing her breast to his hungry gaze. His thumb flicked over her nipple. A shudder passed through her body, and she arched her back, brazenly offering herself, shamelessly accepting the brief stay of reality. Both of their futures teetered on a precipice, but only one of them could achieve the coveted outcome. If Oliver lost the election, Elsa knew—*knew*—she faced a bleak path that would eventually lead her back to the bottle. And as for Norman, without the seat in Commons, he would be cut adrift from any plan for making his livelihood, possibly never to recover from the shame she'd brought upon him at the Christmas revels even once his screening was over. So yes, coward she was, she grasped the procrastination he offered and held tight.

Norman's tongue flicked over the tight peak of her breast. He cupped the mound of flesh in his hand, lifted it higher. Elsa gasped as his lips closed over her and he drew her nipple deep into his mouth, kissing her the way God intended.

• • •

Three days later, one week before the election, it happened.

Stepping out of the Rabbit's Glen where Norman and Alderly had just stopped for their noon meal, they noted a delivery wagon that was, oddly, parked on the green, rather than pulled alongside or in back of any of the shops surrounding the village center. Men Norman did not recognize were offloading bundles of what appeared to be newsprint, tossing them onto the street where a lad cut the twine. As quickly as the bundles were opened, more boys snatched up armfuls and dispersed, scampering down side streets. Soon their hawking cries filled the air, and the papers were distributed to passersby.

"What's this?" Alderly asked. "Papers from London?"

"Ipswich, sir!" cried one of the paperboys, thrusting the broadsheet into Alderly's hands. Norman fished in his pocket for a penny, but the boy shook his head. "Compliments of a concerned citizen, sirs." He gave Norman a copy, too, before trotting to intercept a knot of ladies emerging from the post office.

"Shit," Alderly spat, the paper open in his hands.

Norman snapped his open. It wasn't a periodical of news from Ipswich; rather, it was a printing of one article only—*article* being a generous term, considering the brief number of words on the page. It didn't take very many to proclaim that the Fine and Upstanding Citizenry of Fleck had been taken in by charlatans, one Mr. N. Wynford-Scott and his associate Mr. R. Alderly, formerly of Gray's Inn, London. Both gentlemen, the author declared, had been sent away from Gray's Inn via a discipline action called screening.

"Your humble writer," Norman read aloud, "will spare your eyes, oh gentle reader, details of the misconduct perpetrated by these two malefactors."

The paper advised readers "Be You Not Fooled!" into voting for an infamous London rogue. The writer concluded with a flourish, "Remember, dear reader: a Vote for Fay is a Vote for Fleck!"

Shock numbed his face. Cold skewered his heart. How could this happen? Who could have—?

No. He shook his head against the obvious answer, not wanting to believe her capable of such a betrayal. *No, not Elsa. She wouldn't have.*

"Holy skipping Christ," Alderly ground out. He balled up the paper and brandished it in his fist. "What are we going to do about this?" he demanded, then cast the scandal sheet into the gutter. Already, Fleckers were turning stunned expressions in their direction.

As the pair walked to the rail where their horses were tied, Norman neatly folded his copy of the paper and tucked it into his pocket, his mind still reeling. He stroked Apple's nose before loosing the reins and mounting.

Norman met looks of speculation and scorn with a stiff smile and a touch of his hat brim.

When they were clear of the village proper, Alderly pulled back on his mount's leads, forcing the animal to Apple's plodding pace. "Fay did this," the younger man fumed.

"Undoubtedly," Norman agreed.

"How does he know we were screened?"

Norman shook his head, unwilling to voice the terrible suspicion.

Alderly did the unthinkable for him. "It had to have been Lady Fay." He turned to regard Norman, a curl of his flaxen hair catching on the sharp point of his collar. "Besides ourselves, she's the only person in Fleck who witnessed the Christmas revels. But then"—his brow furrowed—"how would *she* know we were screened? Did you call her as witness in your hearing?"

Norman's voice rose in impatience. "No." He slanted a frown at the younger man. "Look, Alderly, we have spoken of the screening in Sir Seymour's home—who's to say someone else, a servant or visitor, perhaps, did not overhear and spread the tale?" He was casting out wild suppositions now, angry at himself for not asking Elsa directly how she knew about his screening. He'd assumed she learned of it in a letter from Sheri—in which case, he would hunt down the loose-lipped dandy and shove the man's quizzing glass down his throat—but did not wish to give Alderly any more reason to suspect Elsa. Not until he'd learned the truth of the matter for himself.

Was Elsa behind outing the truth of his screening to Fleck? The same woman who had been breathless with the ecstasy they'd shared? Her apology had been sincere, of that he had no doubt. She'd been shattered by the knowledge that she'd played a part in him being sent down from Gray's. If—*if*—she'd shared that information with her cousin, it must have been done in innocence.

But ... But. Oliver Fay had come to Berrybrook Cottage the very morning following that apology, as well as the what-he'd-believed-to-be joking insinuation that her words were, in part, meant to sway Norman into quitting the campaign.

What if, having failed in persuading him, Elsa had put another plan into motion? What if she'd shared with her cousin the information about Norman's screening, knowing that going public with it would sink Norman's chances at winning? Was Elsa that desperate to see her late husband's cousin in Commons? Was she capable of such duplicity?

Yes. He had to be honest. Clever and determined, Elsa was capable of damned near anything she set her mind to. But *would* she betray Norman in such a way? That was the question. Not being able to immediately answer that question in the negative troubled him deeply. He drew a deep breath and let it out slowly. Beneath him, Apple huffed a horsey sigh, echoing his master's unrest.

"Gossipy bumpkins," Alderly grumbled. "Well, what do you mean to do about it?"

Norman felt desolate. Even if Elsa was behind this, would Norman have the heart to strike back against her? He shrugged. "Nothing."

Alderly's eyes bugged; his face went nearly as livid as it had when his head was on fire. "Are you touched in the nob? Of course you must fight back! This is an outrage!"

"Why must I fight back? The story was sensationalized, but the premise is true. We *were* screened and excluded from the Hall. I've only myself to blame. I knew it wasn't right to allow you and Sir Seymour to set me up as some political white knight, but I went along with it. This is no more than I deserve." Easier to blame himself than the bewitching raven-haired beauty.

"It's a dirty trick," Alderly protested. "And you can't tell me there's nothing else to do. What if ... what if we explained that it wasn't our fault? That we were swept up in circumstances—"

"Damn you, I said no!" Norman roared. Alderly flinched; his horse sidestepped. Norman lifted a trembling hand to his brow, unsettled by his own sudden flare of temper. But what Alderly suggested came perilously close to pulling Elsa into this mess. Damn him, too, for still wanting to protect her.

"We shall carry on as we have done," he said, his words clipped but more reasonable in volume. "Speak on the issues, try to assure constituents that they can trust me with their seat in Commons."

Cursing under his breath, Alderly drove his heels into his horse's flanks, urging the animal to a canter, and then a full run.

By the time Norman arrived at the Beaufort home, Sir Seymour was already appraised of the situation and in a fine fettle. "Those damned Fays!" he bellowed, stomping around his gallery. "They knew their influence in the district was on the wane, and instead of taking their decline gracefully, they have resorted to underhanded measures."

Alderly stood to the side, arms crossed, nodding his agreement. "Just what I said, Sir Seymour."

Sir Seymour lifted his hand, finger pointed. "This cannot stand!"

"This *will not* stand," Alderly echoed.

"If I may," Norman interjected, his hands neatly clasped behind his back, "I would remind you that it is my candidacy imperiled by this revelation, and I do not wish to retaliate in any way. Can this not be the end of it?"

The squire looked appalled. "Now see here, Wynford-Scott. It may be your name on the ballot, but it's *my* name that brought you here, that gave you a campaign and opened doors in this community."

Norman bowed his head. "I'm well aware, Sir Seymour. It pains me that everything you've done on my behalf may end with this ignominious gossip, but you cannot be entirely surprised by this turn of events. Our censure becoming common knowledge was always a risk in this contest, one you weighed at the outset."

Sir Seymour sighed. "I know I did," he said in a defeated tone. "I was just so bloody *sure* that we could finally break the Fays' hold on this borough and seat someone willing to fight for progress and reform, instead of another government toady like the Fays have championed for the past generation."

The gentleman's lips twisted in a bitter smile. From the beginning, Norman had appreciated that Sir Seymour was a man of true conviction, not just a spoiler with a grudge against the established powers. And though he did not say it, Sir Seymour must, too, have worried about how this scandal would affect him and Lady Beaufort. After all, they were the sponsors of the "charlatan" Whig candidate. Whatever standing they had in Fleck might also be swept away by the flood of public outcry.

"We have run this campaign on a vision of how a government can better serve the people it represents. I mean to carry on that way until the end," Norman said.

After a moment, Sir Seymour extended his hand. Norman clasped his forearm. "A vision of a brighter future," Sir Seymour agreed. "Until the end."

Chapter Twelve

That night, Norman arranged to meet Elsa at the boathouse where the previous MP, Ben Jonson, had met his mortal fate. The structure was a pragmatic choice, secluded as it was from nearby dwellings, and Norman meant to get to the bottom of the paper her cousin had printed.

She had already arrived when he entered, and her eyes, restlessly scanning the dark water of the lake, reflected stars dancing across the surface. At the sound of his approach, she turned and flung herself into his arms. His hands slipped around her waist, savoring the feeling of her soft curves pressed against him even as his heart limped along, painfully aware that he may be holding his betrayer.

"Norman, I'm so sorry. I told him not to do it. I thought I'd convinced him not to. I didn't know—"

Rearing back, he stared into her face, weighing her words and the pleading writ plain in her eyes. "How did he know? How did you know?"

"The day of the picnic," she answered at once, not pretending to misunderstand. "When your people were there with flowers and singing, Oliver and I came over to ..." Even in the shadows, he saw her face darken with color. Was she blushing? "We overheard Mr. Alderly make reference to your screening. I knew what that meant. I knew I had to have been the reason for it. It's why I asked you to come that night, so I could apologize." Shaking her head, she went on, "I didn't know Oliver had heard, until the next morning."

"When he came to your house."

"Yes." Elsa took his hands, squeezing his fingers as though trying to press belief into them. "He wanted to use the information against you, but I said he mustn't. I would never do that to you." She kissed one hand and then the other.

Norman felt the weight of doubt slip from his shoulders, allowing his heart to soar. Elsa had not betrayed him. He pulled her close and gripped one hand in her hair, holding her tight to his chest.

"I've already told Oliver I will no longer work on his behalf." Elsa still bristled with consternation at Oliver's perfidy, not understanding that Norman didn't care anymore. So long as she had not meant him harm, Norman could confront whatever Oliver Fay cared to throw at him. "In fact," she declared, "I've a mind to come out in support of you. Goodness knows you're the better candidate, and I've always had a secret reformer streak—"

He cut her off with a kiss, sealing his mouth to hers.

Her generous offer caused his heart to flop at her feet and wag its tail in adoration, but he could not allow her to do that. Nothing good would come of it. Norman would lose the by-election anyway, and Elsa risked alienating herself from the community she loved so well by aligning herself with a pariah. Fleck was good for her. She'd been restored to health and flourished here.

She'd tried to argue, but he stopped her every time with a kiss.

From that moment, they didn't speak another word about the election in the boathouse. They met there for the next three nights, speaking of everything else under the sun—when they spoke at all. Mostly, they had sex. Lots and lots of spine-tingling, earth-shattering sex. If either of them had misgivings about carrying on an assignation in the same place where a fellow had died, neither of them voiced it.

Night after night, Norman lost himself in the tight heat of Elsa's body and found himself again when she cried out his name. It wasn't as if he hadn't known he'd been missing out on something wonderful during his prolonged virginity, but every time he joined with Elsa, he was astonished all over again by just how bloody marvelous it was.

He expressed as much one night. Elsa laughed. "You could have been doing this for years," she chided. "You can't convince me no maid ever offered herself to you. And I can think of a good six or seven lonely widows and wives in Town who would be delighted to have such a strapping young man at their beck and call."

"Perhaps," he demurred. "But I cannot think of a single one at whose beck and call I would wish to be. I'd rather be your strapping young man now than any other woman's a decade ago."

There was plenty of such talk, compliments and sweet nothings, but never did they broach what would come after the by-election. Elsa spoke little of her late husband, but Norman had the distinct impression it had not been a happy marriage. He could not fault her for shying away from the topic of matrimony. She may never be prepared to bind herself to another man again.

But for himself, Norman knew this was it. For the first and only time, he was in love. Elsa was the woman for him, her spirited intelligence the perfect foil to his more reserved nature. They were both interested in matters of public service, and he felt certain that she would sparkle once more as a political hostess in London when she was ready to return to Town. He'd keep her in his life in whatever capacity she allowed him, for as long as possible. Forever sounded about right.

• • •

Two days before the election, Norman rose at nine o'clock, hours later than his customary time. Thoughts of Elsa in mind, as they so often were these days, Norman stepped off the stairs and sauntered into the breakfast room, where he found Sir Seymour and Lady Beaufort lingering over their tea. The squire was ensconced behind the morning paper, while her ladyship read through her post. It was an affecting little tableau of domestic tranquility; Norman couldn't help but place himself and Elsa in the scene.

"Good morning, Lady Beaufort. Sir Seymour." His hosts returned his greeting. "Alderly's not yet about?"

"He was up and out quite early this morning, in fact," Sir Seymour answered, setting aside his paper and reaching for a triangle of toast. "Had an errand in Ipswich."

"Hmm. He went there but two days past. Why the need to return so soon, I wonder?" Norman mused.

"Perhaps a fitting," Lady Beaufort suggested. "Believe it or no, Mr. Wynford-Scott, but we here in Suffolk are not without refinement. A gentleman of fashion will find plenty to suit his tastes right here in the county, no need to hare off to London."

"I'm sure that's true," he agreed amiably. "There are no campaign events this morning, I believe? Do remind me if I'm neglecting something."

Sir Seymour crunched his toast and shook his head. "Nothing until tea this afternoon with the Ladies' Auxiliary at the vicarage."

"Very well. I shall spend the morning working on my hustings speech."

Lady Beaufort cut a glance over the rim of her teacup. "You're terribly composed for a man likely to suffer crushing defeat."

"Laura!" Sir Seymour exclaimed.

"Well he is!" she rejoined. Then to Norman again, "You aren't one of those who is deceptively calm right up until the moment he picks up an ax and kills everyone in the house, I hope."

Norman made a thoughtful noise. "Having never perpetrated ax murder against an entire houseful of inhabitants—or even a single individual, I'm afraid—I suppose I really couldn't say. Should this ever turn out to be the case, I'll be sure to advise you."

"Thank you; I'd be most appreciative. Darling, would you pass the salt?"

After a hard month of campaigning, Norman was grateful for a quiet morning. He took a long walk after breakfast and put his mind toward the composition of his speech. Lady Beaufort had not been remiss in her observation: Norman was sanguine about his imminent loss to Oliver Fay, and he also knew his composure did not mask an underlying rage that could erupt at a moment's notice.

Elsa was the reason for his serenity. Having their stolen hours in the boathouse to look forward to made it easier to bear the hostile words flung at him from the same villagers who had so recently lauded his progressive ideals. When his calls for reform were answered with accusing cries of "radical," when another door slammed in his face, Elsa remained the calm harbor in his heart. He could not fear defeat or wither under public scorn, not when he was simultaneously fortunate enough to have the affection of the most beautiful, sensual woman he'd ever beheld.

Later, as he sat in the library, going through the soothing motions of putting quill and ink to paper and turning abstract ideas into concrete symbols, he felt come over him a great sense of ending. At the conclusion of this by-election, Norman would have no reason to tarry in Fleck and would once more have to turn his mind toward finding a means of supporting himself.

... and, perhaps, of supporting a wife?

The nib of his pen skittered across the paper. He quickly blotted the mistake and bent his head to his task, forbidding himself from entertaining such notions. His future was too uncertain right now to take a wife, and besides, Elsa had given no indication that she desired more from their relationship than what existed at present.

Glancing at the tall clock, he began putting away his writing utensils. He'd worked through luncheon and had to hurry to prepare for tea with the Ladies' Auxiliary. As he gathered his papers into a neat stack, the library door opened, and Alderly strode through, a parcel tucked under one arm. His boyish face split into a wide grin.

"I hope that's your victory speech there," he said, jerking his chin to Norman's manuscript.

"Riding high on the purchase of a new article of clothing, Alderly? I've seen delusion like this before. A friend of mine was once so enraptured of a new pair of gloves that he spent three days chasing down beggars just so he could press coins to their palms with his gloves. Claimed it to be a double charity, sharing both his money and the feel of that supple leather."

Alderly raked a hand through his hair. "Better than gloves, my friend." Setting the rectangular parcel on the table, he tugged loose the knot of twine and folded back the brown wrapping paper. It was a stack of papers—a drawing of some sort was on top, but from this angle, Norman couldn't quite make out the depiction.

Alderly took the top leaf from the stack, turned it, and slid it across the table. "You're back in this contest, Wynford-Scott. You're going to win."

A short time later, Norman would have to wrap his cravat around his swollen knuckles and report to Lady Beaufort that he was, in fact, capable of a sudden and ferocious outpouring of violence.

• • •

"You're practically keeping Town hours again, milady," Foster scolded as she drove another pin into Elsa's hair. The morning had nearly passed, and Elsa was only now dressing for the day. "Trouble sleeping?" the lady's maid inquired. Her tone, Elsa noted, was politely neutral.

"A bit," Elsa said just as carefully.

Foster's hands stilled on Elsa's dark tresses. "You should have told me, Lady Fay. I'd have given you something to help you sleep. I'll give it to you tonight, if you'd like."

The vinegar, to prevent pregnancy. Elsa had been careless, she knew. It was just ... somehow, when she was with Norman, she felt as though nothing bad could touch her. Whenever they were together in the boathouse, the rest of the world had a tendency to recede to insignificance.

She wasn't sure what to make of these feelings, as they were unlike any she had experienced before. She'd felt mindless lust often enough, knew the symptoms of carnal infatuation. She'd felt fondness for friends, like Sheri, whom she loved with comfortable affection. This was all of those together, and something entirely new. With Norman, she did not feel reckless, even when he fucked her from behind over the rail of a dilapidated sailboat. And she did not feel staid, even when they did nothing more than hold hands and talk about whether the upcoming season of theater promised to be any good.

Whatever this was warranted more consideration. In the meantime, she must not be complacent. "Thank you, Foster. I would appreciate your sleeping remedy."

"I'll see to it, milady." The maid turned to fetch Elsa's dress from the bed, a robin's-egg-blue muslin printed with roses of yellow and pink. "I'm glad Mr. Wynford-Scott is standing for our seat here. He's a good man, very decent. I hope he wins."

Elsa ducked her face at the warmth sweeping over her chest and rising up her neck. "Perhaps he shall, Foster. Perhaps he shall."

She walked to the village and lifted her face to the sky as had become her custom. In addition to cataloging the myriad wonders of nature, Elsa savored the sensations of her own body: the languor of satisfaction, the loose-limbed sway of her hips, the delicious ache of her flesh at having been well used.

For the first time, she felt like a whole and complete person, in and of herself. Elsa made her own choices. She was not dictated to by a harsh husband, nor driven to destroy herself by her demons. Every day, Elsa chose not to drink. And every night, she chose to give herself to Norman. In the hours between, she could fill her time with meaningful activities. If she never hosted a political evening again, she could enrich her life with friendships. She could help her neighbors. She could find a thousand things to do besides drink. Her time with Norman had taught her that. There were unexpected joys to be had in life, and she wanted to be sober and clear-eyed so she could find them.

A buzz of anticipation hung over the village. The hustings cast its long shadow across the green. Elsa would miss it when it was struck following the polling in two days' time. Until Oliver had printed that dreadful broadsheet, Elsa had truly enjoyed the contest. Campaigning was a different animal than the political hostessing she had done on Harvey's behalf. During her marriage, there had only been one general election. Though she and Harvey had ostensibly campaigned in Fleck on behalf of the Tory candidates, it had been an uncontested election, and so their efforts had been minimal. This by-election, on the other hand ... this had been *fun*.

She had Norman to thank for that, as well. Had he not stood for the seat, she never would have had the opportunity to participate in a hotly contested election, would never have been compelled to think up new and creative ways to promote her candidate, or to exercise her knowledge of Parliamentary and legal matters that had so long lain unused.

A shriek of laughter drew Elsa's attention to where a crowd was assembled in front of the mercantile. A queue of customers streamed in and out in numbers she'd never witnessed there before. A batch of adolescent males formed a tight semicircle in front of the shop window, while little clusters of two and three individuals were scattered in front of the store and around the square, heads bent over some sort of pamphlet.

Elsa's heart sank. What had Oliver done now? Having cut her association with his campaign, she'd no more insight as to what new depths he may sink than the average Flecker. She'd no doubt, though, that he was up to something, some last sally of political scandal to serve as the coup de grace to Norman's candidacy.

She recognized a few residents of Weatherhill Lane in one of the little groups. Little Mary, one hand clinging to her baby brother's, waved to Elsa with her other hand clutching her toy soldier. "Mummy, look! That's her, from the picture!"

Elsa approached the group. Mary's mother glanced up, wide-eyed, and stepped in front of her children. Another woman, one of the spinster sisters, snatched her copy of the paper behind her back.

"What is this? Let me see, please." Elsa extended her hand.

The old woman's lips pinched in a tight knot, and she turned her back on Elsa. The young mother swept Mary and Sammy into her arms and trotted away without a word.

All around, Elsa's neighbors and acquaintances, people she'd counted as friends, were noting her presence. Dove from the Rabbit's Glen hung out the tavern window, her pretty face contorted in a sneer. "Slut!" she yelled. "Swill tub!" The finger the barmaid aimed at Elsa gave no doubt as to whom she referred.

Numb with shock, Elsa spun and forced her way through the crowd jostling for entrance to the mercantile. A man stepped out of the shop with the paper held aloft to his face. Elsa snatched it from him.

"Hey!" he cried. "I just paid a ha'penny for that!"

Clutching her plunder to her chest, Elsa whirled. The press of people caged her in. "Oh, milady," said a jeering male voice. "How much for a dance? Buy you a pint?"

"Bet a half-pint'll do the trick," said another man. "Lusty ones like her flash their goods cheap." Rollicking male laughter followed this comment. A rough hand snatched at her skirt, while a woman shrieked, "She *touched* me! I'll have to burn this dress."

Blood pounded in Elsa's ears. She couldn't breathe, just kept jabbing with her elbows and clawing at limbs blocking her way. At last, she made it through the mob and gasped a lungful of air. She staggered a few steps, then looked at the hard-won paper, now rumpled.

It was an illustration, a lampoon in the style of Cruikshank. In it, a woman poised on one toe atop a table, the other leg kicking up behind her. One hand hoisted her skirts high, while the other clutched a bottle. Three men stood at her feet with leering expressions, while another, much larger, man stood off to the left side, his hands clasped in an attitude of pleading. In the background, flames partially obscured a coat of arms on the wall.

A spidery scrawl labeled the tallest man in the caricature as "Mr. W.-S." A speech bubble above his head read: *My lady, I implore you to stop! You're burning down the Inn!* The woman's reply: *Let it burn, so long as the wine does flow! Excellent hosts, I've a powerful thirst, who will fill me up?* The trio at her feet clamored their offers: *Here's a vote*, said one; *I've a vote and a flagon*, said the second; *My vote and my flagon are bigger than the rest!* boasted the third. Another bubble for the woman, lower, to indicate her response to the men: *I'll take them all!*

Across the bottom was etched the title of the piece: LADY F'S REVELS AT GRAY'S INN.

When she glanced back at the drawing again, she spotted another figure on the right, this one an old man with a long nose. *Bencher* read his label. *D—it, W.-S., there will be h-ll to pay for this!* the man vowed, glaring across the page at the giant on the left.

The bottom dropped out from ... everything. Suddenly, Elsa understood that Fleck would no longer be her safe harbor. The shouted insults were superfluous, the apple core that struck the side of her face unnecessary. *Yes, yes, I know*, she wanted to say, but she could form no words.

Shame poured through her, scalding and thick, obliterating any other sensation, until Elsa swore she'd never felt anything else in all of her days. Her feet were rooted to where she stood in front of the mercantile while the citizens of Fleck bayed.

At last, she put one foot forward, and then another, although she made no conscious decision to do so. Her mind was paralyzed, only peripherally aware of her surroundings. Howls of derision followed her to the door of the Rabbit's Glen tavern.

Inside, she went to the counter and met the proprietor's pained gaze. "Mr. Denny," she said in a calm, detached tone, "a bottle of scotch, if you please."

Chapter Thirteen

With Norman's frantic urging, Apple accelerated all the way to a trot. "Damnation, horse, go faster and I'll give you an entire sugar loaf." Unmoved by his master's attempt at bribery, the beast continued on his jaunty way. It was a brisker pace than Norman could have achieved on foot, but his teeth ground in frustration at the lack of speed.

Maybe she hasn't seen. Maybe it's not too late. When he arrived at Berrybrook Cottage and vaulted from the back of his winded steed, his hopes were instantly dashed.

The front door flung open on Foster, the abigail's thin face pale, heavy lines of worry creasing her forehead. "Thank God! I don't know what to do."

"Where is she?" he asked as he bounded up the front steps.

Foster wrung her hands as if she'd peel the flesh from them. "Locked herself in her room with a bottle of spirits. Why would she do such a thing?" The abigail's voice wavered. "She's done so well these recent months."

Norman slid a folded copy of the hateful illustration from his pocket and silently handed it to Foster. Not bothering with the pretense of not knowing the location of Elsa's room, he took the stairs two at a time and knocked on her door.

Silence.

From the entryway, he heard Foster's gasp of dismay. "My lady," she moaned. "Oh, my poor lady."

"Elsa," Norman called, knocking again. "Open the door."

Nothing.

His gut twisted with worry and a heaping dose of guilt. When Fay had that scandal sheet printed, Norman should have withdrawn from the race. He'd sensed there was a danger of Elsa being exposed, but he'd thought he could mitigate the risk by refusing to speak out on the matter. His silence had left the way clear for Alderly to concoct and enact this dreadful scheme. As a result, Elsa would be ostracized from the town she loved—had already been, else why would she presently be locked up with a bottle of oblivion?

He pounded again with the same result.

"Stay clear of the door," he warned. "I'm going to break it down." He retreated down the hall, pivoted, and braced his shoulders. His enormous body wasn't a boon very often, but just now, he was awfully glad to be his own battering ram.

The door opened.

Relaxing his posture, Norman hurried over. He smelled the alcohol even before he reached her. She leaned against the doorframe, clinging to it for support. Ebony strands had fallen from her coif, framing a colorless face. She blinked up at him with red, bleary eyes.

"Only you, Norman Wynford-Scott, would be so courteous about breaking down the door. I decided I'd better open it, else you'd never forgive yourself for splintering the wood." Pushing off the doorframe, she turned and sauntered back into her bedchamber.

Norman followed, quietly closing the door behind him. The bedclothes were rumpled. On the nightstand stood a bottle of scotch, half empty. A glass beside it, one she had used to serve her chilled tea concoctions, contained three fingers of the amber liquor.

She stopped several feet short of the glass and bottle; her head bowed, her hands fisted in her skirts.

Norman's heart lurched. He went to her, put his hands on her shoulders. She was rigid in his grasp, so brittle he feared she would crumble into pieces.

Gently turning her, he pulled her into his chest. "I'm so sorry, darling. I'm so sorry it happened." Squeezing his eyes shut, he bent his cheek to the top of her head. One hand clasped her hair, while the other held her tight about the waist, a band of protection that was never going to release her. "Whatever happened in the village … Your true friends stand by you, Elsa. Lady Beaufort was beside herself when she saw the drawing. Sir Seymour packed Alderly back to London without even a steak for his eye."

She stirred at that. "What …?"

"And no one is upset with you right now, not I, not Foster. We understand why you felt the need for alcohol. It's just … I wish …" His heart hurt, and he didn't know how to put into words his desire to take her cares upon his broad shoulders. "You don't owe me anything, Elsa, but I want you to know you can always come to me if you feel the compulsion to drink. I will help you however I can. This past month has been a revelation, seeing you healthy and sparkling and full of life, and—again, you owe me nothing, Elsa, nothing at all—but the thought of you going back to how it was before just guts me, Elsa, it does. Think of …" He sniffed, his throat tightened. Elsa softened against him. Norman kissed her hair. "Think of your journal," he went on, "all those ticks, all those days you have been so strong. Keep being strong, sweetheart. And if you feel you've depleted your own strength, you're welcome to mine. God knows I've more than enough."

He lapsed into an awkward silence, feeling there was so much more to say, but that he may have already said too much. She was in no condition for a reasoned discussion. He would have to try again tomorrow. For now, she needed something to eat and then a good rest. He eyed the bed, prepared to lift her into it. "All right, then, let's get you—"

"I didn't drink."

The sound of her small voice stopped him dead. Gripping her shoulders, he held her back, examined her weary face. He smelled it all over her. She reeked. His stomach sank as he recalled Brandon's warning that habitual drunkards could become secretive about their drinking. "Oh, Elsa."

"I didn't!" she insisted.

Sighing heavily, he said, "Elsa, I can smell you from across the room."

Blushing, she stepped back. Her red-rimmed midnight eyes touched his, then darted away. "I wanted to drink," she said. "Intended to. But the cork was stuck in the bottle. I had to wrestle the damned thing with my teeth, and when it finally popped out, half the bottle spilled down my front. But I haven't … Come here." Contradicting her own command, she approached him, stood on her toes, opened her mouth, and breathed heavily into his face. Norman sniffed. There was a faint fume of tea on her breath, and perhaps a hint of bacon, but no alcohol.

"If my eyes are red," she muttered, "it's because I've been crying, not from drink."

He brought his hand to her cheek. "You astound me," he said quietly, "and you humble me. You're so very strong."

She shook her head. "I'm not, Norman, I'm really not. I want it so very badly, you see. I've been lying there on my bed for the past hour, looking at it, smelling it, imagining that first sip burning down my throat." She began to tremble. "Why am I still so weak for it? I thought I was better, but I'm not, I'm not."

"You are," he said in a commanding tone. "Elsa, this is a moment of choice, the very same choice you make every morning: Will you drink today, or no?"

"No?" She sounded uncertain. Her eyes drifted once more to the scotch.

Norman placed himself between her and the liquor. "Brandon gave you a piece of advice. Do you remember what it was?"

"Day by day, hour by hour, and sometimes minute by minute."

"Good," he said with a nod. "Are you going to drink in the next minute?"

"No," she said, more confidently this time. "No, I'm not."

Norman crossed to the window and threw open the sash to dissipate the aroma. He looked at Elsa and lifted a brow. Tucking her chin into the air, she plucked the bottle and glass from the table, held them well in front of her, tipped their contents onto the flowerbed below, and tossed the containers out after it. She turned her back and glanced at him over her shoulder in silent request. Quickly, he unfastened her dress and helped her step out of it, then he opened the door and passed it off to Foster, who'd obviously had her ear to the door. Norman could not rebuke her when he knew the woman was beside herself with worry for her mistress.

"She'll be all right," he assured the maid.

Foster's eyes shone and she nodded. "Thank you, sir." Then she dashed away with the scotch-perfumed frock.

When he turned back into the room, Elsa had already selected a fresh dress from the wardrobe and struggled to pull it over her head. Norman tugged her into it, buttoned her up, and then tied a neat bow in the sash around her waist. "There." He tipped her chin and pressed a kiss to her lips. "I'm so proud of you, Elsa. You spent an hour locked up with your personal devil and lived to tell the tale. You *are* strong. The strongest person I know."

She offered a thin smile. "Quite a compliment, coming from a man with the approximate dimensions and constitution of an ox."

As if to demonstrate his formidable constitution, he swept her into his arms and spun her in a circle until she squealed for mercy. Then he dropped her onto the bed and followed her down. She nuzzled her face into his neck as his arms wrapped around her.

They lay in silence for a time, Norman's fingers drifting up and down her arm. Elsa gradually relaxed completely, and her breathing slowed. A tender sense of possessiveness shook Norman to the core. He pressed his lips to her hair and breathed her warm, floral scent deep into his body.

"Thank you for coming for me."

"I thought you were asleep," he murmured. "I'm so sorry, Elsa," he said a moment later, turning on his side to face her. Her wide blue eyes in their thick fringe of dark lashes were filled with sadness. "I didn't know what he was planning." Norman inadvertently echoed Elsa's words about the scandal sheet. What had this campaign done to them? "Please believe, I never would have—"

"I never thought you had. Not for one second." Her hand came to his face, her touch light as a butterfly. She tucked a strand of hair behind his ear. "The by-election is rather spoiled now, though, isn't it?"

Rolling onto his back, Norman brought the back of his forearm to his brow. "Completely sullied. I don't want anything to do with that damned seat."

She inhaled sharply. "Don't say that," she protested. "You've worked too hard."

A growl of frustration rose in his throat. "But what can I do? Your cousin made sure no one will vote for me, and then Alderly struck back through you ..." He just couldn't puzzle a way out of this quandary. Everywhere his mind's eye looked was rot and dirt.

There was a *bang* as the front door slammed open against the wall downstairs; then the whole house juddered when it crashed home again. "*Elsa*," roared a man's voice.

She bolted upright, her eyes wild, her hand clutched to her throat. She scrambled off the bed. "Oliver," she said when she looked out the window. "It's just Oliver."

Norman frowned. Her response implied more than just being spooked by a loud noise.

Foster's voice floated up the stairwell. "My lady is resting, Mr. Fay, you mustn't go ... Mr. Fay, wait!" Boot steps on the stairs. "I'll fetch her down for you, just—"

Norman rolled off the bed and tucked himself into the corner behind the door just as it opened. Oliver Fay strode into Elsa's bedchamber. She scrambled from the mattress and smoothed her palms down her skirts. "Cousin Oliver." She nodded once, a regal bend of her neck. "I was just resting. If you'd be so good as to wait downstairs while I freshen up—"

"Is it true?" he spat.

From his hiding place, Norman could not see Oliver's face, but he could see Elsa's. She lifted her chin and arched one elegantly winged brow, her deep blue eyes serene as they met her irate cousin. "Yes, Oliver, it's true."

She didn't hedge, didn't pretend ignorance, just met his question head-on with bare honesty. His heart swelled with pride and love for his fierce woman.

"You're the reason Wynford-Scott was screened from Gray's?"

"I just told you so. You're becoming tiresome." Her eyes slid to Norman. He gave her a nod of encouragement. To her cousin, Elsa said in a dismissive tone, "If that's all, Oliver—"

"It isn't close to all," he snapped. "Have you any idea what you've done? You've tainted me with your debauchery."

Elsa strolled to the vanity, plucked a ribbon from a silver box, and wound it around her finger. At Oliver's allegation, she snorted. "Come now, sir, I was not the one who published that illustration. I believe you must give Mr. Alderly credit for tainting you with my debauchery."

Oliver's hands fisted at his sides. The hairs on Norman's nape rose.

"For the past two hours," Oliver ground out, "I've been confronted by voters who say they will no longer vote for me because of our bad family blood. I tried telling them you were not actually family, but to no avail."

Elsa threw her head back and laughed, rich and throaty. "Oh, *now* you wish to distance yourself from me? You were happy enough to claim me as your cousin when you needed my expertise on your campaign."

"And even *more* electors," Oliver went on, gesturing broadly, "say they're fed up with the whole thing and won't vote at all."

"Can you blame them?" Elsa tugged the loose end of the ribbon, dislodging it from her finger in a long curl. "You started this, cousin, with your ridiculous scandal sheet. I told you to leave it alone."

"Yes, but you didn't tell me why I should have done. Now I know. Didn't want your dirty little secrets getting out, did you? Didn't want the village to know that their beloved Lady Fay in her wholesome little cottage is a slut and a drunk."

"Leave now."

Oliver spun, startled, as Norman pushed the door out of his way and stepped into the smaller man's space.

Oliver tipped his head all the way back to meet Norman's eye. "I don't know why, but I'm not surprised to find you here making use of Elsa's readily dispensed favors."

Norman experienced an anger that he felt first in his stomach, and that slowly spread outward from the middle. "Mr. Fay," he said in a deceptively mild tone, "owing to the fact that Lady Fay may harbor some residual familial feeling toward you, I have thus far refrained from punching your teeth into your brain. But the next word you utter—be it a single syllable—will breach the border of my restraint. Leave this house now. Do it swiftly and silently."

Oliver's mouth popped open. At Norman's grim smile, he snapped it shut again, made a hasty egress from the room, and then the house.

Elsa raised her brows. "Impressive, Mr. Wynford-Scott. Who knew you possessed the ability to be terrifying?"

"Did I terrify you?" He stepped forward to place a hand on her waist.

"Oh, no, not me. I was not frightened in the least." She smoothed a palm over his lapel. "I found your display rather thrilling, in fact."

"Did you?" He brought his other hand to her waist and lowered his head.

"I did," she affirmed, "and soon I shall make good on the thrill that's coursing through my flesh, but just now, I must tell you the brilliant idea I've had."

She did, her eyes bright, her gestures animated. And it *was* brilliant, but—

"No," he said, shaking his head when she'd reached the conclusion. "You're so brave, Elsa, and the fact that you would do this for me is humbling beyond words. But it's too risky. You've been subjected to enough scorn as it is. I cannot expose you to more."

She brought her hands to his face and pulled his mouth to hers. "Norman," she said in a husky voice after a kiss that left her gasping, "I love ..." She took a shuddering breath. "I love that you worry for me. But I can do this. I'm strong. You showed me that." She smiled into his eyes, and he was lost.

He smiled ruefully, defeated. "Then we'd better make a plan."

Chapter Fourteen

Shortly after breakfast the following morning, Elsa arrived at the Beauforts' home. Standing in the entry hall, she ran a palm over her hip, smoothing a wrinkle in her white skirts. Today she'd chosen to dress all in white, not as a protest to innocence, but as a clear statement that she was presenting herself without any political affiliation whatsoever.

Laura, whom Elsa had not seen since the day Norman's campaign had horned in on Oliver's picnic, rushed down the stairs and grasped Elsa in a tight hug. "You don't have to do this. Sir Seymour and I stand by you. The village will come around in time. There's no need—"

"I want to do this," Elsa assured her. Stepping back, she smiled bravely into her friend's worried face and attempted to stomp out her own apprehension. "I've come to learn these past few months that one cannot will a problem to solve itself. It must be met head-on, regardless of momentary discomfort. Avoiding issues only allows them to fester. If I want my neighbors to respect me again, then I must act in a manner worthy of respect."

Laura's eyes shone with moisture. "Mr. Wynford-Scott is in the stable yard. I'll walk with you."

The two women strolled into the damp morning air. Low gray clouds threatened rain, but Elsa would not be put off by inclement weather.

They found Norman in the back of a cart, working with Sir Seymour to affix a bronze alarum bell to a frame that had, in turn, been hastily hammered into the vehicle. Norman lifted his head and smiled at her in greeting, that sweet, boyish smile that melted her bones. She lifted a hand in return.

The beast harnessed to the wagon glumly toed the earth. "Well, well, well." Elsa sauntered over, hands planted on hips. "Looks like a certain someone will have to earn his supper for once?" Apple tossed his large head and gazed into the distance, avoiding Elsa's teasing gaze, his demeanor one of wounded dignity.

"All set," announced Sir Seymour. He clambered out of the cart and came to bow over Elsa's hand. "You're very courageous to subject yourself to further scorn, my lady. Whatever comes ..."

"I told her," Laura filled in.

"Whatever comes."

Turning her head, she looked to where Norman stood in the back of the wagon. Behind him, the gray clouds were illuminated from within by the morning sun, setting him against a striking backdrop that accentuated the lines of his jaw and broadness of his shoulders in their dark blue coat. A light breeze teased strands of hair peeking out from beneath the brim of his tall beaver hat, tousling them about his ears and strong cheekbones. She exhaled a little sigh. He was *so* delicious.

Soon, the two of them were settled in the wagon, and Norman snapped the ribbons, setting a reluctant Apple to work.

"Did you sleep last night?" Norman asked as the cart merged onto the road leading into Fleck.

Elsa shook her head. "Only a little. You?"

Norman tipped his hat in greeting to a farmer guiding several cows along the road with a long switch. "The same." He slanted a look down at her. "You know, you don't have to—"

"I don't have to do this," she interrupted, rolling her hand. "So I've been told." With a laugh, she looped her hand through his arm. "Even Apple is committed to the cause now. I'll not be the one to back away. Perhaps you wish to abandon our plan?"

Norman puckered his lips and twitched his head once to the side. "Not a chance."

They rolled on into the village, all the way to the green at the center of town. People going about their business paid little notice of the cart with its passengers and strange cargo consisting of a single bell.

Norman gave Elsa a hand, and she gingerly stepped her way into the back. After setting the brake, Norman hopped into the back with her. Elsa clanged the bell for long minutes until people poured from their houses and shops to see what the commotion was all about. Her head threatened to split from the din.

Once a crowd of several dozen had gathered around, Norman raised his hands for quiet. "Good people of Fleck, I bid you a good morning and beg a moment of your time." His rich baritone poured over the assembly like warm molasses. "Yesterday, many of you saw a caricature that I need not describe further. I have come before you today to disavow that illustration. It was produced by someone attached to my campaign, without my knowledge or consent. However, I wish to personally apologize for the illustration and its distribution, as well as any contention it may have caused to arise between neighbors."

He glanced at Elsa and nodded. Taking her cue, she drew a deep breath, then stepped to stand at his side. He gave her a private smile of encouragement, but Elsa's nerves had already settled. Standing beside Norman, she felt like she could conquer the world.

"For my part," she called out, her voice threadier than his, "I hold no ill will toward Mr. Wynford-Scott for yesterday's incident." She met the eye of one of the men who had made a bawdy remark at the mercantile. He ducked his head, abashed. "I know Mr. Wynford-Scott to be a man of valor and integrity. It is my wholehearted belief that he is the best choice for election to Parliament."

A buzz went through the crowd as Norman shot her a startled glance. Her endorsement had not been part of the plan. Elsa chuckled softly and shrugged. She was a political creature at heart.

"Yeah, but is it true?"

Elsa pulled her attention back to the gathering, her eyes scanning for the speaker. Ah. Mr. Thomson, the baker. "Beggin' your pardon, milady, but since you're here to talk about it, that's what we all want to know. What the picture showed, did it happen?"

A rumble of agreement circled the cart. Elsa and Norman were isolated in the midst of gossipy villagers hungry for the juiciest scandal to hit the borough in years. Norman's mouth hardened; she saw his shoulders pull back, ready to do battle defending her.

It wasn't necessary. Elsa knew Fleck. She'd known this was coming. She lifted her chin, refusing to appear weak. "Yes, it happened." An excited murmur swept through the assembly. Elsa raised her hand for silence. When she had it, she continued, "That illustration depicts what I consider to be the lowest point in my life. You see, for some years, I have struggled with the habit of drunkenness, and that night at Gray's Inn was the culmination of a period of ever-increasing consumption of spirits. I am not proud of what happened, but after that terrible night, I made a drastic change in my life. Since that night, for 115 days, I've not had a single drink of intoxicating liquors." There was a smattering of applause, but most people just looked uncomfortable. "Mr. Denny," she addressed the tavern keeper standing near the rear of the crowd, "I see the look you're giving me. I bought scotch from you yesterday. As you may imagine, I was feeling very low after certain events, and I felt driven to drink." Someone in the audience gasped. "But, I did not. Thanks to the intervention of a dear friend, I remembered my promise to myself, and I threw the liquor away."

There was a rousing cheer, and the smile Norman beamed at her radiated pride and admiration.

The crowd dispersed after that, with a few people approaching the cart to shake Norman's hand. The abashed man shuffled over and apologized to Elsa for his behavior.

Back on the seat, Elsa waved as they pulled away from the green to continue their tour of disavowal and confession. Norman was quiet, only clucking directions to his reluctant draught horse as they wended their way through the village.

For Elsa, the experience of public confession set something inside her into motion. Pressure built up in her ribs. More than anything, she wanted Norman to know her. Only a full accounting would do. "I have these awful voices inside me sometimes," she blurted, "Guilt and Shame, telling me how wretched I am, how little I'm worth."

Norman's startled eyes flew to hers, his brows drawing together in a hard line. He pulled Apple to a stop in the middle of the narrow lane and turned to face her. Though she held his gaze, Elsa shifted nervously. He would call her crazy now or demand additional information.

He didn't.

"Where did those voices come from?" he asked instead, pinning her with a fierce gaze.

"I don't ... They're just there."

"Since when? Did you parents tell you you were worthless? A governess, or a tutor?"

She shook her head and lowered her eyes, her chin quavering. This was a mistake. *Please don't ask me about him. Please don't—*

"Was it your husband?"

The weight of years bore down on her shoulders, pressing her into herself. Elsa covered her face and curled downward until her forehead came to rest on her knees. Her shoulders shook with the force of her sobs.

Norman plucked her from the seat and settled her into his own lap. His body curved protectively around her, sheltering her while she cried.

"I never had a babe," she gasped. "Every month, when my courses came, he beat me. He stuffed my bloody rags into my mouth so the servants wouldn't hear and he ... he ..."

"*Shh*, it's all right," he crooned, rocking her side to side. "You don't have to tell me. That's all over now, Elsa. You're safe. He can't hurt you ever again." For a while, he simply held her, his chin tucked over the top of her bonnet, with one hand cradling her ear and the other stroking up and down her back.

"You're so brave," he murmured. "My beautiful, brave Elsa. You did nothing wrong, nothing to deserve such treatment. Many women are barren; that's no moral failing, it's simply—"

She laughed bitterly. "I couldn't begin to tell you whether or not I'm barren because, you see, Harvey was impotent. He couldn't reach completion."

Norman's body stilled around her; a dangerous energy pulsed through him. Then his hand resumed its path up and down her spine. Elsa expected him to ask more, maybe a reckless shred of her heart even wanted him to press—to ask if that's why she'd bedded a dozen men since then, desperate to prove to herself that his inability hadn't been because she was undesirable, as Harvey frequently claimed—but Norman didn't. He didn't. He just held her and kissed the top of her head and her temple and her cheek and then her head again.

"This is why it was so important to me for Oliver to win the seat in Parliament. The only thing I've ever been good at is politics—helping a man's political career. If I can't do that, I fear succumbing to those voices again, sliding back into my drinking habit." She drew a shuddering breath. "That was my fear, anyway. Ever since I left Oliver's campaign, I've determined that it doesn't matter if I'm never involved in politics again. I won't allow this thing to best me."

Elsa's tears seemed to have knocked loose the last of the plaque of sorrow and guilt and shame that had clung to her heart for a decade. Snug in Norman's arms, she felt washed clean. Reborn.

Norman's breath hitched in his throat. "Let's go back to Sir Seymour's."

Elsa lifted her face as a gentle rain began to fall, replacing her tears with nourishing, life-giving water. "No. We started this, and we're going to finish it." When his look of bewilderment made no signs of abating, Elsa slid from his lap, took the ribbons from his hand, and snapped Apple into motion.

At Weatherhill Lane, they repeated their joint statement to a new batch of onlookers. Once again, the "Is it true?" question arose, and once more, Elsa spoke the truth.

Afterward, a wisp of an old woman tottered in their direction. "Lady Fay!" Elsa leaned over the side of the cart and clasped her hand. She recognized the woman as one of the spinster sisters who resided on the lane. After an exchange of pleasantries, the woman said, "Lady Fay, I want to apologize to you about my behavior yesterday, giving you the cut as I did."

"Thank you," Elsa said with a gracious nod. "I accept your apology, and I appreciate—"

"It was bad of me, milady. Hypocritical."

"Oh dear, I don't think—"

"I'm a drunk."

Uncertain what else to do with that information, Elsa nodded and gave a compassionate smile.

"That's why Agatha lives with me, so I won't take to the bottle again." The woman's lined cheeks creased in a frown. "I was touched by what you said. You're so brave. Isn't she brave, Mr. Wynford-Scott?"

"A veritable lioness," he answered in all sincerity.

Elsa gave the spinster a hug before the woman went on her way. It was strangely comforting to know that she wasn't alone in this struggle.

For the remainder of the day, they traveled the width and breadth of the borough, slogging through the rain and mud, stopping to repeat their statement to whoever would listen. Every time, someone would ask Elsa about the picture. And every time, she told the story of her struggle. Often, she was approached afterward by people she had known for years who had kept hidden their own struggles with destructive habits. Middle-aged men and young mothers, crones and fresh-faced youths, it seemed no segment of the populace was without representation in the people who stepped forward to say, "Me, too."

Despite the blanket Norman wrapped her in, by day's end, Elsa was dirty, wet, and chilled to the bone. She'd never felt better in her life. When Norman brought her home, he handed her down from the cart and swung her around in his arms.

"Well, we've done what we can," she said when he finally set her on her feet. "The rest is in the hands of the voters."

Norman tipped her face and kissed her until she was boneless and clinging to him for support. "You gorgeous, magnificent creature." His eyes were soft with wonder, desire, and something she dared not name. "Whatever happens tomorrow, you must see that you are loved. By Fleck," he added hastily. "Your friends will not let you fall, Elsa. And neither will I."

Resting a hand on his broad chest, she felt the strong, steady beat of his heart. How she adored him. "Let's go win an election," she said.

Chapter Fifteen

The morning of the Fleck by-election started with more rain, but inclement weather did not impede the people of the village and the outlying countryside from flocking to the hustings in their hundreds. Four hundred thirty-seven men had the franchise in this borough, and while not all of them had come, there was a greater turnout than Norman had anticipated. It was difficult to say for certain exactly how many voters were present, as numbers were greatly augmented by the women and children in attendance.

By midmorning, the rain had tapered off, leaving tatters of gray clouds streaming across a pale sky. There was a fairlike atmosphere around the muddy green, with street vendors hawking food while a drum and bugle band blared out marches, attracting a score of children to form up an impromptu regiment and drill their way around the legs of adults. Dogs barked, babies cried, neighbors shouted greetings to one another. The clamor was immense.

Differentiating the gathering from a typical fair were the unmistakable trappings of politics. Tory orange and Whig blue were everywhere Norman looked, in flags and banners as well as in ribbons and other trimmings party supporters had added to their apparel. He noted, with a pang of dismay, that there was far more orange in evidence than the color of his own party, though a great many folks wore no party's color at all. A few individuals carried flags painted with slogans in support or protest of a candidate or cause.

Flanking the hustings, carts festooned in buntings of the sponsoring party kept the populace in a steady flow of beer and port, and thirsty Fleckers bounced back and forth between them, showing no loyalty in regard to whose ale they drank up.

Norman peered at all of these goings-on from the relative quiet of behind the hustings' corner post. At the far end of the hustings, Oliver Fay, in his orange hat and gloves, paced and gesticulated, practicing his speech. It was like the backstage area of a theater, with the players waiting for the curtain to rise.

A hand slipped into Norman's and squeezed. He looked down at Elsa and lost his breath, as happened all too frequently when he saw this woman. Today she was splendidly turned out in buff and blue, a public declaration of her shift in loyalties, both political and personal. Her indigo eyes were serene, providing the steady confidence he sorely needed. She tilted her head. "All right?"

He nodded. "Just anxious for it to be over."

"This is just the beginning! Once you take your seat, that's when the hard part starts."

Norman groaned. Elsa laughed.

A villager approached to shake Elsa's hand, not Norman's, congratulating her on her brave speech yesterday. Their joint declaration had caused quite the stir, but it was Elsa's disclosure of her battle with drunkenness that had everyone rapt. Norman was furious to his core that the late Lord Fay had abused Elsa, robbing her of the confidence her vibrant character so rightly deserved. And yet she had persevered, surmounting the insecurities he'd planted in her mind and besting the habit that had undoubtedly been the result of the scoundrel's mistreatment. Incredible woman. He was once more overcome by his absolute love for this indomitable creature. "Elsa."

She turned at the sound of her name, smiled at him over her shoulder. "What is it?" she asked, her brows drawing together. "You've the oddest look on your face. Are you going to be sick?"

There was a loud trumpeting from the hustings, a signal repeated three times. The roar of the great gathering on the green gradually subsided.

"It's time," she whispered, pulling his cheek down for a kiss. "Best of luck, Norman. I know you'll be spectacular."

After one last squeeze of his hand, she nudged him forward. Both Norman and Oliver Fay came to stand at the base of the hustings stairs while, on the platform, the village clerk called for order. Elsa slipped into the crowd. Though Norman tried to keep her in sight, she was quickly swallowed in a sea of blue and orange.

"We shall hear from each candidate standing for our borough's vacant seat in the House of Commons. First, Mr. Oliver Fay."

The Tory candidate once again leaned heavily on his position as a native of the community, renewing his assertion that "an outsider" could not possibly have the best interests of Fleck at heart. His speech earned a roar of approval from the crowd.

"And now," said the clerk, "we shall be addressed by Mr. Norman Wynford-Scott."

Polite applause accompanied his ascent to the platform. Norman shook the hand of the clerk, then looked out over the audience. In the back third of the throng, a banner fluttered wildly.

HONORABLES FOR WYNFORD-SCOTT.

His friends were here? He raised his hand in salute, though he could not make out their faces, and heard a single voice bellow "*Noooooooorm!*" Henry. Chuckling to himself, Norman began his brief remarks.

"Good people of the borough of Fleck, thank you for coming to participate in today's polling. This past month, it has been an honor and a privilege to meet so many of you and to come to know and love this wonderful community. My esteemed opponent would remind you that I am not a native to this district, and though this is true, your warmth and generous hospitality have ensured that Fleck will always be in my heart, regardless of the outcome of today's vote."

Cheers and whistles greeted this statement.

"Throughout this contest," he went on, "I have spoken with many of you about the challenges and difficulties facing your borough, and I hope you have a better understanding of what is possible when the government and the people work together for the greater good. This past week—and the last few days, in particular—have been difficult. Someone very dear to me was the target of a vicious political attack, but instead of lashing out with anger or malice, she saw that challenge as an opportunity to reach out and create a greater understanding with members of this community. From her example, I have learned a valuable lesson, one I think we all would do well to mark: Courage and honesty are necessary to effect positive change. That is how an individual can change, and that is how a village can change, too. Whatever comes, it is my prayer for Fleck that her people will have the courage and honesty necessary to be the strong community I know it is capable of being. It would be my great honor to work at your side to help Fleck meet its challenges and fulfill its tremendous potential. Thank you."

A hearty round of applause followed his remarks. Then the clerk once again called for quiet.

"By a show of approbation, please indicate your preferred candidate. Mr. Fay." To Norman's ears, the Tory's share of applause and cheers was deafening, with men and women alike hooting their approval and stomping their feet. "Mr. Wynford-Scott." Norman received a fair portion of support, as well, plus one banner enthusiastically waving back and forth.

"There is no clear winner," announced the clerk.

Norman stepped forward. "I request a polling of electors."

The clerk nodded. "The polling will proceed in an orderly fashion. Electors, please approach the hustings."

A surge of men pressed through the crowd to climb the hustings stairs. The clerk took his place at a table with the borough registry. As each man approached, he swore an oath of loyalty to the Crown, and swore that he was an inhabitant of the borough of Fleck before stating for which candidate he cast his vote. The first elector voted Fay.

Norman's nerves would not permit him to remain on the hustings. He descended the stairs and made his way into the thick press of bodies. "Excuse me," he said, "I beg your pardon. Please watch your toes." Slowly and carefully, he made his way to the banner his friends held aloft.

"*Noooooorm*," Henry yelled again as he approached, and then Norman was surrounded by their smiling faces, receiving manful hugs from Brandon and Sheri and Henry. Elsa was there, as well, though she stood apart while the men greeted Norman and offered their congratulations.

A few moments of his friends monopolizing his attention was about all Norman could take before he had to give them his shoulder and turn to the one person whose opinion mattered more than all the rest put together.

Seemingly without thought for their audience, Elsa flung herself at Norman. Her arms came around his neck as he hauled her off the ground in a fierce embrace.

"You were wonderful," she said into his ear. "Did you mean what you said?"

"That and more." His emotions were beating their way through his chest, demanding to be given voice.

He gently set her feet on the damp earth and pulled back so she could see his face when he spoke to her.

"Well, I must say," Sheridan interrupted, sauntering over to clap a hand on Norman's arm and another on Elsa's shoulder, "it's a relief to know two of my closest friends have not killed one another. There was some concern over the possibility, and some speculation after you left London, Norm, but it seems my worry was for naught." The smile he gave the large man was a little too stiff to be entirely benevolent. "Delightful to see you getting along so ... peaceably."

Norman held Sheri's appraising gaze, but from the corner of his eye, he saw Elsa blush.

Sheri then offered the pink-faced woman his arm. "Elsa, my dear, I think I spotted a little cobbler's shop just up the way. Tell me whether it's worth my coin to invest in the provincial economy via a new pair of shoes."

No sooner had he led Elsa away than they were replaced at Norman's side by Brandon and Henry.

"Exciting stuff." Henry bobbed his head to the hustings. The line of electors wrapped around the base of the platform and across the green. While they waited, volunteers for each campaign hoping to earn a last-minute pledge delivered voters mugs of ale and port. "Never thought I'd see one of us standing for Parliament," Henry went on. His green eyes crinkled on a smile. "This has been good for you, Norm. You seem more ... oh, I don't know, at ease, I suppose, than you were before."

Biting back a laugh, Norman shook his head. "This has been one of the most fraught months of my life. At the moment, my innards are knitting themselves into a scarf."

"Still ..." Henry eyed him thoughtfully. "There's something."

Brandon slapped Norman's back. "Lady Fay." Norman startled, thinking the surgeon was naming the source of the change Henry claimed to have noticed. "It was her to whom you referred in your speech, was it not?" At his nod, Brandon grunted. "How does she fare?"

"Remarkably well." Norman rocked back on his heels, unconsciously scanning the crowd for a glimpse of her. "She's maintained her sobriety for 116 days."

Brandon lifted a brow. "That's a very precise accounting."

"She keeps a tally in her journal." When Brandon's other brow raised to join the first at his hairline, he rushed to explain, "I saw it day before yesterday. There was a near thing, you see, when that horrible illustration was distributed around town. Did you hear about that? Anyway, Elsa—Lady Fay, I mean—was terribly hurt and came close to surrendering to her compulsion. I offered my aid, but she had already mastered the impulse. Just astonishing fortitude she has. I played only the smallest part."

Henry and Brandon exchanged amused looks.

A man passing by shook Norman's hand, complimented his speech, and said he'd just cast his vote for a Whig for the first time in his life.

"The journal?" Henry pressed after the elector went on his way.

"The, um ... oh, the journal." Norman cleared his throat and tipped his hat in greeting to an imaginary acquaintance to buy himself time. In admitting knowledge of the contents of Elsa's private journal, he had perhaps betrayed the degree of intimacy they shared—a fact she may not want to become known. "After the crisis passed, we discussed how well she'd been doing. She showed me the count she keeps as a way of motivating her to abstain each day. It was something you said that inspired her, Brandon," he said to deflect attention.

"Oh!" Brandon tilted his head. "I'm delighted to have been useful, but Lady Fay deserves all the credit for doing the hard work."

Time ticked by slowly. Norman asked after his friends' wives and businesses. Brandon reported a surprising uptick in goat-related injuries in Middlesex, while Henry bemoaned a cargo detained in port by a harbor official Henry was convinced was under the pay of the East India Company to stifle the shipping behemoth's competition.

"Any word from Harrison?" Norman inquired.

Henry shook his head. "Last I heard, the ship had docked in Cape Town. That letter came weeks ago, and of course the news was months old, at that point."

Norman sent up well wishes for their absent comrade, wherever he might be. Then he returned his attention to the green, which had been churned up by thousands of feet milling about on the wet grass. The line for polling had diminished to the point that it only wrapped halfway around the hustings. It wouldn't be much longer.

His stomach flipped at the thought. He wished Elsa was here to tease him or distract him with conversation, or one of her erotic kisses that made him forget his own name, much less any other concerns.

"Where the devil is Zouche?" he blurted at last.

"Probably found some widow whose wood needs chopping," Brandon mused. Not too long ago, Norman would have thought Brandon was employing a creative euphemism, but since marrying, the attentions the former rake gave to other women were now strictly social or charitable.

"I hope he's not roped Lady Fay into stacking kindling," Norman groused.

"What of the future?" Henry's question seemed to come from nowhere; Norman cocked his head. "If you win the seat, I mean," Henry clarified. "Will you resign it again in two years to resume your place at Gray's Inn?"

"I don't know." Norman's wide shoulders rolled on a sigh. More and more, the only certainty he saw in his future was Elsa.

Brandon posed the reverse of Henry's question. "And what if Mr. Fay claims the victory? What will you do in the interim before you may be considered for the bar?"

"I don't ..." Norman lifted his hat, ran his fingers through his hair, replaced his topper. "I don't know, all right?"

"Fine, fine." Henry lifted his hands in an appeasing gesture. "Settle down, big man. No need for agitation. We'll learn shortly whether we need to help you devise a plan." Only ten men remained in line at the hustings.

His friends' questions brought to a head the unease that had been building inside him over these past weeks. At last, he spotted Sheri and Elsa heading in their direction. Their progress was as ponderous as one of Mr. Yelverton's suppertime lectures back in the great hall at Gray's Inn. Impatient, Norman struck out from the opposite direction to meet them in the middle. "Excuse me. Madam, would you please ...? Thank you." After a small eternity, Norman looked up and found there were still fifteen feet separating him from Elsa. With a huff of frustration, he cupped his hands around his mouth and bellowed, "Clear the way!"

His voice carried farther than he'd intended, for all across the green, people scrambled like startled hens, uncertain of the source of the command. Those directly before Norman quickly fell back, opening a corridor, at the end of which stood the most heartbreakingly beautiful woman he'd ever beheld. With a smile of welcome for Norman, she dropped Sheri's arm.

Three strides carried him the rest of the way. He took her hands. "Elsa."

"Look, Norman, the electors have finished." Sheri pointed to the hustings. "The clerk seems to be tabulating the results."

Norman did not look away from Elsa when he issued his threat. "I swear to God, Zouche, if you interrupt me again, I will tie your tongue in a knot."

• • •

Elsa clapped a hand to her mouth to cover an inelegant snort. Sheri *had* been remarkably chatty, even by his own loquacious standard. After dragging her from shop to shop—not to make any purchases, because all the merchants had closed for the by-election, but only to gawk through the windows—and declaiming over every architectural feature he found interesting, Elsa had finally had enough.

"What's gotten into you?" The village streets were abandoned, as everyone in Fleck had crammed onto the green. Her question bounced off the close-set stone houses.

Sheri's fingers went to his waistcoat. "I don't know what you mean."

Elsa slapped his wrist. "Don't you dare pull that quizzing glass out on me, Sheridan Zouche, and quit playing coy. You're chattering like a magpie. Something's amiss." A dreadful thought occurred to her. "Is it Arcadia?"

"Arcadia is in perfect health. She sends her compliments."

"Then what?"

Sheri released a sigh of long suffering. He led her to a bench in someone's front garden and gestured for her to sit beside him. "Do you remember when I proposed to you?"

She drew back and regarded him, bemused. "I do. But it's too late to do anything about that, my darling Chère. Though your wife grew up in a harem, she would take exception to any attempt you make at establishing one of your own."

Sheri's lips quirked at her reference to Arcadia's childhood in India. "Flattered though I am that you would consent to be my second wife—"

"I refused you, if you'll recall."

"—that was not the object of my inquiry. I was thinking about what you told me that day, that you would only marry again for love."

His brown eyes settled on hers. "Is there to be a wedding, Elsa?"

She ducked her face and examined her hands folded demurely in her lap. "There's ... no, Sheri, there's no wedding."

"Might there be?" He nudged her with his shoulder.

Lately, Elsa had wondered that very thing. After her unhappy union with Harvey, Elsa had embraced her status of financial and social independence and vowed she'd never again marry for anything less than love. After several years of enjoying the company of lovers in her bed but experiencing no deeper sentiment, she'd begun to think Elsa Fay was not meant to love, or to be loved. But now she rather suspected that had been Guilt and Shame talking, for in recent weeks, her heart had blossomed with love for her quietly dignified and mildly stuffy Norman. It still thrilled her to know that no other woman shared her knowledge of the sensual, erotic, not-at-all-stuffy side to him. If she had her way, no other woman ever would. She slanted a look at Sheri and gave him an enigmatic little smile. "Perhaps. We shall see."

"Be happy, my dear," Sheri said, pressing a brotherly kiss to her cheek. "That's all I ask."

"I will. But certainly," she said, rising to her feet, "the only announcement you can expect today is the one that shall be coming down from the hustings. Let's return to the green."

And so she was taken entirely by surprise when Norman dropped to one knee right there on the muddy green with most of the borough looking on.

"Elsa, I love you," he began, and just like that, her eyes began to fill. "I don't know what's going to happen here"—he jerked his chin toward the hustings—"or what I'll do if I don't win. The only thing I know for certain about my future is that I need you in it." A chorus of *awwww* rose up around them. "You're utterly marvelous in every way. Your intelligence astounds me. Your wit brings laughter to my days. Your strength inspires me to be better, to try harder, because no one has to try as hard as you, but you do it, every day, without complaint." Elsa brought her hand to his cheek. He turned his head and pressed a kiss to her palm. "You are so beautiful, Elsa. I've thought so for years, but you've become even more so to me since I've come to know your keen mind and loving heart. When I look at you, you're radiant. An angel."

Somewhere nearby, a woman sobbed, "*I just love weddings!*"

"I've little to offer but my heart and my promise to spend the rest of my life as your friend, your lover, your helper, your partner in all things." In the absolute silence that had fallen over the green, she heard the racing of her own heart as it galloped toward joy. "Is that enough, Elsa? Will you marry me?"

She nodded. "Yes. Absolutely, yes."

A thundering cheer erupted. Norman's face split in a wide grin, and he jumped to his feet. "*Yes? Really?*" she read on his lips, for she could not hear his voice over the deafening approval of Whigs and Tories alike. "*Yes,*" she mouthed in return.

Then his arms were around her, and he dipped her back. Elsa squealed and threw her arms around his shoulders. "I LOVE YOU," she yelled, determined to be heard.

His fingers tightened on her back in acknowledgment; then his mouth swooped down on hers. Elsa brought a hand to his jaw, loving the feel of the muscles working there as he opened his mouth and delivered a hot, passionate kiss that made her head whirl and her body ache. She clung to him all the harder, feeding the kiss back to him and arching against his chest.

The crowd once more grew silent, and only then did Elsa fear they may have become a mite bit indecent in their embrace. Norman must have had a similar thought, for he lifted his head and rolled his lips inward, looking rather abashed.

"The votes have been tallied," called the clerk. Elsa startled. She'd forgotten all about the blasted polling. "With a final count of 172 to 143, the vacant seat in the House of Commons for the Borough of Fleck goes to Mr. Norman Wynford-Scott!"

The crowd went wild again, and Norman crushed Elsa to his chest with renewed intensity. Laughing, he spun her in a circle. The hustings, the green, and hundreds of faces all became a blur, a whirlwind of color and sound and a bellowed cry of "*Noooooooorm!*"

In the center of it all was her one fixed point, this giant among men, her heart, her hope, her love.

Epilogue

When Elsa's monthly courses did not arrive, the plan for having the banns read were tossed out the window and Norman rode hell-for-leather for London and a special license, then turned right around and returned to Fleck, accompanied by The Honorables and their wives, as well as his father, stepmother, and litter of half siblings. Poor Apple still had not quite recovered from his brief, glorious career as a proper horse, but Norman had upped his ration of sugar lumps to aid the beast's convalescence, and Elsa rather suspected the animal of malingering.

The wedding ceremony was small, attended only by those companions from London and a few of Elsa's closest friends in Fleck. Sheri escorted the bride down the aisle and gave her away. Norman's father stood up with him, and Elsa was curious to see that while there was an unmistakable resemblance between father and son, the elder Wynford-Scott did not share his offspring's prodigious height. But he had Norman's kind eyes, and when her new father-in-law smiled at her so sweetly and hugged her and thanked her for making his son happy, tears pricked the corners of her eyes. Of course, everything made her cry these days.

On the upside of marrying in haste, her request that the hustings be left intact for the time being had been humored. So after the ceremony, the church bells pealed and the doors were thrown open onto a glorious spring morning. On her husband's arm, Elsa crossed the green. Everyone in the borough who cared to attend showered them with rice and flower petals. The hustings had been transformed one last time into a bower dripping with flowers, greenery, and swags of airy tulle.

Norman clasped her hand tightly as they mounted the stairs. "Careful, darling," he couldn't help saying. "Mind your step."

She slanted an indulgent smile at her husband, and her heart melted at his look of anxious concern. The coming months might be as difficult for him as for her.

On the hustings platform, their waves were met with cheers and shouted wishes for health and happiness. Norman pulled a purse from his pocket, and they tossed pennies to the children gathered at the front of the crowd.

There was music and dancing and an abundance of food—but no alcohol. Even Mr. Denny had shuttered the Rabbit's Glen for the day out of respect for the newlyweds' wishes for sober festivities. As it happened, there were no complaints, as all felt they were well done by with Mrs. Wynford-Scott's creative concoctions to sample.

Elsa danced with Norman, then Sheri, and then she lost count of the villagers she'd spun circles with, until Norman claimed her once more—only to make her sit down and rest a few moments. While they shared their little respite, the local tanner hurried over and tugged his forelock.

"Congratulations and felicitations on the day, missus. You're the prettiest bride since my own Sal, and that's the truth," the man said, his slouched hat clutched to his chest. "I wondered if I might have a word, sir. You said to let you know if ever there was anything you might be of help with."

"Of course," Norman said with a nod. "What can I do for you?"

"Well, you see, sir, I'm a Roman Catholic, so I didn't get to vote for you in the by-election, even though I wanted to and would have done. I'm an inhabitant of the borough and head of my household, but I'm denied the franchise on account of my faith. And well, Mr. Wynford-Scott, sir, that's wrong." The fellow screwed up his mouth and nodded. "So, what are you going to do about it?"

Norman glanced at Elsa. She nodded. *Go on*, she silently said with a tilt of her head. Norman clapped the man's shoulder. "What do you know about petitioning Parliament?"

Hours later, Elsa was gasping in her husband's arms, her body singing from the exquisite orgasm that had her seeing stars. "God!" she exclaimed, turning her head to the sweaty and rather pleased-with-himself man who'd rolled off her and lay at her side. "I still can't credit that you were a virgin until I had my wicked way with you. You're awfully good at it, you know."

He grinned impishly. "I had an excellent tutor."

"And you always were quite the scholar. I should have noticed your latent potential sooner. I'm fortunate no other lady scooped you up."

"*Damned* fortunate." He grabbed her around the waist and rolled onto his back, pulling her onto his chest.

Laughing, naked, and utterly replete, Elsa took her husband by the face and kissed him soundly. "I love you," she said when she lifted her head to catch her breath. "I love you."

Later still, she sat on the edge of her bed, opened the drawer in her little nightstand, and withdrew her journal. The book naturally fell open to the pages where she kept count of her days without liquor. She turned to a fresh page, smoothed her hand down the crease, then took up her pen and made a single mark.

Norman's whisker-roughened chin came to her shoulder blade, his hand rested lightly on her belly. He kissed her neck. "What's this, love? Why are you starting your count again?"

"This," Elsa explained, tapping the tally mark and feeling the wonder and love of all it represented, "is the first day of the best of my life."

THE END

Author's Note

Dear Reader,

If you're like myself and other historical romance lovers, there's a fair chance you've learned a lot about our favorite time period just through reading wonderful stories set in the Regency era. You know what a reticule is, what it means for a young lady to make her bow, and how a man who's been to Gentleman Jackson's has passed his time. However, when we start venturing too far beyond ballrooms and estates, our understanding may get a little murkier. *Valor Under Siege* required a fair bit of research and learning on my part, so I thought I'd pass along some information regarding the British legal professions and the electoral process during the Regency era that may be new to you.

Just give me a moment to swap out my writer's cap for my history nerd chapeau…

For Americans and other non-British readers, you may know that a barrister and a solicitor are both practitioners of the law, but you may not understand the difference in their scopes of practice (as they existed during the Regency. If you want details on current British legal practice, look elsewhere!). In exceedingly brief terms, *lawyer* applied to anyone who practiced the law. A *solicitor* or *attorney* was a lawyer who specialized in British civil law. If you needed to draft a will, sign a contract, or find loopholes in that pesky entail, you'd hire a solicitor. Men who wished to become solicitors were educated in civil law at universities. Because they charged fees for their work, solicitors were (gasp!) in trade. While they could be respectable, upstanding members of the community, they were not considered gentlemen.

Barristers were lawyers who argued cases in court—trial lawyers, if you will. Criminal defense or prosecution, lawsuits, etc., were matters handled by barristers. Their specialty was British common law, which was learned at the Inns of Court, a system of law schools in London that still exists today. Gray's Inn, where Norman studies and resides at the beginning of this novel, has been an institution of legal scholarship since at least the late 1300s, and possibly earlier. Students at the Inns of Court had already completed a university education (or passed an examination demonstrating their proficiency in classical learning). A minimum of four years at an Inn was usually required before one could be called to the bar, but my research shows that eight to ten years was a typical length of time for young men to spend in their studies before finally becoming barristers. Clients did not directly engage the services of a barrister. If you needed an advocate to plead for you in court, you would first hire a solicitor, and the solicitor would then engage the barrister on your behalf. Barristers did not receive direct payment. Their fee was passed through the intermediary of the solicitor as a "gift" or "consideration." In this way, they were not technically (gasp!) in trade, and could retain their status as gentlemen.

On the election front, the process I describe in *Valor Under Siege* may seem strange to you. Elections during the Regency were carried out under what we now call the Unreformed system, which was basically a hodgepodge of local traditions. The rules regarding who could and couldn't vote varied from borough to borough (though in all cases, only men had the franchise). My fictional borough of Fleck is what was called an *inhabitant borough*, meaning all adult male householders residing within the borough and not receiving poor relief were eligible to vote.

Though women were not permitted to cast a ballot, they were highly involved in Regency politics. Political hostesses like Elsa played a vital role. Their parlors served as neutral territory for political adversaries to hammer out a compromise. Debates spilled over from the floor of Parliament into their dining rooms. And, of course, their own influence could push a waffling Lord or MP into voting the way she—or her politician—wished.

Women actively engaged in canvassing. Female family members of candidates were expected to take part in winning votes for their menfolk. Though giving gifts to constituents strikes modern readers as dodgy—if not downright corrupt—Regency voters expected to be treated, and treated well, in exchange for their votes. A candidate might write a letter of recommendation to help the son of a voter get a desired post or hire the carpenter to fix the leaky roof on another voter's house. Complimentary food and drink were par for the course, both during the campaign and at the election itself. Most anything short of outright buying a vote was fair game. Kissing voters during canvassing, as Elsa does, was another accepted practice. In the home, the vote was regarded as held in common. Father might be the one casting it, but you'd better believe Mother (and probably the children, too) made her opinion known. Families held their own debates to settle which way their vote would be cast.

The actual election was a bit of a holiday for the whole town. As depicted here, there was often first a "vote of approbation," in which everyone, registered voter or no, could cheer for their favored candidate. If there was a clear preference, the loser conceded defeat, and that was that. If, however, there was not an obvious winner, one of the candidates would request a polling of electors. At that time, the registered voters would make their way to the hustings, swear an oath of allegiance, and state their vote. No secret ballots here; your vote was public knowledge. Realistically, the polls would stay open for days, allowing voters to come cast their ballots at their convenience. For the sake of the story, I've shortened the voting period here to one day.

As ever, I have endeavored to present accurate information in this novel. There's bound to be an error or two, and while I take ownership of any such mistakes, I do beg your indulgence. I hope you've enjoyed learning a little about Regency politics as much as I did in writing *Valor Under Siege*. Please let me know what you think! I love hearing from you.

Best Wishes,
Elizabeth

Acknowledgments

I wish to thank Rose Lerner for the wonderful class on Regency-era elections, and other members of the Beau Monde who answered my many questions. Even the stupid ones. *Especially* the stupid ones.

As ever, thank you to my brilliant editorial team at Crimson Romance: Tara Gelsomino, Julie Sturgeon, and Brianne Bardusch. Thanks to the magical art fairies who have, once more, graced my work with a beautiful cover.

To Jason and my three stupendously magnificent children, thank you for your unflagging love and support. Your willingness to overlook my deadline-induced funk and gently point me to the shower is greatly appreciated. Michelle and Sarah, thank you for always being the cheering squad I need.

For my readers, my deepest gratitude for your continued enthusiasm and kind words. Your lovely letters and reviews mean so much. Thank you for spending time in my world, and for allowing me to be part of your day. I hope I can give you a smile when you need one most.

Finally, my compliments and abject apologies to The Honourable Society of Gray's Inn. Sorry for burning your hall. It was a really good party?

About the Author

Elizabeth Boyce's first taste of writing glory was when she won a gift basket in the local newspaper's Mother's Day "Why My Mom is the Best" essay competition at age eight. From that moment, she knew she was destined for bigger and better gift baskets. With visions of hard salamis and tiny crackers dancing in her head, she has authored seven Regency novels and novellas, resulting, thus far, in two gift baskets from adoring fans (AKA amazing friends).

Elizabeth lives in South Carolina and shares her artisanal cheeses with her husband and three children. She sneaks some to the cat when no one else is looking.

More from This Author

Duty Before Desire
Elizabeth Boyce

August 1817, London

Lord Sheridan Zouche was having trouble with his linen. A thin, damp fog wreaked havoc with his cravat, to say nothing of the sorry state of his collar. Grimacing, he plucked at the wilting material.

"Devil take it," he muttered. "Anyone know if Dewhurst carries a looking glass in his bag?" he called out. "On second thought, no. Perhaps it's better if I don't know how shabby I appear."

"Where the hell do you think you are?" snapped the giant at his side. Norman Wynford-Scott jostled Sheri's shoulder with an oversized paw. "For once in your life, would you be serious?"

Witnessing the normally unflappable man in a veritable lather did wonders for Sheri's spirits. "Right you are," he said, leaving his neckcloth to its fate. He spun sharply on boots freshly blackened and polished with champagne to an immaculate shine and addressed the remaining occupants of his coach. "Step lively, lads. This way. Hop to."

Henry De Vere clambered out, rubbing sleep from his deep-green eyes. "Shouldn't be chipper at this ungodly hour. It's deuced rude." To their immediate north, the Thames was a hard, steel gray in the pre-dawn gloaming. Henry's jaw cracked on a yawn.

"The secret is not to go to bed. At least," Sheri said with a smile, "not to sleep."

Glowering darkly, Henry muttered invective against the menace of confirmed bachelors. Married just two weeks ago, he'd spent most of the ride through Mayfair and Chelsea grousing at Sheridan for robbing him of his domestic comforts.

The last occupant of the coach, Harrison Dyer, descended from the carriage with a long, flat box tucked under one arm and a grim set to his stubbled jaw. "Tyrrel is here ahead of us." He indicated with his chin the black carriage at the far end of Battersea Fields.

Two men stood near the vehicle while a third, solitary figure, dim in the gray mist, paced a short distance away. A distinctive limp identified the man as Lord Tyrrel. The orange ember of a cigarillo intensified, then faded, as Tyrrel drew on it.

"I'll speak to his men." Harrison clapped Sheri's back and strode to meet the seconds of the offended party.

It had been deuced bad luck that Tyrrel walked into his wife's bedchamber two nights ago. The man hadn't been expected back from his hunting trip for another week, and he'd not made so much as a peep as he entered the house. It was well known that her ladyship had a string of paramours over the last five years, of whom Sheri was just the most recent.

Having already spent several nights together, Sheri and Sybil had moved beyond the fundamentals of coitus and were becoming a little more creative in their bed play. That particular evening had involved various foodstuffs. Sybil had been lying on her stomach, and Sheri had scooped dollops of blancmange in a line down the column of her spine. Naked and aroused, he'd been poised above her on hands and knees, licking and nibbling his way up her back, at the moment her husband entered the room.

Sybil had gasped and started to move, setting all the bits of dessert to quivering like frightened baby bunnies. Perhaps he lacked some vital instinct for survival, Sheri reflected, or maybe he was just too accustomed to his dissipated pastimes. In any event, when Lord Tyrrel happened upon them, Sheri didn't make a run for his breeches; rather, he'd laid a calming hand on Sybil's haunch and met the furious, shocked glare of his host with a steady, amused gaze. Then he'd offered the man a spoon.

He was more than a bit nonplussed over being the instrument by which Tyrrel chose to restore his manly honor.

A dull rumble announced the approach of another carriage. Within seconds, a hackney coach pulled in behind Sheri's equipage, and Brandon Dewhurst hopped out, surgery bag in hand.

"Sorry I'm late," he said. He spoke to the driver, then joined Sheri, Norman, and Henry. After another moment, Harrison returned from his *tête-à-tête* with Tyrrel's representatives. In the center of their protective ring, Sheri slowly turned to meet the eyes of each man. He couldn't help but feel a lump of gratitude in his chest.

Tasked with naming his seconds for the duel, Sheri had quickly dispatched notes to his tight-knit group of friends, the Honorables. They'd been drinking companions at Oxford, meeting frequently at The Hog's Teeth tavern, facing the crucible of those final steps into adulthood around a rough-hewn table. "The Honorables" derived from the fact that though each man was the scion of an aristocratic family, none of them would inherit a title. They were each The Honorable Mr. So-and-so.

Technically, he, *Lord* Sheridan, second son of the Marquess of Lothgard, was not honorable—literally and figuratively—but courtesy title notwithstanding, he was legally a Mister, just like his friends.

Now, on the dueling ground of Battersea Fields, Sheri had never felt the appropriateness of the name more. Pressing a hand to his chest, Sheri bowed. "Thank you all for coming, gentlemen."

Henry lifted his hat and swiped a hand through his hair. "Was that a note of sincerity I detected? Don't tell us you're actually worried."

"He should be," Norman snapped. "Tyrrel is reputed to be a crack shot." Standing well over six and a half feet tall, the large man's disapproval seemed to fall quite a distance before it reached Sheri.

With a dismissive flick of his hand, Sheri scoffed. "How good could he be? He returned home early from his trip. I'd wager he challenged me after already having been bested by every beast in Scotland, who laughed him over the border with his tail 'twixt his legs."

Crossing his arms, Norman muttered, "Unless he came home early because he shot them all and had nothing left to do."

Squinting at the lightening sky, Harrison said, "Nothing to fear, Norm. Tyrrel intends to shoot wide. It's satisfaction he wants, not blood. Our Lothario will be seducing the ladies tonight." His brandy eyes flicked to Sheri. "It's time."

Brandon held up a hand. "Just a moment." He produced a flask from the inside pocket of his great coat and unscrewed the cap. "A dollop of Dutch courage."

Sheri took a swig of the gin. Nerves he would never admit to had kept him awake for nearly twenty-four hours, so he appreciated the stringent vapor of juniper that curled up the back of his nose and sharpened his focus.

After passing the drink around, the circle broke up. Harrison met Tyrrel's second at the weapons table to inspect and load the pistols, while Brandon took a position off to the side, surgery bag at the ready. Norman loped to the center of the field and fished out a handkerchief, as Henry and Tyrrel's other man paced off the distance.

With all the fellows busy at their appointed tasks, Sheri was left alone. A pang of loneliness, or maybe nostalgia, ached in his chest. Turning so the others couldn't see him, he fumbled at his waist to detach the fob that secured his omnipresent quizzing glass to his person by means of a silver chain. The silver fob was round, a little larger than a guinea, and puffed like a delicate sea biscuit. Embellished with the Zouche family crest, the fob reflected the weak morning light in undulating gray lines.

Pressing his thumbnail into a recess on the edge, Sheri popped the fob open, revealing a miniature portrait of a young girl, which he cradled in his palm. She smiled at him shyly, her lively brown eyes hinting at impishness. Not for the first time, Sheri felt a rush of gratitude to the portraitist who had managed so perfectly to capture the way Grace's lower lip curled over her teeth when she smiled and the stubborn lick of brown hair that liked to escape her ribbons.

"Miss you, Grace," he said as he always did, as he always had done. *Miss you, Sheri!* she used to call back when he took his leave of her cottage. She hadn't mastered many words in her twelve years, but those three had always rung out clear and true.

"I won't ask if you've got any sway up there," he murmured. "I don't suppose I've a single favor to call in, even if you had. But if you could spare a few moments to be with me now, I'd be much obliged. You'd laugh yourself silly at the scrape I've gotten myself into this time, Grace, you really would. So maybe linger a bit for the entertainment, if nothing else." He smiled sadly, a poor imitation of the expression captured in the tiny portrait. "And if things go badly here, then we'll see each other soon. We'll play snakes and ladders, all right?"

"Sheridan!" called Henry.

Sheri snapped the fob shut and returned it to its place on his waistcoat, then went to his mark.

Twelve paces away, Tyrrel joined Sheri on the field of honor. The challenger gave Sheri a long, hard stare.

Beneath the other man's scrutiny, a vague feeling of embarrassment stole through Sheridan at being caught up in something as sordid as a duel. In his long, storied career of fornicating, this was the first time he'd been called out. On the surface, it seemed remarkable that after sleeping with dozens of married women he'd not once been called to task for it, but Sheri was meticulous about discretion. He was interested only in seeking pleasure with enthusiastic partners, not in causing trouble for the women he bedded, their lawful husbands, or—most importantly—himself.

Inside his kid gloves, which he'd purchased for the occasion of his first duel, Sheri's palms began to perspire.

The seconds broke away from the weapons table, each making for their respective principal. Harrison held the gun—one of the two he always carried about his own person—across his flat palms and presented it to Sheri.

It didn't look like much. The stock was fashioned of dark wood, with a brass cap on the end of the handle he supposed would be good for coshing one's opponent over the head, should one's shot go astray. The barrel, he believed it was called, was simple and unadorned.

"You get the lucky one," Harrison said. "This is the same pistol Brandon used to put an end to the scoundrel who abducted Mrs. Dewhurst."

That had been last fall, back when Mrs. Dewhurst was still Miss Robbins. Sheri had a particular fondness for Mrs. Dewhurst. Maybe the gun that had defended her life would, indeed, serve him well. He would take all the help he could get right now.

Gingerly, he took the thing in his hand. It was heavier than he'd expected. "I just depress this lever here, do I?"

Harrison snorted. When Sheri didn't respond in kind, the man's eyes widened. "Tell me you know how to shoot a gun, Zouche."

"Never touched one before in my life."

"What?" Harrison blurted. "How … ?" He cut himself off with a sharp gesture. "Never mind. Doesn't matter." Turning in a tight circle, he blew his lips out in exasperation before leaning in to hiss,

"Why the devil did you choose pistols if you've never fired one? Are you trying to get yourself killed?"

Raising a russet brow, Sheri ticked off items on his fingers. "My other option was fencing, which: One, takes too damned long. Two, I do not engage in exercise resulting in effusive perspiration before three o'clock. Three, I've a distaste for practicing fancy footwork with another man—I prefer my dancing partners to be female. Four, it's piratical and uncivilized in these modern times. And five, I plan to delope, in any event. I tupped the man's wife, which he and I and everyone else knows. Drawing his blood would only further humiliate the poor bastard. Let Tyrrel have his tantrum, and then we can all tell him what a fine, brave boy he is and return to our own beds."

Harrison tipped his head into his hand. A heavy sigh poured from him. "Yes, Sheridan, you just depress the little lever. Be sure to point the gun well away from your own foot."

The seconds cleared the field. Norman stood between the combatants and to the side. He rattled off the rules of the duel. Then he raised his arm, holding aloft a white handkerchief.

Tyrrel turned to the side, his right foot leading. Sheri imitated the stance.

Norman released the scrap of material. It seemed to be a long time in falling.

Lord Tyrrel lifted his arm, gun pointed skyward.

Sheri's abdomen released a knot of anxiety he hadn't known he'd been holding. He pointed his own weapon to the ground, at a forty-five-degree angle away from Tyrrel.

The handkerchief alighted on the dew-silvered grass.

With the lightest squeeze of Sheri's finger, his pistol erupted. The noise slammed into his ear with the force of a pugilist's fist. A gout of turf spurted into the air much closer to Sheri's feet than he'd intended, startling the hell out of him. Bluish-white smoke snaked from the gun to mingle with the thinning morning fog.

"Oh, my god!" screeched a feminine voice. "I'm come too late!"

All heads swung to the woman bearing down upon them, one hand anchoring her fashionable hat in place, the other lifting the skirts of her perfectly *en mode* dress free of the damp grass.

"Tyrrel," Sybil cried, "did you kill him? I'll never forgive you if you did." This dramatic declaration despite Sheridan standing not ten feet away from her, whole and unharmed.

The pretty woman stopped at his side, chest heaving in a manner calculated to draw attention to her generous bosom. "My love, you're all right!" Looping her arm through Sheri's, she cast a scornful look on her husband. "I'm leaving you, Tyrrel. Lord Sheridan and I are eloping."

This was news to Sheridan.

"Is that so?" came the aggrieved reply from down the field.

"My lady," Sheri murmured, "might we discuss this at a more convenient time? Perhaps when your husband and I are not locked in a contest of honor?"

Her pale brows drew together; she tightened her grip on him. "But, Chère, I love you so. No man has ever made me feel like you do." She shouted down the field, "Do you hear that, Tyrrel? Lord Sheridan satisfies me in ways your dull, little brain could never imagine! And as for your—"

"Sybil," Sheri hissed. He shook her once, trying to silence her goading. "Stop it. Now."

"—no larger than my thumb and veers to the right, but Chère's endowed perfectly." She laughed, loud and jeering. "Why, our infant son has more in his clout than you've in your drawers."

A choked sound pulled Sheri's attention back down the field, to the man who had not yet taken his shot. Twelve paces away, Tyrrel's mouth twisted in a bitter sneer. He lowered his arm, training his pistol on the adulterous pair.

Instinctively moving to shield the woman, Lord Sheridan Zouche perceived the flash of Tyrrel's shot an instant before the bullet hit him.

•••

That night, Sheri lay on his stomach, lengthwise, across an otto- man bench in the bedchamber of his rooms in Upper Brook Street. His arms dangled to either side. The fingers of his left hand curled lightly around the club foot at the bottom of a walnut cab- riole leg, while the fingers of the other grazed the page of the book open on the floor beneath him. He read with his chin propped on the generous cushioning, but the entertainment did little to dis- tract him. His manservant, French, had set a snifter and bottle of brandy on a silver tray on the floor, in easy reach of his wounded employer. The air was lightly perfumed by the handful of bou- quets he'd received—along with a veritable hillock of notes—from various women of his acquaintance, expressing shock and dismay at the news of his injury and wishes for a speedy recovery.

Beneath a bandage Brandon had wound about his hips, the stitched gunshot wound throbbed—even the silk of his dressing gown felt heavy on his sensitive skin. Thank God Sheri had only been grazed, but the gash burned like the very devil. He reached for his glass and propped up on an elbow, wincing at the sudden, sharp pain that darted down his leg.

He returned his beverage to the tray and closed his eyes, his cheek resting on the cushion. Sheri couldn't remember ever hurting so much. Not that he'd imagined being shot would be a lark, but neither had he anticipated the painful throbbing that enveloped most of the right side of his body.

Brandon had left him some laudanum, but Sheri didn't want to take it unless the pain became unbearable. So far, his discomfort fell somewhere between terrible and beastly. Nothing he couldn't live through.

He wished he had some company—female, preferably. Idly, he wondered what his friend Elsa, Lady Fay, was doing this evening. The beautiful young widow never failed to liven his spirits.

As if in answer to his wish, his door slammed against the wall—but it wasn't Elsa come to minister to his wounds. Sheri's eyes popped open in time to see his older brother striding into the room, with French trotting just behind him.

"The Marquess of Lothgard," called the harried servant.

"Thank you, French," Sheri drawled. "If you'd be so good, perhaps a preparation of the medication Mr. Dewhurst recommended? I sense the imminent approach of a rather large pain."

French nodded and backed out of the room.

The marquess stopped several feet short of the ottoman. Sheri lazily pulled his gaze up his brother's form, noting, with a touch of envy, the fine breeches gracing his lordship's limbs. Sheri's new pantaloons had been a casualty of the morning's carnage—a senseless death.

He craned his neck to meet his sibling's thunderous expression. Eli's brown hair was a shade darker than Sheridan's, and his eyes almost black to Sheri's coffee-hued irises. The elder Zouche folded his arms across his broad chest, straining the shoulder seams of his evening coat. Every line of his noble form bristled with a sense of umbrage.

"Evening, Lothgard," Sheri said. "Kind of you to blow in for a visit."

His brother tapped a manicured finger against the opposite elbow. "It's all over Town that you were shot in the arse this morning."

"I did suffer an indignity to my fundament, it's true. However, the injury is not life-threatening, so you may put away your smelling salts."

Eli scoffed. "More's the pity. They say you deloped."

Sheri, silent, returned his gaze to his book.

"*And* that Lady Tyrrel made quite the memorable entrance."

When Sheri still made no response, his brother's toes appeared in his line of sight. Eli kicked Sheri's book, sending it skittering across the rug. "Blast it, Sheridan, look at me when I'm speaking to you."

Propping on his elbows, Sheri lifted a brow. "Shades of Pater," he remarked. "How many times did I hear just those words before the strap landed on my backside?"

Eli's face—much like Sheri's, but fuller, the skin slightly loose about the jaw, now that he was approaching forty—reddened. "Perhaps you should have better heeded our father's lessons. Not only did you bed a man's wife, you once more insulted his honor by refusing him a proper duel, and then making a scene with his wife! You may as well have spit in his face." The marquess's hands clenched and released at his sides. The heavy gold signet ring adorning the fourth finger of his right hand caught the light of a nearby candelabrum, flashing a rich yellow. "You're thirty years old, Sheridan. When will you behave like a grown man?"

Slowly, and with no small degree of discomfort, Sheri rolled onto his side and rose. He stood an inch shy of Eli's six feet, and he felt the disadvantage of being in a state of undress while the marquess was exquisitely garbed. Still, Sheridan was younger than his brother by nearly a decade, and for all his lackadaisical airs, he kept his body in prime condition with an hour of vigorous exercise each day—his preferred activities of dancing and bedding women depended upon physical stamina, after all. If Eli thought to intimidate him with paternalistic chiding, he would soon find Sheri was not so easily cowed.

"What masculine accomplishments do I lack, brother? Should I have cut Tyrrel down, as our sire would have done? Pray, enlighten me."

The hard lines around Eli's mouth softened a fraction. "Dammit, Sheridan," he muttered. With a heavy sigh, he retrieved the book he'd abused and idly flipped through the pages.

When Eli spoke again, his voice sounded altered, as though he parted with the words unwillingly. "When I heard about the duel," he said, "my first thought was how you'd always refused to touch a gun, and I wondered if you hadn't managed to shoot yourself in the rump."

"I had a quick course in handling the thing."

Eli snapped the book shut and met his younger brother's eyes. "You've become an embarrassment, Sheridan."

"The gossip will blow over in a few days, Lothgard."

"Not just the duel." Lothgard grimaced. "Deborah"—his wife—"tells me the ladies all call you Chère …"

Sheri couldn't suppress a smile at the mention of his French nickname amongst many of the *ton*'s ladies. "It's just a silly little—"

"While I've heard the men," Lothgard continued, "call you *Share*. Share Zouche."

Sheri shifted his weight to his left foot. The right side of his body throbbed. "Honestly, that one is undeserved. There was only the one time." He frowned. "No, twice. But everyone involved had a fine time … Oh, I suppose there was a third occasion, but there was a great deal of drinking involved that particular night …"

His glib recitation tapered off as Lothgard's face grew more and more pained with every word. He didn't look angry anymore, just … disappointed.

A ripple of defensiveness coursed through Sheri. How dare Lothgard come in here and moralize at him?

"Your reputation is abysmal," Lothgard said. "You are known only for your sexual exploits, rather than for anything of worth."

Sheri crossed his arms. "I contribute a great deal of worth, Lothgard. In fact, had Tyrrel walked into that room an hour earlier and witnessed the act his wife begged me to perform with a cucumber, he'd have thanked me for sparing him the task." He lifted his chin. "I should receive the Royal Guelphic Order for keeping Lady Tyrrel contained to her own boudoir while his lordship was away, rather than letting her menace an unsuspecting male populace."

Lothgard drew back. Squeezing his eyes shut, he pressed his third finger between his brows, as though suffering the headache.

Feeling the beginnings of victory, Sheri stooped over for his glass of brandy. Offering his brother a silent toast, Sheri brought the glass to his mouth.

"I didn't want to do this, but you leave me no choice."

Pausing with the snifter at his lips, Sheri raised a brow.

His brother opened the door. "French, please bring her ladyship here."

Sheri stiffened. "You didn't."

His brother smiled evilly. "I did."

"Elijah?" said a gentle, uncertain voice.

Sheri groaned. Just like that, he was defeated.

"Here, darling." Hopping into action like a footman, the marquess held the door wide to admit French escorting a petite woman. When she saw Sheri, her big brown eyes instantly filled.

"Oh, Sheridan!" She approached him in a rustle of evening silks, one gloved hand pressed to her cheek.

Delicate of health and guileless as a calf, his sister-in-law, Deborah, had always been a great favorite of his. Eleven years ago, when Sheri couldn't tell Eli's infant twins apart and suggested, in all seriousness, that they tattoo the boys' names onto the bottoms of their feet, Lothgard had erupted and called him a buffoon. Deborah had merely laughed her tinkling fairy laugh and tied different-colored ribbons about the babies' ankles until their uncle could distinguish them. Ever since, Sheri had doted on the woman.

"Pray, do not fret, Deborah," he said, gently squeezing her hand to reassure her of his vitality. "Tyrrel missed my heart by a mile. I may lose my leg yet," he joked, "but you can be sure I'll have the most fashionable peg leg in London. Something silver-plated and gold-tipped, I imagine, engraved with scrollwork, possibly set with rubies and sapphires. Or maybe I'll allow some promising artist to paint it with a masterpiece that follows me wherever I go. It would be the latest sensation—wearable art for amputees. I predict wounded soldiers will soon be clamoring to have their wooden limbs frescoed with depictions of their battlefield heroics. What do you think?"

In a tense, silent moment, Deborah's lower lip quivered while the water level in her eyes rose to alarming heights before the flood finally spilled over the dam of her lids. She emitted only a small, plaintive whimper, worse by far than a loud show of distress. She did nothing to stem the flow of tears down her face, only stood there and quietly cried, her eyes still locked on Sheri's.

Lothgard wrapped his wife in his arms and drew her away from his brother, glaring accusingly at Sheri over her head while making soothing sounds.

A hot coil of guilt twisted in Sheri's gut. "Forgive me, Deborah. I was simply making light of the situation, which, obviously, was the incorrect course." He raised a hand, then let it fall uselessly to his side.

Deborah lifted her face and wiped her nose on a handkerchief Elijah had provided. "I can take no more, Sheridan," she said in a watery voice. "Anyone else, I'd know they were funning, but you very well might go out and have some gaudy false leg made and parade it all around Town, flaunting the fact that you'd lost your leg in a duel with your lover's husband.

"Do you never think of your nephews, Sheridan? What kind of example are you setting for them?"

His ass throbbed, and that hot coil twisted tighter, pinching his innards. He dropped onto the ottoman, sucking a breath through his teeth at the flare of pain. His discomfort was making him cross. "It was a jest," he ground out. "What would the twins know about it, anyway?" Sheri demanded. "I don't make a habit of discussing my private affairs with your offspring, my lady; do you?"

His eleven-year-old nephews were called Crispin and Webb. Sheri had thus far refrained from telling Eli and Deborah that he'd always thought the boys' monikers sounded like the name of a legal partnership. He could very nearly see the engraved brass plate now: *Crispin & Webb, Solicitors at Law.* In his current state, he very nearly let loose out of spite.

The marchioness swayed on her feet. Eli helped her to a chair. Never possessed of a strong constitution to begin, the twins' birth had very nearly killed Deborah, and she'd never quite recovered from the ordeal. She passed her days navigating from one resting spot to another. Pain was her constant companion; any activity more strenuous than a sedate stroll was beyond her, but she put on her sweet smile and did her best to move about in Society. Sheri was glad he'd kept his spiteful remark between his teeth and was sorry he'd ever thought to lash out at her.

Husband and wife exchanged a look. "Things have not gone well, I take it?" Deborah asked.

Hands clasped behind his back, Lothgard once more looked the formidable nobleman. His nose sliced a negative through the air. "Sheridan won't hear a word I say."

"He's always gone his own way."

Lothgard blew out a snort. "Down the devil's highway, more like."

"I worry about your mother, too—what must she make of all this?"

There they went again, treating Sheridan like a recalcitrant child, speaking as though he were not in the same room.

"Our mother," he interjected, "is too busy kicking up her heels in Bath to pay any heed to London gossip. If I have in any way discombobulated her, you can be sure she'll let me know."

"Yes, you can be sure she will." Eli stood behind Deborah's chair and rested his hand on her shoulder. "Both of us wrote to her today."

"What, both of you? One missive wasn't enough?"

Deborah parted her hands in her lap. "We wished to assure your lady mother that we were aware of the situation."

"And that we would handle it," Eli pronounced down the length of his aristocratic nose.

"Handle?" Sheri echoed. "How must I be handled?"

In her soft, soft voice, Deborah said, "You must marry, Sheridan."

For a while, no one spoke. In the silence, the aroma of flowers became oppressive. Sheri's head began aching in earnest, his skull beating in sympathy with the angry pulse of his wound. He wanted that laudanum, after all.

He opened his mouth to formulate an argument, but the marquess cut him dead with a look. "Your days of indulging your every base desire are at an end, Sheridan. If it were just myself, I'd cut you loose and let you fornicate your way through all of England." At his wife's gasp, he winced. "Sorry, my dear," he hastily apologized. "But it's not just me," he went on, addressing his brother once more. "It's Mother, and Deborah, and the boys. You're ruining our family's name and causing them embarrassment. Deborah has persuaded me to grant you one last chance: if you wish to remain an acknowledged member of this family, you will do your duty and wed."

Damn Elijah!

Knowing there would be no winning with his brother, Sheridan turned to his sister-in-law. "Sister," he began, his tone conciliatory, "please forgive me for causing you any shred of humiliation. You know I'd never willingly do you harm."

The woman's lower lip trembled. She made a little, muffled sound.

Sheri went to where she sat and, repressing his own whimper, knelt before her like a penitent seeking absolution. He took her hand and pressed a kiss to the back of it. Her nose reddened. "I see now that things have gotten out of hand. I'd no idea Lady Tyrrel would make such a to-do this morning, and I recognized at once that there would be scandal. I see now, though, that this is not the first time my behavior has brought you grief, is it?"

Sniffling, Deborah shook her head. "Oh, Sheridan, if you'd heard what the ladies all say. Half of them think you're the Lord's gift to womankind, while the other half think you're the devil incarnate. No matter which side they fall on, every one of them loves nothing better than swapping tales about you: *Where will Chère Zouche be tonight? Who is he wooing now? Have you seen his new coat? Can you credit the way he looked at Lady Whistleton at the ball? Do you suppose he's taken her to bed?* It never ends!" She cast a hurt look at the flowers arrayed around the room, stand-ins for the women who'd subjected her to their tattle.

"Well, it ends now," he vowed, squeezing her hand and gazing earnestly into her eyes. "There's no need to bring marriage into things; I will be a reformed man without all that, I swear."

Deborah shook her head. "I pity you, Sheridan—truly, I do. You're missing out on the good things in life, and you don't even realize it. Goodness knows you love women and they love you right back, but we're nothing more to you than …" A fierce blush flooded her face. "Bed partners," she finished in a whisper.

"That isn't so," he protested. The pain in his flank drove him to hands and knees, his face almost to the rug, so that now he was practically groveling at Deborah's feet. "I live to make women happy—not just *that* way, either. Don't look at me like that," he yelled. "Your pity is insufferable."

His affairs had been for the pleasure of the women he bedded— his own, too, naturally—but he'd never once touched a woman selfishly. A woman's pleasure was Sheridan's greatest joy. To think that all the time he'd been pleasuring women in his bed, he'd been hurting Deborah every bit as much.

A guttural moan vibrated in his throat. Perspiration damped his hairline.

"Perhaps we should take our leave, my dear," said Eli.

Yes, Sheridan cried to himself. *Begone, and take your witch of guilt with you.* It was just the pain that had his mind in such a muddle, he assumed. Once he felt better, his mind would set itself to rights.

"Sheridan?" Deborah's hand touched his chest. Sheri's eyes opened; he found he was laying on the floor, his sister-in-law crouched beside him.

"Deborah," he rasped. "I'm so sorry. Every bit of unhappiness I caused you, I wish I could take it for myself."

She smiled sadly. "I think you shall." She took his hand. "Don't you love me, Sheridan?"

"You're the sister I always wanted," he replied in a rough voice. Grace was never far from his thoughts. "I couldn't have picked a better sister for myself. I'm grateful every day that Elijah chose you."

Her angelic smile was a blessing. His eyes started to drift closed. *I really must summon French with that medicine.*

"Do you acknowledge that you have caused me a great deal of social embarrassment with your indiscreet behavior?"

"Of course, darling, I already did."

"And would you like to make it up to me?"

"If I can, certainly." There were several jewelers Sheri patronized when he needed to make amends with a woman. Through the haze of pain, he wondered whether Deborah would prefer a new fan or a pearl bracelet.

Her face filled his vision as she leaned over him. Sheridan sensed the bulk of Elijah behind her, physically supporting his wife. "Then get married, Sheridan. You've made every woman in the *ton* happy, and now it's my turn. Find a wife. Tell me you will, Sheridan. You've never once broken your word to me. Tell me you'll marry and be a good husband and stop your wicked sinning."

"Yes, Deborah, I shall marry."

A moment later they were gone, and Sheri was on the floor, gutted and raw by the promise he'd made. He wouldn't go back on his word to Deborah—not ever. It would be the end of any relationship Sheri hoped to have with his brother and nephews in the future—not to mention with Deborah herself.

Even now, the flowers and letters filling his chamber, which had marked the happiest part of his life, were the funereal arrangements for that same time of life. It was over. Gone. Dead.

Sheri would marry.

Somewhere in the back of his mind, a rallying thought: hadn't he always been prepared for this eventuality? *In Case of Crisis, Wed* . . .

Sheridan stiffened. Yes, he would have a happy bride in no time.

Quickly, he rose to his feet. And just as quickly collapsed on the ottoman. His leg felt like hot, liquid lead. "French," he bellowed. "The laudanum. Now."

He might not have a happy bride in *no time*. But soon, he thought, rubbing his hand over the battered rump. Soon.

For more by Elizabeth Boyce, check out:

Honor Among Thieves

"Intriguing and unique, with likable, human characters ... mixed with competition, sexually charged scenes, and danger, this latest from Boyce is highly recommended for historical romance lovers." — Library Journal

"... a romantic version of a very grim (or Grimm) fairytale where the danger and horror of the journey is balanced by the exquisite and hard-fought peace of the ending." — Heroes and Heartbreakers

"...an unflinching look at the violent part of the Regency rarely seen. Boyce's prose is magnificently gritty and heartfelt, imbuing this romantic suspense with the perfect mix of light to calm the darkness ... " —Erica Monroe, USA Today Bestselling Author

Truth Within Dreams

"If you enjoy an historical romp, or a little madcap short story, *Truth Within Dreams* will fit the bill." —Long and Short Reviews

Once a Duchess

"Sparkling characters, a fast-paced plot, and beautiful descriptions of Regency England made this moving story of love lost and found once again, a book I couldn't put down. A delicious debut by an author to watch!" —Danelle Harmon, author of *The Wild One*

Once an Heiress

"*Once an Heiress* combines everything readers love about historical romance with a twisting, suspenseful story that will have you on the edge of your seat ... I loved every second of *Once an Heiress*—it had the intrigue I love about historical romance combined with an excellent storyline that kept me on my toes."—The Romance Reviews

"If you like historical romances with a strong heroine that doesn't stick to society rules and a scarred hero with a wonderful hidden heart then you will like *Once an Heiress* by Elizabeth Boyce." —Harlequin Junkie

Once an Innocent

"*Once an Innocent* by Elizabeth Boyce is a fantastic espionage romance that has some surprising action and gripping drama. If you are a 007 fan, you will be entertained by this novel."—The Romance Reviews

In the mood for more Crimson Romance?
Check out *Dark Season by Joanna Lowell*
at CrimsonRomance.com.